BUTTERFLY

D1648843

BUTTERFLY

Gwendoline Butler

Chivers Press • G.K. Hall & Co.
Bath, England   Thorndike, Maine USA

This Large Print edition is published by Chivers Press, England, and by Thorndike Press, USA.

Published in 1997 in the U.K. by arrangement with Severn House Publishers Ltd.

Published in 1997 in the U.S. by arrangement with Chivers Press Limited.

U.K. Hardcover ISBN 0–7451–8978–4 (Chivers Large Print)
U.K. Softcover ISBN 0–7451–8979–2 (Camden Large Print)
U.S. Softcover ISBN 0–7862–1020–6 (General Series Edition)

The text of this Large Print edition is unabridged.
Other aspects of the book may vary from the original edition.

Set in 16 pt. New Times Roman.

Printed in Great Britain on acid-free paper.

British Library Cataloguing in Publication Data available

Library of Congress Cataloging-in-Publication Data

Butler, Gwendoline.
  Butterfly / Gwendoline Butler
    p. cm.
  ISBN 0–7862–1020–6 (lg. print : sc)
  1. Large type books. I. Title.
[PR6052.U813B87   1997]
823′.914—dc21   96–52559

PART ONE

THE SIXTIES

CHAPTER ONE

Butterfly was created in 1964. At the same time, Charlotte Chaudin, the gifted young woman behind this exquisite new designer label, had decided to re-create herself.

One had to edit, she reasoned, cutting out some facts, adding others, in order to survive. But inside herself she spoke the truth.

The twenty-one-year-old Charlotte Chaudin was a bright young designer, fresh out of college. She worked in the couture house of Madame Anstruther Breen in Bond Street, but already had made her own mark on the fashion world, branching out with her own designs under the name of "Butterfly."

Charlotte was a pretty girl, with big eyes. She had lovely dark hair. And this was what hurled her into the world of Jehan.

Hurled and caught; words that came naturally when thinking of that passionate, violent figure.

Jehan Treharne—self-named, his real name a careful secret which everyone knew and no one mentioned—was one of the new breed of hairdresser. With a string of successful shops in London (he called them shops; no nonsense about "salons": his father had been a scissors and razor barber) Jehan had tasted real money. And it had been the taste of blood to a tiger. He was off and running when he met Charlotte.

As the affair progressed, a friend, Diana de Marche, had taken Charlotte aside in warning, saying, 'It would be a pity to be eaten up, darling.'

But at the time, it hadn't felt like being eaten. Though later, the blood would be real, when Jehan started to hit her.

It was then that she decided it was time to fall in love with someone else...

Not a great idea really...

She met Tony Beauclerc one evening at The Rondo Club, quarrelled violently with Jehan that same night, because he said, 'You might as well go to bed with a polecat as that bloody aristo' (Jehan was ferociously egalitarian at that time), and was with Tony the day after.

Jehan was on his way that day to New York. He no doubt expected her to be broken into little pieces when he flew westward. She wasn't. But crackles of his anger reached her across the Atlantic. Nothing I can do about that, she thought, anger is the other side of love.

This was Jehan's first bite, of course, but she didn't know it at the time. It seemed so sunny in the world outside. Inhabitants of the fun world swinging in London?

* * *

Everyone was hot that night of the Great Ball at Beauclerc House, overlooking Hyde Park, and all the windows were open to catch what breeze there was, scented with the mixed sweetness and sharpness of a London summer. It was almost the last house in private hands in Park Lane, and its days were numbered. It was almost midnight. The dancing had been going on for nearly two hours. Soon, supper would be served, alfresco in a marquee made to look like a birdcage in the garden, or more formally in the library, if you chose it. All the decorations had been designed by Charlotte; even the food had been specially selected by her to blend in with their colour scheme of apricot and peppermint green. Strong colours, but Charlotte was a strong person. This was her last chance to stage a big ball in the old house. Her first as well as her last, because Tony Beauclerc had never let her get her hands on its furnishings.

'What was good enough for my grandmother is good enough for me,' he had said, when Charlotte showed a desire to decorate the Beauclerc town house.

'You don't wear the same clothes your grandfather wore.'

'But I go to the same tailor. Anyway, hands off.' It was a warning. The art deco of the Seventh Duchess must remain.

Since their relationship, although strong and passionate, was not that of marriage, Charlotte

5

did lay off. She had thought Tony would do anything for her, but apparently not that. He loved her more than she loved him, she was quite sure, which gave her confidence, but lovers could not redecorate houses, although wives could. Perhaps it was built into their marriage contracts. Who cared about marriage? Certainly not Charlotte, who was simply happy to be with Tony and to leave far behind her the bruising violence of her relationship with Jehan.

In retrospect it had been more of a collision than a love affair.

Better to be loved, she thought with contentment, than to love. I love Tony just enough, and he loves me more than enough, which suits me fine. Perhaps I *will* be a duchess one day. Who knows?

But now, Beauclerc House was to be sold at last, thus Tony and Charlotte were giving a final, huge party in a home already emptied of most of its fine furniture.

It was the party of the season, of the year which was 1967.

'Interesting people, no matter where they come from, are what counts,' said Tony firmly, earlier that evening, before the guests had arrived. 'None of that old nonsense about class and who's in society. I can't bear it. So old-fashioned. We're all equal now.' He did not mean it, did not even believe it, but it was the mood of the time.

6

The room where they were talking was on the second floor, above the ballroom and the library, both of which were arranged for the party. A staircase lined with flowers in tubs had been specially built to lead from the library to the flood-lit garden. Charlotte had her own flat overlooking the Thames.

'It's a good thing you've got me, Tony, to keep your feet on the ground. Without me you'd float away like a balloon.' She said it lovingly.

Tony gave her a bright, blue stare from his slightly prominent eyes, the eyes which Gainsborough had painted in the Fourth Duchess. 'Think so?'

'Know so.' She strolled about the room, a restless spirit, as always. 'Don't look at me like that. It's not one of your kind looks.'

'This better?' He kissed her throat.

'Yes, much better,' she murmured. Her throat was a specially sensitive area, as Tony knew. Her first lover, Jehan, had once tried to strangle her, she had confided, and even this had been almost a pleasure for a while.

When she designed a dress or a blouse, Charlotte gave the neck a little flutter of frills or lace, unconsciously underlining what was to her an important feature. Her own neck was white and soft.

Tony kissed her again. She could not see his eyes, but he was looking over her shoulder in a particularly concentrated manner, as if assessing something. You could see that look in the very first Duke, who had made a fortune out of the South Sea Bubble when all the other speculators had gone down into penury.

'Our guests will be arriving any minute,' she said.

'So they will.' Suddenly he released her.

Below them they could hear the steady plod back and forth of the caterers' feet (Searcys, of course) and the voice of Smithers who had been butler to Tony's father and was now major-domo in chief to Tony himself.

'That must have been the band arriving.' Charlotte had been listening. 'I've got Tommy Jackman for the main band, with a steel band in the garden—oh, and did I tell you I'd got the Stones for the last two hours? Hope they come.'

Upstairs were several floors of bare room after bare room. You could almost feel the echoes of emptiness as if the rooms were ringing to their own chimes like a glass that has been struck once, then goes on ringing.

'Let's go upstairs.' Tony stroked her hair, the soft, silky black hair that always had a shine on it, as if Charlotte polished it with a silk handkerchief.

'We ought to go down.'

'Upstairs,' he insisted.

'There's nothing upstairs.'

'I know a room. I'll show you.' He was leading her by the hand, Charlotte demurring

8

softly, but willing to be led. 'There's a bed up there.'

It was a servant's room, high up in the eaves, with a small window overlooking an inner court. It had a square of carpet, an old-fashioned wash-stand, and, as Tony had said, an iron bedstead.

'How did you know about this?' Charlotte was looking around her in amazement.

'Never you mind.' He was undressing her, shaking away the delicate chiffon frill of hand-painted silk that she wore across her breasts.

'This is my home, after all.'

'Don't tear the silk.' Charlotte moved her shoulder carefully.

'I'll buy you another.'

'You can't buy another in time for tonight. Jassy Behren designed and painted the bodice especially for me. See it's a butterfly.'

'Your breasts are my butterflies.' He was kissing them.

'Oh Tony, this is against all the rules.'

'You're laughing. You know it isn't. We make the rules.'

'Those are our guests downstairs arriving. I can hear them.'

Tony laughed. He always laughed when he made love, but gently and softly as if he was happy. He had taught Charlotte to laugh too, something which she had not learnt with Jehan. Charlotte believed she made him happy.

9

She hadn't laughed a lot with Jehan, he had been so desperately serious himself. Also, he had been her first lover, with whom, for a good part of their year or so together, she had been tentative and unsure. Beside Jehan's frantic creativity (hair, faces, total look), he had influenced them all with the snip of his barber's scissors. Charlotte had felt a minor character. But deep inside herself she had also felt that a hard kernel of talent inside her was waiting to crack open.

I'll be a whole waving forest one day, she told herself one day when Jehan had been particularly dismissive, when he's a burnt out match; a bit of spent tinder.

It was only when she was angry with Jehan she had such thoughts, at all other times she respected his talents.

At Jehan's side she had moved into the world inhabited by people like Tony Beauclerc. She found they liked her, and when the break came, they took her side against Jehan.

She had already won a prize for a suit design from The British Style Centre together with a contract for its production. Possibly it was this success, the feeling that Charlotte was about to draw ahead of him that had made Jehan so violent towards her. The spirit of the times had caused people like Jehan and Charlotte to be asked to dinner at places where they would once have used the trademen's entrance, but their invitations had 'talent' marked on them, and talent was the price they had to pay. It made for competitiveness and the sharp cutting edge. Jehan had felt this pressure and had passed it on to Charlotte with the back of his hand.

In the end Jehan had hit her that once too often, had blacked her eye and stormed out of their shared apartment, never to find her there waiting again.

Tony Beauclerc had offered to horsewhip him for her.

'No, thank you,' Charlotte had said.

At least, this is what the newspapers had reported. It was not one of the stories that Charlotte told herself, but pictures of her, looking pale, enigmatic sunglasses hiding the black eye, appeared in the London *Evening Standard*, suitably headlined.

'She's a bloody masochist,' Jehan had said some time later, when he met Tony in Blades. They were both being fitted for more or less identical anthracite-grey silk suits. 'You'll find out.'

It was her vitality that drew people towards Charlotte, as well as her talent. Also, her elegant, slant-eyed beauty which she emphasised with kohl, long before anyone else was using it.

Jehan's name was never mentioned between Tony and Charlotte, but the expression on her face at times of love-making sometimes said

11

much. It was a sad look. Tony, not an imaginative man, wondered if every one of her lovers would leave a legacy on Charlotte's face, and what his bequest would be.

She was laughing now, as he took her, utterly confident of her power over him. She had come a long way since she had arrived on the London scene in Jehan's company, from an origin about which she was vague, providing different details of how she had grown up at different times.

Charlotte thought about Jehan more than she admitted, although now was hardly the moment, with Tony forcing her to a shuddering climax, and the noise of the band tuning up down below. This is no time to be bouncing about on a broken-down bed in a servant's room, she thought, giving a soft laugh.

A few minutes later, they ran down the stairs to the burgeoning party. Charlotte's skin above her butterfly dress was as pale as ever under her gleaming hair, but Tony had a pink flush under his tan. Diana de Marche, who knew him, noticed and drew her own conclusions.

Tony and Charlotte went round their friends, greeting them carefully. For Diana there was a special welcome because she unconsciously exacted one, no one overlooked Diana.

All was light and movement, with the band

banging out its strident rhythm, women with flowery silks swinging from their shoulders (pretty, meadowy prints were newly in fashion) as they shook and twisted opposite their partners in the dance. The men, too, were showing a flash of colour, here a bright brocade waistcoat, there a lace jabot at the throat. The influence of the continental designers was making its impact on the traditional style of Savile Row. The men at this party still bought their clothes, in the main, at the tailors their fathers and grandfathers had used, but they were also buying clothes at new firms with bright new young men at work. Perhaps the standard of tailoring was not so meticulous, but there was a dash that their generation demanded.

As for the women, they were shopping everywhere: Paris, Rome, Florence, but just lately London was setting the pace.

Charlotte usually designed and sometimes made her own clothes; she was dressing a small discerning circle. Tonight's dress from Jassy Behren was a present from a friend. Jassy had wanted to make sure of an invitation to this party of the year and to bring a companion. Jassy got her invitation, but her friend didn't. Tony put his foot down, as he said, 'No. I'm not a prude, darling, but that lesbian is entirely too much.'

'Jassy loves her.'

'That's Jassy's problem.'

Jassy still came to the party, and indeed could be seen now, talking hopefully to Diana who was friendly to all and loving to none. So many generations of selective breeding lay behind Diana that she was related to everyone she wished to be related to and obliged to be polite to none.

Charlotte put down her glass and spun on her heel. 'Let's dance.'

'No.' Tony's eyes had switched to the door. 'There's someone I want to talk to.'

Charlotte's gaze followed his, to the tall, thin man wearing dark-rimmed spectacles; he looked elegant, but cold. Her expression changed, the joy in it dimming. 'Oh, him. Charles Scrope. I didn't ask him.'

'Well, I did. Not that Charles needed to be asked. As one of my oldest friends, and my estate trustee to boot, he knows he's always welcome.'

The Beauclerc estate straddled London, solidly based in rich, thickly-populated areas of the city. Charles Scrope was a landowner himself in Norfolk, and his family had been associated with Tony's for generations. The first Beauclerc Duke had hired an earlier Scrope as steward. Charles had been at Eton with Tony, then Cambridge, after which he had shot off to Harvard, while Tony had stayed at home. Charles was reputed to be one of the best brains in the City.

The reproof, reprimand even, registered

14

with Charlotte, who was irritated. 'Not with me, he isn't. He doesn't like me.'

'Doesn't matter whether he does or not.' Tony was indifferent.

'He stopped you buying me Redmond & Bruce.'

For some months since, this had been a contention between them. Redmond & Bruce was an old established couture house now past its prime. Redmond had long gone, but there was still a Bruce at the helm: James Bruce, son of the company's founder.

Earlier in the year, it became known that the major shareholder in Redmond & Bruce, an anonymous sleeping partner, was soon going to be open to offers. Charlotte had gone there, ostensibly to buy a dress, but really to look things over with a view to persuading her lover to buy it for her. She would repay the loan, naturally. Tony had refused, however, and, as far as Charlotte knew, the shares had not yet changed hands.

'No one stopped me. No one stops me doing anything I want to do. It was something I was never going to do for you.' His voice had a cold flick in it. 'Besides, I did see you got the basement floors in the same location to set up on your own.'

In the garden floor of the eighteenth-century house in Mayfair where Redmond & Bruce hung on to their place in the fashion world, Charlotte had established a small business where she designed and made hats, blouses and soft dresses, what the trade calls "flou"—under the Butterfly name.

'Excuse me, will you? I must go across and talk to Charles. We have some business to discuss.'

'Business? This is party time!' But the protest was unavailing. Tony had gone, was already threading his way through the dancers, giving a smile here and a wave there, but easily avoiding stopping to talk, and never losing sight of his objective.

He looked like a man going somewhere purposefully. More than one person present thought so.

Diana detached herself from her partner, who was boring anyway, and came across to talk to Charlotte. 'Have you heard the news about Jehan?'

'He's killed himself?' said Charlotte hopefully. While he was alive she always had the fear that she might go back to him.

'No!'

'He's got married?' Not much protection there, but some.

'No. He's gone bankrupt.'

Charlotte felt a pang. Apparently it was still possible for her to feel sorry for Jehan. 'I'd almost rather he'd done either of the other two things. I did love him, Diana.'

'Try and forget him.' Diana was a realist.

'I do, most of the time.' Charlotte's gaze

16

flicked towards Tony, still deep in conversation with Charles Scrope. Diana's gaze followed her; she sketched a minute shrug.

'You won't try to help him?' The realist speaking again.

Charlotte took her time in replying, although she knew her answer.

'Probably. My own money; my little business is doing well. Tony won't like it, of course.'

'No,' Diana said briefly. 'I shouldn't let that worry you.' She turned back her gaze to Tony. 'Not that I'm in favour of you helping Jehan, but just don't let Tony be the arbiter. It's not good for him.'

A waiter offered a tray of drinks. Charlotte waved him away. 'Oh, Tony's easy. The only thing that he hasn't agreed to since we've been together was to buy Redmond & Bruce for me. And I think that was because he was frightened my work might come to mean more to me than he does.'

'And would it?'

Charlotte just shrugged.

Diana said, 'Has he mentioned marriage?'

'No ... It's on his mind, though. I can tell. He keeps talking about what the estates mean to him, and how he loved the big house as a boy.'

'All the family love that place. Always have. Full of old cousins.'

17

'I've hardly been there,' said Charlotte absently. 'I suppose I'm a London person.'

When the next waiter came round she took an egg stuffed with caviare. She loved them; they were as far away from the food of her childhood as she could get. When one was eating an egg stuffed with black caviare one was a different person from the girl who had gone hungry to bed.

'Supper will be served in about an hour,' she said. 'Buffons are doing the food in the garden tent, and also breakfast.' She had decided to use two caterers, Buffons as well as Searcys. 'But I want to talk to you about sleeves.' Charlotte's work was never far from her mind. 'I've got a brilliant idea for sleeves for the spring. Could you get some photographs in *Vogue*, do you think?' Diana had contacts everywhere.

'My question is answered.' Diana's tone was dry. 'Work does come first.'

'Not always, not all the time.'

'Often enough.'

Charlotte said suddenly: 'How did you find out about Jehan?'

'He told me himself,' Diana replied. 'It will be in the newspaper under his real name of James Edward Henty,' she went on. 'Did you know he was called that?'

Charlotte nodded silently. There was a pause, and then she said: 'Thank God I got out. I might have stayed, even married him, and

18

missed Tony. You know how we came together, Tony and I? He saw me crying, walking up and down the Embankment. We had met the night before, at the Rondo Club, and he remembered seeing how upset I was as Jehan and I left, in the middle of an argument. I didn't tell Tony we'd been arguing about him!' Charlotte smiled. 'Anyway, he thought I was going to throw myself in the river. I wasn't. I was mad with anger and Jehan had given me a black eye, but I was not planning to jump. Tony was so sweet. We took off from there.'

'For Paris, as I remember,' said Diana. Tony had been going to dine with her that night; she hadn't seen him for a month.

'Yes. Then Venice. I'd never seen Venice. I loved it. You ought to see it with a lover. I saw my first Fortuny dress in Venice. *What* a designer.'

Back to her real love, thought Diana. 'So … How are things between you and Tony?'

'Oh … Fine. Fine.'

There was an awkward little silence.

'You don't mind me asking?' Diana queried.

'No, indeed.' Diana's being *kind* to me, thought Charlotte. That was vaguely worrying.

People were passing up and down the great staircase, while the ballroom shook to movement, the whole house vibrated to music and lights.

Although the press had not been invited,

19

several journalists had found their way in, and photographs were taken. Photographs may not lie, but they do not always tell the accurate truth.

The staircase had been lined with red and white flowers in huge porcelain tubs. In the great days, a footman had stood on each step, but even Tony could not afford this now, nor were the footmen to be found, not of matching height and size such as had been the requirement of the old Duke. They had considered hiring out-of-work actors, but had decided it would be a show-off, so Charlotte had stationed an army of flowers.

Charlotte started towards the upper flights of stairs.

'Where are you going?' asked Diana.

'To change for supper. I have a dress like a golden birdcage,' called Charlotte over her shoulder. 'I think that's only fair, don't you? Jassy's dress first, then mine.' But Charlotte knew this was not the truth. Inside she was saying: I have to get away and think over Jehan's losses, and I see Tony coming.

It was this change of dress that caused the trail of ruined dresses to start.

Tony kissed Diana on each cheek. 'Where she's off to?'

'To change her dress.'

Tony nodded. 'To one of her own design, I expect. She never misses a trick. Proper little professional. I *think* I admire it.'

'But you didn't buy her Redmond & Bruce.'

Tony frowned. Certain areas were closed territory. 'No. What a lot you know about, Diana.'

'Yes.' She put a slight emphasis on the word. 'What about you slipping up and changing into something fresh?'

'Oh—an English gentleman doesn't do that sort of thing,' said Tony lightly.

'But you're not an English *gentleman*, are you, Tony? You're an English duke.'

There was a silence.

'I see you do know something.'

Diana shrugged. 'Jamie Bruce is a friend of mine. Has been for years. Naturally he knows.'

At this moment Charlotte reappeared in her dress like a golden birdcage by Tony's side. He put an arm around her bare shoulder, looking at her affectionately. 'You've been quick.'

'Come and eat in the library.' She smiled.

The library had been turned into a Turkish tent, hung with carpets and embroideries brought back by Tony's great-great grandfather when he had been Ambassador to the Sublime Porte in Istanbul and had talked to Disraeli about peace in Europe.

Gilt tables were placed here, close, because the library was not a huge room, where many must be seated. Someone had suggested making the food purple, red and gold to match the decor, but Charlotte's innate good taste had prevented this, so she had ordered a classic

21

hot weather menu: watercress soup, salmon mousse and smoked turkey, with a cold raspberry soufflé as pudding.

It was late in the season, the strawberries were over and raspberries better anyway, Charlotte said. They drank champagne again, but there was claret and hock for those who chose. So, in a way, they got the purple, red and gold colour scheme anyway.

As soon as Tony and Charlotte had seated themselves, the tables around them filled up. Everyone greeted the two of them politely, some even affectionately, although they had all said hello to their host and hostess as they arrived. It was that sort of party: polite, in spite of what the papers were to say later. Besides, they wanted to be asked again, even if not to this house where no more parties would be held.

There were people from Tony's orthodox world. Old friends like Diana and Charles, relations like the Loungueville twins, wild as wolves, and mad with it, but seen everywhere, and distinguished members of *la jeunesse d'orée*, like Sigismund de Rath and Bellina Vigny. But with these mixed denizens of Charlotte's world of fashion. One of the model girls for Hartnell had entered, having borrowed a white satin *robe-de-style* from the house. She was hoping no one would step on it or spill wine. No great beauty, yet no woman wore a gown the way she did. Charlotte admired her, too. All her guests had been chosen for their professionalism.

A group quickly gathered together at Tony's table. Charlotte had taken her own table close by so that conversation passed easily back and forth between the two parties.

She raised her eyebrows when she saw the crowd Tony had with him. Only to be expected, she thought. What she called the Chelsea Gang had settled around him.

She knew where the origin of this little group lay. To begin with, they were born into the same set of families, with long connections. Their parents and their grandparents had known each other, played with each other, then married each other. There was the implied assumption that their descendants would do the same.

If their backgrounds were similar, then so was the way they had been brought up. They had cut their teeth on similar teething rings purchased at Asprey's or Tessier's, while their nannies had met and gossiped together; they had gone to the same dancing class, Madam Vacani's or Miss Ballantine's, learning to point a pretty toe, then to bow or curtsy according to sex. Both sexes naturally learnt the all-important steps of the Scottish dances, a skill Charlotte still lacked and always would.

They had all gone on to different, but similar, schools, then universities, reuniting at parties and holiday times. No wonder they joined formation in adult life; it was just another party.

When they had all finished eating, Charles Scrope who had, somehow, got a seat at Charlotte's table, stood up and asked Charlotte to dance.

She agreed, although she did not count him among her friends, and was surprised he should ask: almost unconsciously she realised that there were those who lined up on Tony's side, and those on hers. Charles might be called the captain of Tony's team.

Charles was a good dancer, and the dance, a jolly quick-step from the Twenties called "Blue Eyes," was easy to move to. She found she was enjoying herself; that is, her body was, for she still found no desire to have her mind communicate with Charles. What could they say to each other, except to discuss Tony?

'I'm glad your business is doing so well,' said Charles. 'I saw the balance sheets the other day. Splendid. I congratulate you.'

'Thank you.' Better not ask how he had seen her accounts. Charles saw everything connected with Tony and money. 'I suppose a good balance sheet is like a poem to you.'

Charles moved her expertly out of a tight corner between two couples converging from opposite directions. Then he said: 'Not really, but everyone has their own skills. I just like to use mine, as you do also. I was congratulating you on the expertise with which you do so. You

24

have a business head as well as creative talent, an unusual combination.'

'Sorry. Ungracious of me.'

'You could never be that.' He smiled overhead as they danced. He knew she did not like him, and he understood why. 'Charles—Charlotte—we do rather well together, don't we?'

'Mmm,' Charlotte murmured without committing herself. Charles is being nice to me, she thought. First Diana, now Charles.

Charles relinquished her at the end of the dance. 'I enjoyed that, thank you. Don't forget, if you ever need advice, just ask me.'

'About money?'

'About anything.'

'Yes. Sure.' But who needed advice when they had Tony?

She went across to him in a sudden rush of affection, and pushed her arm through his.

'Forgive me a moment,' he said, disentangling himself. 'Smithers wants a word.' He went off with the old servant.

Diana was pushing her way through the crowded room towards her. Behind her some sort of commotion seemed to be taking place at the door to the ballroom.

More gate-crashers Charlotte supposed, only surprised that they should arrive so late. But there were one or two other parties on that night. Some people, not the most loved, went the rounds.

Diana got to her. 'It's Jehan. He's come here, he insists on seeing you.'

'What shall I do?'

'Normally, I'd say go and speak to him. Calm him down and get rid of him ... But I simply don't trust you with him.'

Charlotte was white. 'No, that's all over.'

'So you say.'

'I must let him go out as a person with dignity,' said Charlotte tightly.

Diana watched her walk towards the door. She was stepping carefully as if walking through a mine-field.

Tony suddenly appeared behind her. 'What's up?'

Diana shook her head. She wasn't going to say. It was his party, his woman, let him find out. 'I think she's dealing with unwanted guests.'

'Can't the servants do that? I suppose I'd better go.'

Diana put out a restraining hand. 'I shouldn't. Look Tony, here's Imogen weaving this way, drunker than ever. Let's get out of her way. Dance with me.'

They danced in silence for a while. Then Tony said: 'It's Jehan Treharne, isn't it? I've always wanted to give him a black eye.'

'He might give you one. He's very big.'

Outside the ballroom door Charlotte was face to face with Jehan. He was flanked on either side by one of the servants hired for the

26

evening, while Smithers, the Beauclerc butler, stood by.

Jehan looked an angry man. A big man, with a thatch of black hair, and broad shoulders, Jehan was normally well-groomed, with shirt, suit and shoes in immaculate order. Where once he had had the sheen of a healthy animal, now he looked dishevelled.

'It's all right, Smithers. You can leave us,' Charlotte said.

She led Jehan into a small room which had been the last Duchess's sitting room, a place of pale blue and gold, now empty of its French furniture.

She closed the door and stood with her back to it, hanging on to the door knob in case she wanted to escape fast. She thought it might be necessary; she couldn't bear to see Jehan like this. It touched her more deeply than she wanted to admit.

'What is it?'

Jehan looked around. 'Isn't there somewhere to sit? And couldn't I have a drink? God, I'm tired. Do you know what I've been doing for the last forty-eight hours? Going about from debtor to debtor trying to rake in some of *my* money to stave off bankruptcy. *Me*. Jehan Treharne.'

He continued angrily, 'Now I come to this bloody place and there's nowhere to sit!'

'What do you want from me?'

For answer he threw a shining emerald and

27

diamond jewel upon the floor. It was in the shape of a lizard with emeralds for eyes, while the body was of pavé diamonds and cabochon emeralds.

'I gave you that object. You can't say I wasn't generous. And when we split you threw it back with the rest. Not because I asked for it, but because you said you did not want anything of mine.'

Charlotte licked her lips as if they were dry. She bent down to pick up the jewel which was surprisingly light in her hand. Only, perhaps to her, the surprise wasn't so great. 'Yes, I remember.'

'Only, it's not real.' He spaced out the words slowly and bitterly. 'Not any longer, although it was when we bought it. When I tried to sell it today, took it back to Asprey's, they kindly told me it was paste. All the stones had been replaced by imitations. What you gave me back was a fucking fake! You've *taken* from me. And I need that money now.'

The bracelet had been a gift, but some gifts should not be taken for granted. And there *had* been some anger in her heart when she had sold the stones. She sighed. 'I think you may have the wrong idea of the way things stand. All right, I do live here a lot of the time. But I don't live on Tony, any more than I did on you. This time I've had the sense to take my own apartment, which I pay for. I keep myself, Jehan.'

'Out of the business *he* bought.'

'I'm shall pay him back. It was a loan only.'

Jehan took hold of one of her wrists, hard. With her free hand, Charlotte groped for the door handle again.

'Charlotte—' he was turning her wrist. 'You don't get the point. I want the money. *Now.*'

She struggled for control. Any sign of fear from her only produced more violence in Jehan. She kept her voice level.

'Jehan, I know you can't help being violent. I know it goes back to things in your childhood which you've told me about. Contrary to what you say, I don't like it. Let me go.'

Jehan tightened his grasp, but stopped twisting her wrist. Charlotte gritted her teeth. Tomorrow, as she knew of old, she would have a bruise, stretching right up her arm, and the knowledgeable would shrug and refer to Jehan's love-twist.

The door opened quickly, pushing Charlotte forward, and Tony came in. He closed the door behind him with care.

'Your guests are outside waiting for you, my dear.' He did not sound friendly.

'Oh, but—' began Charlotte.

'Mr Treharne is leaving.'

'Tony, listen, please.'

'Mr Treharne is leaving,' he repeated, and turned to Jehan. In a tone of inherited insolence which had taken generations to produce, he said: 'Let me show you out.'

'He thinks I owe him some money,' said Charlotte hastily. 'That's all he came for.'

'No. You don't owe him anything.'

'Perhaps I do.' Charlotte was troubled.

'Then he can send in his account like any other tradesman and it will be settled in the usual way.'

There was a silence in the room, while outside the party throbbed on. It sounded as if the Stones had arrived, and were performing. The noise had reached that level.

Jehan and Tony stared at each other. It was Tony who dropped his gaze first. He masked the movement by shaking his head and turning away. 'Please go.'

Jehan had pulled himself together. 'Right, I'm going. But I know where I am now. I was down and you kicked me. Thanks. I shan't forget.'

'Jehan—' began Charlotte.

'Don't make a speech,' he was full of cold rage, 'I'm your enemy now. And if I can do you any damage, I will. You can take that from me.' He buttoned his jacket and tidied himself up as if putting on armour. At the door he paused, and gave Charlotte a last look.

Sometimes you sow dragon's teeth, she thought, and sometimes they are sown for you. I think that's just what happened to me now. I might have saved the situation between me and Jehan, but Tony's intervention tipped the scale.

For some reason the image made her laugh. Tony looked at her. 'Occasionally I think you *must* have Japanese blood in you.'

'Why?'

'Because you baffle me.' He took her arm. 'And you laugh when I don't expect it. Come on, Madame Butterfly.' He sounded half affectionate, half exasperated as he led her back to the party.

*　　*　　*

The party was ending. By this time most of the guests had crammed themselves into the garden, which was big for London, but still not the size of the grounds at Buckingham Palace.

Charlotte stood watching, letting the emotional reverberations of the scene she had just been through die away.

She turned back to look into the house. In the ballroom a few dancers were slowly moving around, as if they were no longer interested in what they were doing, but did not know how to stop. Their livelier fellow-guests had departed for the garden and the Stones, leaving them behind. The band which had been playing in there all night had mysteriously halved in size. No one knew where the missing performers had gone to, or if they would come back.

The flowers on the great staircase, that once proud army of red and white, were wilting, their bright petals falling to the pale carpet like

31

exclamations with little punctuations spots of white lilac.

It's strange, Charlotte thought, how people disappear as a party draws to an end. For a while you feel the party will go on for ever, never stop, and and then, suddenly, people are gone. One isn't conscious of them saying goodbye, or walking through a door, they are just no longer there.

From the marquee in the garden, floated the mingled smells of coffee, bacon with a hint of grilled kipper. Here was where most of the remaining company were now gathered. Presently, they too would go home, leaving the odd drunk asleep in the garden.

Tony appeared throu⸝ h the door. 'I was searching for you.'

Charlotte drank some orange juice. It was still cool and iced even at this late hour, a tribute to the excellence of her planning. She caught sight of her face reflected in a looking-glass, and at once opened her handbag. 'I must repair my make-up. My face has gone all peculiar.'

'You look delightful,' said Tony, whom drink and fatigue always made amorous. He studied her speculatively.

'It's dawn.' Charlotte yawned. 'Even Diana has gone. Without saying goodbye. Or perhaps she did and I've forgotten. Could be. There's a kind of mist in my mind over the middle of the night. Did we really have one? I can't seem to

32

remember ... Let's leave, Tony.'

'Yes,' he said, without hesitation. 'I want to make love to you.'

'Let's go to my apartment,' suggested Charlotte dreamily, 'and make love by the open window overlooking the river. I love the river.'

They left hand in hand.

* * *

They made love by the opened window with the river sounds floating through, just as Charlotte had wished. The birds, who never ceased their chatter all that summer night were whistling and calling on the trees outside.

Ten minutes later, Tony opened his eyes, sat up briskly, then started to get dressed. Charlotte watched him silently.

He sat down on the edge of the bed to address her. 'There's something I have to tell you.'

She opened her eyes wide.

'I'm going to be married,' he said.

Charlotte stared. Silent. Bewildered. Stunned into immobility.

'The announcement will be in *The Times* tomorrow.' He thought about it. 'Today really, I suppose.'

At last Charlotte managed to say, 'Who?'

'The Princess Sophia von Rothenberg ... Her mother was my father's cousin. You've

33

seen her at Redmond & Bruce. She worked there for a bit.'

'*That* was why you wouldn't buy it for me,' said Charlotte from between stiff lips; she felt half paralysed.

'I wouldn't buy it for you, because I already own it. Or most of it. However, as you will now realise, I hope to be selling my interest soon. All my finances will have been gone into on my marriage. I must reorganise, Charles says.'

'Charles says, Charles says,' shouted Charlotte.

If she hadn't managed to shout she might have burst into tears, and that she would not do. I haven't known him at all, she realised, I have never known the real Tony. How can he sit there, talking cold-bloodedly in this way to *me*?

'Leave my keys when you go,' she said.

'Charlotte—' Tony began.

'And you'd better go now.' She rolled over, her face pressed into the pillow.

'Goodbye darling,' she said under her breath, but she wouldn't look as he left.

Suddenly she wasn't saying goodbye to Tony at all, but to herself. 'Goodbye, happy Charlotte, goodbye.'

At the moment all she felt was anger and humiliation. Later the pain would come and she would discover exactly how much she had loved Tony. There would be plenty of pain.

Poor old Madame Butterfly, indeed.

CHAPTER TWO

Somewhat to her surprise, almost against her will, Charlotte had slept for two hours after Tony had left. She thought about some of the things her friends had done when similarly abandoned:

Cut off the trouser legs of his suits.

Burn down the house.

Pour concrete all over the place.

Or I could run up a great red phallic flag, she mused.

And then she laughed. Sanity was coming back. It was the first step in her recovery.

She went into the kitchen and made some tea. Her eye fell on the calendar. It was the third Wednesday in the month. How could she have forgotten? No she had not forgotten, the thought of this third Wednesday had always been there.

She washed the cup and the teapot and tidied the kitchen. When she made these Wednesday visits, she wanted everything behind her and to be clean, neat, and orderly. In a universe that could appear to be very disorderly, she felt the need to exercise what control she could.

Charlotte dressed herself carefully in a printed cotton dress with a full pleated skirt. The dress was red and white because this was the colour that appealed to those she going to visit.

She took a bus at the end of the street which deposited her a few hundred yards from where she wanted to go.

There it was, quiet brick building with a board proclaiming it the Adelina Clinic for Sick Children.

Founded at the turn of the century it had been called the Princess Adelina Home for Crippled Children. Times and attitudes had changed and the hospital's name with it. But then, and now, it was always affectionately, 'the Addie'.

The Adelina was housed in a building of dark brick but it was not a place of gloom. Inside it was painted in bright primary colours: red, blue and daffodil-yellow. Nor was it silent, but rang with shouts and laughter.

It was a small hospital as these things go with only four wards: the Edith, the Lucy, the Victoria, and the Peter. Boys did get a bit of a look-in as one small patient observed.

The porter opened the heavy swing doors, smiling at her. 'Morning, Miss. Punctual as ever.'

'I nearly forgot this morning.'

'Not you, Miss. You're here, aren't you?' He smiled. 'I see you've brought your usual presents.'

'Yes, I stopped on the way.' Under Charlotte's arm was tucked a number of brightly coloured children's comic magazines.

36

She knew that a few of the staff thought such comics too frivolous, but she thought they did the children good. A laugh was a laugh however ill you were.

Not all the small patients stayed in the Addie for long. Some came for a week or so to give their parents a rest, others stayed longer for treatment, and one or two came to die. In this last category there were few, because the Addie seemed to inspire survival even in those terminally ill.

Just a few children lived in the Addie. Charlotte was one of their favourite visitors. She spoke to every child as she walked through, but there was one child she held always in her mind.

Sarah was not always awake, she slept a lot, resting her difficult body, but she had plenty of energy once alert, moving and manipulating her limbs to do what she wanted; she was a fast mover. She was highly intelligent, and her closest friend was Maisie, who no longer had speech; was trapped inside her own private prison. For her, brightness, joy, comprehension, ebbed away a little every day.

Charlotte liked to take Maisie on her lap while she talked to Sarah. Sometimes the two had an animated conversation, but sometimes they were silent. Charlotte valued these wordless conversations in which body talked to body, in which Maisie, as she pressed heavily into Charlotte, could join.

APPOMATTOX REGIONAL LIBRARY
HOPEWELL, VIRGINIA 23860
07/97

Touch counts, Charlotte told herself, stroking Maisie's face. 'This for love,' she said, as one finger traced a line down Maisie's cheek, 'this for love.'

Sarah leaned forward, bending from the hips, into position, so she could imitate Charlotte, dividing her strokes up between Charlotte and her friend Maisie.

'Goodbye you two,' Charlotte said, gently pressing each head. Sarah looked at her alertly. 'I'm not crying for you, baby, but for myself.'

Charlotte had no illusions. One day she would go into the Addie and be told in a quiet voice that Maisie was dead. Or Sarah. But she thought Maisie would go first.

She took a different bus, and got out near Park Lane. Then she walked to Beauclerc House. With relief, she saw that there were no cars outside.

For a minute she paused to stare upward at the building: a plain brick front, typical of its period with three windows on each side of the big door, and above, another two rows of windows, regularly spaced, but as classical perfection demanded, diminishing slightly in size toward the roof. In the roof were more windows, evenly spaced. The flagpole was above.

She had never had a key, but she knew from experience that the basement door down the concrete steps was not locked. One pushed hard until it gave.

The huge kitchen was empty; no cooking had gone on in it for years. Tony had installed a modern, smaller kitchen on the ground floor.

She made her way upwards through the silent, empty house with the debris of the party still about it, to collect her things. After packing them up, she went through the small door which led to the roof. She stepped out on to the platform for the flagpole.

Her favourite view of London lay before her.

Above, a pale blue sky.

Then, she turned her back on it, and left Beauclerc House for the last time.

*   *   *

Once in her own flat, she took a shower (she loved the Addie, but somehow you had to wash it off), sprayed on some Guerlain—L'heureblu it was just now—and made a large pot of tea.

The telephone rang at intervals but she ignored it. Her door bell rang several times, once persistently. She ignored that too.

She was drinking a cup of tea by the window, wearing a silk dressing gown from Charvet which had belonged to her now ex-lover. It smelt of him, of them both really, because a breath of Guerlain hung over it. Suddenly the door clicked behind her. Diana stood there.

'How did you get in?'

'A key, you fool. You gave me one ages ago in case you died in bed!'

39

'I have done,' said Charlotte turning round to look out of the window. 'Don't think I haven't. This is Lazarus you see.'

Diana ignored this. She always ignored Charlotte at her worst, her wildest and damndest, it was the reason they stayed friends.

'Where have you been?' demanded Diana. 'I was ringing and ringing on the phone before I burst in. But I only did that because I was worried.'

'I was out. I went to see someone.'

'Oh? Anyone I know?'

Charlotte shook her head. 'No.'

Diana did not persist; she knew that look on her friend's face. Something hidden there; one day she might find out what. But whatever it was, it was not a case of joy. 'I was worried; I thought you might have topped yourself because you had found out about Tony's engagement.'

'I thought of killing *him*!' Charlotte replied. 'Or perhaps I shall kill her. Have you noticed the way she holds her arms? Straight by her side.'

'That's because she was a model!'

'She looks as if she was waiting to be hanged. I thought I might do the job for her.'

'And you look so gentle and good!'

'I *am* gentle and good. I am also angry!'

'I'll say.'

Charlotte sank into a chair, suddenly

40

deflated. She guessed there was a whole world of emotion and pain to be discovered yet. A kind of city of feeling, stretched out for her to walk in all its multitude of highways, twisting paths that came to one spot, and culs-de-sac from which you could not climb out.

'I can't believe the way Tony behaved!' she exclaimed. 'Everything going on behind my back, settled and cut and dried, with no hint, no warning to me. *Then* telling me this just the night before the announcement.' A night in which they had made love twice, but she didn't say this to Diana, who had probably guessed anyway. 'It hardly seems human.'

'Tony isn't an ordinary human being,' said Diana slowly. 'That's something you have to remember. Brought up the way he was, with all that money, all that tremendous family background, encouraged to see himself as someone special, you could hardly expect he would be ... I'm not excusing him.'

'You almost expected him to behave badly,' accused Charlotte.

'Yes, I did.'

'You realised that in spite of all this equality and emancipation we're supposed to have, he put me and Sophia into two different categories; I could be treated in one way, and she in another.'

'It's quite unconscious, or almost so.'

'It's bloody Victorian,' said Charlotte angrily, brushing away a tear, with the back of

41

her hand. 'I ought to get dressed.' She looked around her. 'Tidy things up a bit.'

'Looks all right.'

Charlotte picked up an ebony hair brush and, walking into the bedroom to dress, said, 'I wonder if I will be able to afford to stay on here?' She had taken a short lease, paying the rent (which was high) herself. This had been manageable while her business flourished. Now she had to ask herself how much of that she owed to her relationship with Tony? How many customers had come to her because he was what he was, and she was known to be what she was to him? In the bathroom she had come across a blonde tortoise-shell comb with a matching hair-brush. Male objects. She gathered them up together with a couple of linen handkerchieves. Inevitably Tony had left things about. There was a little leather notebook and pencil on the bedside table. Nothing written in it, though. She added it to the other objects which she placed in a box.

Oh, Tony, she had thought, as she put the lid on, will I ever be able to look at the little everyday things you used to handle here without thinking of you?

They stared at each other: tall, leggy Diana, and shorter, slighter Charlotte, out of the two different social pockets, but friends.

'I feel a fool,' said Charlotte.

'I'd feel the same—oh well, you know about me and Albert Glasdeer; everyone does. I made a real fool of myself there. Which you have *not* done, darling Charlotte, if it's any comfort to you.'

'You knew yesterday what was coming, didn't you?'

'Not the timing,' said Diana quickly. 'Not that.'

'And Charles Scrope. He knew exactly.'

'I expect so. Old Charles always knows everything. He's not as bad as you think, you know.'

Charlotte sat down; she felt sick. She might actually be sick.

Diana was silent for a short while, then asked, 'What will you do?'

'Get on with living. What else is there to do?' Charlotte replied. '... And then there's Jehan. He wanted money from me, did you know that?'

Diana mutely shook her head.

'Well, he did. He had a right to ask, I suppose. Anyway, I've sent it. I shall have to see the bank about it. The cheque will about clear me out. And don't say, ask Tony.'

'I wasn't going to ... But you *could* see Charles. He's a wizard about money.'

'If there's a man I hate, it's Charles Scrope,' said Charlotte fiercely.

'Ah well, you have to know old Charles to like him,' Diana concluded.

She looked at Charlotte seriously for a moment, then suddenly and unexpectedly grinned. 'You do and say nothing my pet. Just look elegant and lovely. *I* will do what's necessary. My first job as your publicity agent.' She leaned forward and picked up the telephone. 'Isn't it lucky *I* adore the telephone?'

*   *   *

The next day the press was, in some ways, as bad for Charlotte as Diana had forecast. Reports revelled in the callous way Tony had abandoned her in order to marry the more 'suitable' Princess Sophia von Rothenberg.

Nevertheless Diana had done her work well, because side by side with the gossip paragraphs, most newspapers ran a serious account of Charlotte's style. They had been handed out to them by Diana, together with photographs of some garments.

A lot of unexpected people also telephoned with messages of friendship, or sent flowers. One of these was Charles Scrope.

He called before she left her apartment the next morning, not saying very much, but once again offering help.

'Thanks,' said Charlotte. She wondered if Diana had been on to him, but on the whole she thought not. She did not accept his offer.

When she went into work that day, resolved to be composed and bold as if nothing was being said against her, she expected a flood of

44

cancelled appointments. But it was not so. She was news.

In fact, as the day went on, and Val, her secretary, came and went with her appointments diary, Charlotte realised more work was coming in than on a normal day; far more. It was exhilarating.

She studied the list of appointments. Diana read it over her shoulder, giving a soft whistle at the sight of one or two of the names.

Charlotte handed the appointments diary back to Val. 'If they all come through with orders, then I am doing well.' Part of the response was due to curiosity, but there was another element of a desire to support, that was more complicated to assess. One couldn't tell how long all this attention would last. It might die down pretty quickly.

But the telephone continued to ring, and more casual customers dropped in to look over Charlotte's current collection than was usual. She forced herself to chatter away in her usual fashion. No one had the bad manners to say anything to her, either about Tony, or Jehan.

Mid-afternoon the following day, Val took a call, made an excited noise, and said: 'Please hold on, I'll get her.'

To Charlotte she said, 'Virginia Grace's secretary is on the line—she says Virginia would like to show some of your clothes in her half-hour slot after the early evening news. Can we get them round?'

Virginia Grace was a rising figure in the television world, coming to the front as a sharp and amusing figure. Quick with the apt word, she had been awarded her own programme. It was still a 'for women" show, (and Virginia Grace would move away as soon as she could) but it was granted prime viewing time and audience figures were good. She was reputed not to like rivals. But who did?

Charlotte did not answer for a moment.

'Can we?' pressed Val. She was very keen: her mother watched Virginia Grace every night. So did her boyfriend.

'Yes,' said Charlotte. 'Certainly we can. But only if I go along and appear as well. Tell her that and then come back to me.'

Val was soon back. 'She says yes.' She gave a sigh of satisfaction. 'You have to get the clothes round straight away, and be there thirty minutes before the show starts for a run through.'

Charlotte chose the models to present, carefully selecting a wide range of garments with an automatic efficiency that allowed her to think about other things while she did so, then dispatched them round to the TV studios in a taxi.

She had been surprised how she was able to push thoughts of Tony into the back of her mind. Sooner or later she would have to take her memories out of the deep freeze and deal with them. She suspected that there was going to be a lot of anger and resentment there to deal with when the anaesthesia wore off.

'Are you all right?' Val looked at her. 'You gave a shiver ... Want me to come too?'

Charlotte shook her head. Now she had to put all other preoccupations behind her and give her total concentration to the interview ahead.

*　　*　　*

Two hours later Diana arranged herself comfortably in front of her television set. She was sitting on the floor with her feet drawn up beneath her, a drink in one hand and a cigarette in the other. Once she had fixed up with Virginia that Charlotte was to have a place in the evening's interview rota, she had deliberately kept out of the way. She knew Charlotte would ask how she should handle Virginia, and that was a question she did not want to answer.

Charlotte's was the last interview of the evening, a good slot because Virginia saved her best energies for this one, in order to go out on a high note. But this meant the person waiting had time to become tense. Diana could see Charlotte *was* tense at first and felt tense herself as she watched.

Charlotte had changed into a dark blue and white spotted dress with the round white organza collar that was her mark that season,

47

and already much copied.

Virginia did the introduction with her usual skill, managing to imply but without actually saying so, that Charlotte was newsworthy apart from being a designer of beautiful clothes...

*　　*　　*

The venture proved to be a great success. Orders came flooding in; as did other media interest.

In the next few months Charlotte was able to see her dreams take a tangible shape. At moments she felt she could reach out her hand and touch success; at other times, it moved before her like a marsh light.

Though her order book was healthy, her bank book was still in the red: Jehan had cashed her cheque; her debt to him was paid, but it had cleaned her out. And though orders were coming in fast, raw materials, and the labour to fulfil the orders, had to be paid for first. Nor were her customers quick to pay. Clients such as these expected credit.

During this period, despite her success, Charlotte found that she sometimes felt sick and weak. She told herself it was just anxiety and tension. She would not admit to a private wretchedness over Tony.

Underneath, however, all the time, there was the distant cry of her body wanting to be heard.

It was important to keep this deadened into quietness by work. So Charlotte worked very hard. Diana helped her, by setting up all sorts of activities.

But there came a point when Charlotte's constant nausea caused her to consult her diary and, with a growing sense of disquiet, check the date of her last period...

* * *

Charlotte retained hidden inside herself the memory of what had subsequently taken place. One day she would take it out to examine, but not today.

Some things were with her now: the smell of disinfectant, the feel of warm blood. Physically nothing too bad, but emotionally much worse than she had expected.

The doctor had listened to her, and agreed that, if the circumstances were as she said, she was right to end the pregnancy.

During this time, Tony's wedding took place. So august an occasion was it that it might almost have been called his nuptials. It was almost the only word left unused by the newspapers who reported at length on the romance and marriage of the couple, together with their high births and combined great wealth.

There were plenty of photographs also, and a television interview in which Tony explained

49

that his bride would take on great responsibilities as his wife, but her birth and education had prepared her for this. (One year at a Swiss finishing school, and eighteen months at Redmond & Bruce, Diana had remarked, if that's an education).

Charlotte observed, with some hollow pleasure, that the bride's wedding dress, a design from Germany, did not suit her. She had a slender but difficult figure, of awkward proportions. 'Give her ten years and she's going to look like a giraffe,' Diana commented. Charlotte knew that Diana attended the wedding and bore her no ill-will for this act; Diana had to keep in with all parties. Always had done, always would.

She contented herself with dressing Diana superbly well, with the result that a number of discreet enquiries were made about the source of Diana's clothes.

Charlotte accepted the episode wryly as good business coming out of a private grief. It was all part of what was happening to her just now.

*   *   *

Charlotte had thought about money in the past, but never so often and never with so much concentration as she did now. She saw that the possession of the right amount at the right time was going to be vital to her success. How she was to acquire it had yet to be arranged. She had seen her bank manager once again, but the sum of money he was willing to advance was, Diana (and her own instincts) told her, not enough.

Seeing Diana more regularly than in the old days, she noticed that Diana, though generally equable and calm, underwent a mood-change in the late afternoon, becoming either dreamy and remote, or excited and euphoric. Inevitably Charlotte came to associate the change of mood with the cannabis Diana smoked at that time of day. She wondered if Diana knew how apparent her mood swings were.

'How many of those do you smoke?'

'None until after four o'clock. Four o'clock's tea time. Joke.' Diana giggled.

'I wish you wouldn't.' Charlotte disliked drugs.

'So *you* say.'

'Oh, everyone knows. The stuff's more harmless than drink. And I need it.' Diana could be self-righteous when she chose. 'I couldn't get on with my life if I didn't get some relief. It doesn't do me any harm, just cheers me up and soothes me down. It's not addictive; I'll stop the minute I so desire.'

'I wish you'd stop now. You have so much natural vitality. I don't know how you can risk it. To be naturally well and whole; a healthy body: it's the greatest blessing.'

There was an intensity in Charlotte's voice that embarrassed Diana.

'And naturally unhappy. You forget that,' she replied sharply. 'That's what I get relief from.'

Diana could have said that she was only modestly gifted when most of her chosen friends were extremely talented, but all she said was: 'I'm in love. Rottenly, wretchedly in love.'

'Oh, Diana.' They touched hands. 'Who?' Charlotte asked eventually, although she knew she shouldn't have.

'Rather not say.'

'Right.' But I'll watch, and find out, she decided.

Val walked in, and put a pad with notes of telephone calls on Charlotte's desk.

'Charles Scrope called, asking to see me,' Charlotte exclaimed. 'Lunch somewhere. Wonder what he wants?' He had left a number.

'I saw him at the wedding,' Diana said.

'Naturally.'

'He wasn't Tony's best man. Not quite grand enough. I think Charles minded that ... he seemed out of sorts ... I know what we'd like from him.'

'What's that?' Charlotte enquired.

'Money. Not his, although he has plenty. But all the lovely money he has access to. See what you can do, Charlotte.'

'Oh shut up.' Charlotte drew the piece of paper off the pad and threw the note away.

'One day I will get in touch with him. Maybe.'

Diana picked up the note, and carefully replaced it on Charlotte's desk.

CHAPTER THREE

There was one other person whose future was altered with Tony's marriage; altered drastically for the worse because of it, and that was James Bruce of Redmond & Bruce.

James Bruce had started his career in Savile Row, apprenticed in the old-fashioned way to a gentlemen's tailor. He had enjoyed the work but had soon realised where his real ambitions lay: he wanted to dress women. He liked women, and he thought he could create beautiful clothes for them.

Once again an apprenticeship was necessary. He chose to go to Paris, where he worked for a time in the House of Dior. There he learnt, somewhat to his surprise, he was still a tailor at heart, but that he could turn this to good account by making structured clothes, suits, coats and evening dresses for women.

What he could not do was what Charlotte was so supremely good at: creating a flowing softness that flattered the figure.

Later, one day in the Redmond & Bruce salon, he had seen a woman wearing a dress so delightful and so original that he had enquired about its origin, as he did not recognise the style.

'Oh a girl called Charlotte Chaudin,' came the reply.

James Bruce had made up his mind at that moment that he would like to work with Charlotte Chaudin. But that had been before his life had been turned upside down, and she had become a threat: to his future at Redmond & Bruce.

Charlotte thought about James Bruce occasionally, as having been her fellow traveller in the journey that had derailed them both. She had met him briefly when she had gone to Redmond & Bruce on that one occasion, and had received the distinct impression that he was not well disposed towards her.

Charlotte had been puzzled, but now she could understand. James Bruce had always known more of what was going on than she had done. To begin with he must have guessed that she wanted a major stake in Redmond & Bruce. But more probably he had already guessed Tony's intentions towards Sophia. How stupid she must have seemed to him in her ignorance. Probably the whole of London had known what she had not. That thought stung, even now.

Now, when Charlotte thought of James Bruce it was with the preparation laid for a solid dislike. It was certain that they would meet again as they worked in the same small territory, but Charlotte thought she could manage by tactfully avoiding him. It was really better there should be a kind of no-man's land between them on which neither trod. She hoped he would see it the same way.

Meanwhile, in the busy pre-Christmas party season of 1967, Butterfly's need of capital reached crisis point.

One morning, she had asked Val if the order of silks and wools from Duchesse Bros. had come in. These fabrics were needed to make up several of her most original models. She had used their fabrics a lot lately.

Uneasily, Val explained that no fabric had been delivered, because the bill for the last consignment was still outstanding.

Charlotte now recognised that she had to take Diana's advice and telephone Charles Scrope.

Expecting to be switched from secretary to secretary, she was surprised to find herself talking directly to Charles. He had left her the number of his private line. At once he asked her to lunch with him.

'Thursday week,' he said apologetically. 'I've got to go to New York in between. I hoped I'd hear from you sooner. I rang last week.'

'I've been busy,' said Charlotte evasively.

'Yes, well, I want to talk to you.'

Charlotte knew that she had to talk to him,

55

and about how to raise money, but he was there before her. 'I know you need money.'

Diana, thought Charlotte, she's told him.

'And I'm prepared to help. I'll transfer a sum of cash to you immediately. But also, you must expand: Tony hasn't sold his interest in Redmond & Bruce, yet. I suggest that with my help you buy it.' His last words on that momentous call were: 'Go and see him. James Bruce.'

Whether Charles heard Charlotte wail she would never know.

She had allowed herself almost to forget that James Bruce worked on the floors above hers; it was a fact she had wrapped up and consigned to semi-oblivion together with Tony's once beloved image, and Jehan's violence. Awkward facts *could* be put aside, Charlotte had discovered in her dangerous adolescence, if you were firm enough with them.

Charles must have contacted James Bruce immediately after their conversation: within an hour James had come running down the three flights of stairs from his establishment to hers, and banged on her door, coming in before he was asked, to encounter Charlotte at her desk.

'I've had Charles Scrope on my phone setting up a meeting between you and me. Why couldn't you do it yourself?'

'Well, you know,' began Charlotte.

'Too much of a coward, I suppose,' he exploded.

56

'Do sit down,' said Charlotte nicely. 'You are scattering all my papers.' They were in her tiny office, a mere slip of a room, so once in, he was inevitably very close. Although by no means as tall as either Tony or Jehan his physical presence was formidable. There had never been a man in this feminine sanctuary before, Charlotte suddenly realised. Tony had never ventured inside. This man seemed to fill it.

'Charles has got a bit ahead of himself, I'm afraid. He didn't tell me either.'

'I know you want Redmond & Bruce!' he accused. 'You wanted it before, but Beauclerc wouldn't give it to you. You didn't know that Beauclerc already had the majority interest in Redmond & Bruce at the time, did you?' He smiled cynically. 'But you do now, of course...'

Charlotte opened her mouth to speak, but got no chance.

James continued, 'Beauclerc bought out my previous partner, a few years ago. Charles Scrope fronted for him. It was a good arrangement at the time. Beauclerc was to be a sleeping partner, continuing to leave the running of the business to me.

'Wonderful, until Beauclerc decided to marry my fiancée himself. Did you know Sophia was going to marry *me*?'

To her horror, Charlotte found tears forming in her eyes.

57

'Obviously not,' James commented, tightly. 'And now Beauclerc is selling his majority shares to another designer, I shall lose creative control of my company too,' he concluded, accusingly.

Charlotte forced herself not to fight back. A deep sense that it was not then appropriate halted her.

She invited him to sit in the one comfortable armchair, and fetched him a stiff drink.

He had a genuine reason for anger, she could see that clearly enough.

She let him drink the whisky, while she sipped at tonic water and summed him up. He had curly black hair cut very short, and blunt features. The hair cut was attractive; Charlotte could see why it had been deemed suitable by antique Roman sculptors to use for the Emperor Augustus.

He doesn't like me, she thought, and I'm not sure if I like him, but this man is going to be tremendously important to me. Old ties and loyalties seemed to loosen. She was surprised at herself for this instantaneous reaction, surprised and a little shocked.

She watched James Bruce warily. 'You and I are going to have to work together, James,' she said in a voice of utter conviction. 'And, who knows? You may get to like it,' she challenged.

*   *   *

The following week she went to her lunch with Charles Scrope, and a whole new chapter in her life was opened.

CHAPTER FOUR

One of the things Charlotte was discovering was that everyone in her present world had more in their past than she realised. They had complicated lives. Charlotte was pursued by her own demons, but somehow she never expected other people to have theirs as well.

She got a hint of what Charles Scrope's demons were when he took her out to lunch.

Charlotte ordered the steak and kidney pie; she was hungry.

Charles watched her tucking into her meal with amusement. 'You're certainly not weight-conscious.'

'I don't need to be,' Charlotte replied. 'I burn off calories like magic. I suppose it'll catch up with me one day. But not yet.'

'I believe a little more weight would suit you.'

Charlotte looked up in surprise. It was the first time she had realised that Charles had really noticed her as a woman. He looks quite nice when he smiles, she thought.

'You are only eating avocado salad,' she pointed out. And he was eating it with a kind of delicate precision that told her something: a man of appetites who could control them to suit his ends. A lot of pride there, she decided. Was that what powered the machine? It might be worth finding out.

He was very hungry. She wondered if he was as hungry as that about sex. And as disciplined? It might be hard to contain all greeds. Perhaps it was money that moved him most.

'This *is* a business lunch?'

'I wanted to talk to you, Charlotte. To meet you, to see you. Does that surprise you?'

She considered. 'Not now I think about it. But there is business? You weren't kidding about that? Because it is tremendously important to me.'

'I was not kidding. What a word to use.'

Neither of them mentioned Tony. Still, his presence was there between them.

'We'll eat first,' Charles said. 'Then we can go to my office. Then I thought you might like a look around the Stock Exchange.'

Charlotte was surprised. 'Not particularly.'

'Charlotte, you're a designer, a creative artist, but if your business is going to succeed then you have to know about money, too,' Charles explained.

'I can buy advice.'

'Of course. Me. But you must also judge for yourself.'

Charlotte continued to eat her steak and

kidney pie while debating whether a creme brulée or apple ice-cream should follow it as pudding. An inner resistance to pressure stirred deep inside her. This man was pushing her. He had too much power already, why should she give him more? 'I'll think about it.'

'Think about it now.'

Charlotte stopped eating to give him a direct look. She found his straight blue gaze surprisingly attractive. 'You're bullying me.'

'Certainly I am. Will you come to the office and the 'Change.'

Charlotte smiled. 'Maybe.'

Charles beckoned to a waiter. 'Please take away this wine and bring some champagne.'

'Champagne doesn't go with steak and kidney pie.'

'Champagne goes very well with you and me.'

The champagne, when it came, which was soon, was an excellent vintage. It was a flamboyant gesture. He was not the sort of man who ordered champagne, Charlotte thought. Why did he do it then?

'Did you design what you are wearing?' Charles asked.

'Yes. Naturally. Do you like it?' She didn't really care if he did or did not. She looked down at what she was wearing, a dark blue and white spotted shift. The spots were the size of large coins and did not overlap with each other. A white organza collar was tied in a large bow at the neck. She had no hat, no gloves, but she wore large pearl ear-rings.

The thing that made Charlotte's dress totally different was that under the shift she wore a stiff underdress striped boldly in black and blue so that when she moved the slightly transparent shift floated over the stripes as if spinning. Across the room she had seen most of the women study it, and all the men.

She knew she had something marketable in that dress; it was a dress women would buy and men pay for with hard money.

'Clever,' said Charles, coolly.

'Brilliant,' she corrected.

'You asked me a question I didn't answer: I do like it, and you in it.'

Charlotte looked at him sceptically over the top of her wine-glass as she drank. He wouldn't get anywhere with her with talk like that. Not unless he meant it. That would give her such a jolt she might succumb. She laughed gently into her wine.

'What are you laughing at?' he asked at once.

'I was thinking you aren't being very clever about me.' Doesn't like being laughed at, she decided. What man does? 'I mean, are we having a business lunch or is this round one of your seduction scene?'

'Very funny, Charlotte,' he said, tightly.

'Sorry.' Charlotte sipped her wine. The room was crowded, many of the people eating there were known to her. One or two had waved or smiled as she came in. She appraised the room. She knew about half a dozen people there, two of them, one man and one woman, really well. Of those six people none of them went back to her time with Tony or Jehan. They were friends entirely of her own making.

She realised how far she had moved on in these last few months. For now, she felt vital and strong, able to take on Charles Scrope if she had to. 'Yes, I'd like to see your office, talk business and, maybe see the Stock Exchange. I don't suppose I'll ever be a quoted company, but who knows?'

He leant forward. 'It's what you ought to aim at.'

Charlotte laughed. 'How far ahead?'

He shrugged. 'Say five years. Eight or ten at the most. If you haven't made it by then, forget it.'

'Ten years? I can't think that far ahead.'

'Oh you can. I read you better than that.'

Their eyes met and it was Charlotte's gaze that submitted. 'I admit it,' she murmured. 'I do have long range ambitions.'

From across the room a tall, beautiful woman was approaching their table. Charlotte had no idea who she was. The woman stopped at their table and subjected Charlotte to a long stare, swaying slightly as she did so.

Charles stood up.

'Sit down, Charles,' she said. She rested one

hand on the table to steady herself, and spoke to Charlotte.

'I'm Diana's sister . . .'

Charlotte raised her eyebrows in surprise.

'Good Lord. Did you think Diana was alone? Is that the impression she gave you? No, no . . . there are four of us. And I'm the one that drinks.'

It was evident that she did . . .

'I just wanted to have a closer look at you,' she continued. 'At the woman who is breaking Diana's heart . . . You do know that Diana is in love with you, don't you?'

'Oh, go away Phoebe,' said Charles. 'You do talk rubbish.'

'Yes,' said Charlotte, not amused. 'That's simply not true about Diana, and I don't think she'd like you to say it.'

'Don't tell her then.'

'I shan't.'

'Anyway, now I've had a closer look, I shall clear off.' But she lingered, saying, 'That's a lovely dress, by the way. Perhaps I should tear it off your back.'

She put a thin white hand on Charlotte's arm. Charlotte sat very still. If she tries anything rough, I'll knock her out, she thought.

Charles looked at the head waiter who came hurrying up with a short sable coat. 'Here's your coat, m'lady. There's a taxi waiting for you.'

'Oh good,' said Phoebe. 'What's happened to the man I was with? Did he run away?'

'Waiting for you, m'lady. Let me help you.' They departed for the door, tact and dislike manifesting itself in equal quantities in the head waiter's stiff back.

'You mustn't take any notice of Phoebe,' said Charles vaguely.

'*Is* it true about Diana?' A whole new perspective was opening up before Charlotte's eyes.

'Well, she's said to be that way, but if it hasn't bothered you, I shouldn't worry now.'

'Fancy me not knowing, though.' Charlotte was aggrieved.

'But Charlotte, you never do notice anything unless you are brought face to face with it.'

'That may have been true in the past, but I'm working on it.' She stood up, decidedly. 'Let's go and see your office and talk business.'

If Charles was disappointed that no more personal note was sounded, he did not show it, but drove her to his office in a modern building of stark white stone in a street near the Mansion House.

'Our old office was blown down in the Blitz. We rebuilt here. A shame to lose the past: the Scropes had been in Farthing Lane since the fifteenth century, moving up and down it a bit, but probably a good thing as well: the bombs blew away a bit of dust. I think we're much more efficient now. Quill pens are out and computers are in.'

All the same, his own particular office, with a view of the old Roman wall, was furnished with fine English furniture, the walls hung with Piranesi prints, and the floor covered with a splendid Persian carpet.

'Not an antique carpet,' he said, as he saw Charlotte admiring it. 'But good of its kind. A kashan. Large for a kashan. That makes it more valuable, but it's still a work-a-day piece. This is an office, after all.'

'Nice colours.' Charlotte was thinking that she might make a winter town suit of just those colours: blue and red, when suits came back in, as they surely would.

Over in one corner of the room was a leather sofa facing outwards to a view of London.

They sat side by side on the sofa and talked. Charlotte slipped her shoes off and tucked her feet underneath, at once relaxed and stimulated by her companion. There was a lot she didn't have to say to Charles because he had seen all her accounts, knew how her books balanced, and what her profit margins were. Considering what a small little affair it must seem to him, he had put a great deal of effort into understanding how it worked.

'You must expand,' he said, flipping over a sheaf of accounts. 'If you produced, say, twice as many garments, then your make-up costs would drop by 20–25 per cent and the outgoing on materials by about 40 per cent. So you could reduce your prices and still make more profit.'

Charlotte nodded; the logic was inescapable. 'Yes, but my customers don't mind paying,' she countered. Not quite true, but some of them were price snobs. To drop her price might be to devalue herself in their eyes.

'I am suggesting you enlarge your market. Bring in a new sort of client.'

Charlotte looked at him with interest. 'Go on. I'm not sure if I want a new sort of client, but tell me what you are thinking.'

'I was thinking that the way forward for you is to get out of strict couture and into mass production.'

'Cheap and cheerful?'

'No. Certainly not. Clothes that are mass produced, but designed by you and still in smallish numbers. More than you do now, but not chain-store stuff. You market yourself or use special outlets, which you franchise.'

'I have already been thinking on those lines myself,' said Charlotte slowly. 'But I'm a designer. I would want to keep tight control of design and production.' She would let no back-street sweat shop make up her designs.

'Of course. What you mustn't lose is your own quality. You are unique. You say something no one else does.'

'Thank you. You make things sound very easy. I don't know if they are.'

A tray of tea was brought in, the China was

Spode and the teapot was silver, with cream in matching jug, and lemon on a sliver dish.

'Will you pour? If you'd like some, that is.'

'Oh, I would, talking business always makes me thirsty. Or, perhaps it was the champagne.'

'No, no,' he was very serious, 'champagne never has that effect. Only poor wine does that.'

He seemed quite different from the man she had known only as Tony's closest ally and adviser. Tony's name was not mentioned. Impossible, however, to avoid all reference, however oblique. On one wall was a large scale map of an area of Norfolk. It was an old map, probably of the late eighteenth century.

Cup in hand Charlotte went over to study it. '*A map of Norfolk drawn at the command of His Grace, the Duke of Beauclerc with special attention to the Ducal Estates. Andrew Underwood, High Holborn, London, 1804,*' she read.

'Interesting.' Charlotte kept her voice carefully aloof. To her surprise it was not difficult.

She admired the map, observed the size of the estate with surprised attention, and found a question: 'Does he really own all that land? Still? Even these days?'

'Oh yes. Every acre, and more.' Charles tapped an area of the map. 'Land was bought here in the late 1940's and a small industrial estate built on it. And here, new land bought as recently as ten years ago before prices rose so much.'

'Clever old Tony.' She looked at Charles. 'No, clever you.'

'It was my father's advice in fact.' Charles turned his back on the map, and went to take some more tea. 'He thought ahead of his time did my guv'nor. He foresaw what we then read in 1957. And that estate was almost the last bit of business he did for the Beauclercs before he died.'

'But surely in the late 1940's you were too young to take over?' Charlotte queried.

Charles nodded, and bit into a biscuit. 'I was still at Eton. There was a bit of a hiatus. An uncle took over.'

'How long have the Scropes managed the Beauclercs' affairs? Right back to the very beginning?'

'And well beyond,' said Charles firmly. 'Even before the Beauclercs were given a Dukedom by George III there was a Scrope running the estates. The Scropes have a longer history than the Beauclercs. They were landed gentry when the Beauclercs were just butchers in Cheapside. Did you know the first Beauclerc to come to public notice was a butcher?' His tone was crisp.

So that's his demon, thought Charlotte. Or one of them, at least. Pride. Personal pride, family pride. The Beauclercs are upstarts beside the Scropes.

And yet she was sure that a genuine friendship existed between Tony and Charles.

Charlotte walked across the room to pour herself some more tea. A masculine appreciation of the deep, underlying links which held them together was what did it, she decided. Each of them had a vested interest in the other, and on this they could build a friendship.

Perhaps she and Diana, being of a new breed of working women, were creating such a friendship, she mused. Then, she remembered the incident in the restaurant and, recalling Diana's own particular demon, wondered.

'What you've got to do,' said Charles, breaking in on her thoughts, 'is buy Tony's shares in Redmond & Bruce.'

Charlotte nodded. But she had severe doubts about James Bruce. Not an easy man.

'Moreover, the company has a very lucrative link-up with the Casteline scent manufacturers. The house scent "Heather" is made by Casteline.'

'News to me,' Charlotte commented. 'Terrible name for a scent.'

'It makes a large profit, of which Redmond & Bruce gets a share,' observed Charles drily.

'You open my eyes.'

'And when it palls as "Heather", it will get a new packaging, a drop of some different colour in the essence, with a new name, and go on making money.'

70

Charlotte sighed. 'I don't think James Bruce will go for a change to mass production. He is couture, through and through. He'll never accept it.'

'You don't tell him.'

'Buy it, you mean, without saying what I have in mind?' Charlotte shook her head. Not her style. 'I couldn't do it.'

'You'll bring him round. He'll see sense. He is a businessman, a thought he hates to admit to.'

Charlotte stood up, held out her hand to Charles to cement the bargain, and said, 'I'll do it.' She might regret it, but at the moment it looked a good idea.

Charles took her hand, using it to draw her towards him. For a moment he held her against him, then he kissed her gently.

In spite of herself Charlotte found herself kissing him back.

Charles released her. 'We've skated around that a long while before finally getting there.'

Regretting her response bitterly, Charlotte picked up her gloves. 'I'll give the Stock Exchange a miss, if you don't mind. I expect it's old and musty. I understand they are going to rebuild it, anyway.'

'Of course. As you wish.'

Charles saw her to the street, hailing a taxi for her.

Before she got into it Charlotte said, nervously, 'All I want at the moment, all I'm fit

71

for, is a business arrangement. Let's leave it there,' she said.

Charles didn't answer.

When he went back into his office his secretary raised her head from her desk for a moment, then pursed her lips with the expression of one who could read the situation and knew it well, she went back to typing fast. Charlotte should have seen that look.

The taxi driver gave Charlotte a curious look as she climbed in. Staring at her face in the mirror set on the taxi partition, she saw she was trembling.

*   *   *

It might have been difficult seeing Diana again after meeting her sister, especially as Diana would have certainly learned of the episode through her friends, some of whom would have been witnesses.

The network of Diana's friends, a word which sometimes seemed synonymous with enemy, was large and close-linked. One of its most efficient services was the passing on of information. Usually this was valuable to Diana, but she had to accept the other side of the coin when the news was painful.

Charlotte thought she could read Diana's knowledge of what had happened in her greeting, when they met next day in Charlotte's office: Diana was wearing dark spectacles, and too much make-up to disguise her pallor.

However, they had a programme to discuss: Charlotte's new collection was ready to show; there would be a private viewing for old customers and friends at a date to be worked out by the two women. It mustn't clash with any other shows that might detract from its impact. One or two important personalities must be consulted, so Diana said; also she had some commercial tie-ups to consider.

When they had finished, and Val had brought in coffee, Diana said: 'How was your lunch with Charles Scrope?' She did not mean the food. 'Oh yes,' Diana confirmed. 'I heard about your lunch with Charles. You might have told me you were going,' she said, feigning brightness. 'I could have got a para, in the *Mail*, and a picture in the *Standard* probably.'

'That's why,' Charlotte joked.

Diana shook her head. 'All publicity is useful.'

'Yes, I know. But I've had my share. I want to be quiet for a while. Personally, I mean. This was a business lunch.'

The awkward moment had passed. She would never hint to Diana of anything Phoebe had said. It had dropped into a black hole between them. It would always be there, she couldn't forget it, but what happened to their relationship depended on Diana. She was quite sure that Diana's good manners and good

73

sense would keep them out of trouble.

'So what did you decide?' Diana, who had in fact been crying with misery for most of the night, kept her voice hopeful. On business matters she *was* hopeful. 'You came to terms with Charles? He'll back you to expand?'

'I don't know why I bother to answer: you always know already,' despaired Charlotte. 'You always know everything. Yes, we agreed. He wants me to take over Redmond & Bruce as a base. I am to have the controlling interest.' But the money would be borrowed, his money.

Diana's hand was unsteady as she took notes. 'So it will be you and James Bruce as a team,' Diana speculated aloud. 'Did Charles have any other moves to make?'

'No.' Charlotte was firm.

'He will,' said Diana thoughtfully. 'Oh, he will.' She gathered all her papers and possessions together. 'Guess what? I've got a new client. I am taking over Virginia Grace's publicity. She's leaving her TV outfit, (that's confidential, by the way) and going free-lance. So I've got two clients now.'

Thus Charlotte and Diana played out this important scene in their lives with a holding back of full confidence on both sides.

*   *   *

In the New Year of 1968, Charlotte and James Bruce met face to face to fight out the future of

74

Redmond & Bruce. But to Charlotte's surprise there was no real battle. After their previous heated encounter, she had expected to have to argue her way through to him as through a hedge of prejudice: she had her case prepared. She had rehearsed her argument the evening before, walking up and down her living-room floor.

It was one of those evenings when her apartment seemed empty, a vacuum sucking at the life inside her instead of enhancing what she had.

Walking up and down, shouting aloud her arguments as she would deliver them to James Bruce, relieved the pain. She wasn't sure what the anguish was about, since surely she had come to terms with losing Tony? The truth was, she wasn't really good at living alone.

The shouting must have worked as therapy, because she felt surprisingly light-hearted as she ran up the stairs from her basement office the following day, to James' office on the upper floors, only to discover that there would be no fight.

She had a few minutes to wait for James who was with a client, a space of time she used to make a quiet, pre-proprietorial survey of his establishment. James and the customer were in a fitting-room so that the main salon was open to her inspection.

Redmond & Bruce had gone in for dark plum and gold as a colour scheme, which was sumptuous, but dark. Also, Charlotte decided, somehow seedy. The whole effect was of a slow running-down, with carpets not replaced when worn, nor paint renewed. In daylight this would probably have been more marked, but Redmond & Bruce was an artificial world lit by glittering chandeliers suspended from the ceiling.

That will end, decided Charlotte. I will let the daylight in. It was an instinctive decision and one sided: what James Bruce might have to say did not come into it.

Charlotte concluded later that the reason for this was that she had expected opposition from James, so that her aggression was up. When it did not materialise she was almost shocked.

Instead, when James emerged from his fitting, he took her into his office, offered her a glass of sherry, and welcomed her to the firm.

'Thank you!' said Charlotte, dazed. 'But no sherry. It's too early in the day.'

'Whisky? Gin?' said James exuberantly. He had a quality of healthy vitality that was showing now.

'I thought you'd fight me.'

'So I would have, once. But when you came to see me earlier—and talked about working *together*—well, you convinced me. We shall do well together. Three cheers for haute couture. I shall have a drink, anyway.'

In fact, they drank some whisky together, and Charlotte felt more than a little tipsy. She

76

also felt ashamed because she had not told him about the plan to move out of couture, and now she wasn't going to.

'I'm absolutely delighted,' James went on. 'A fresh infusion of capital and talent. I've got a lot of ideas. I expect you have, too...'

CHAPTER FIVE

James and Charlotte worked splendidly together, which was more of a surprise to Charlotte than to James. He had intended to make a go of the partnership. He wasn't a devious man, but he knew what he needed. Redmond & Bruce had been headed for the rocks of bankruptcy when Charlotte came along with youth, push and money.

He had been desperately unhappy himself over the loss of Sophia, but that was something not to think about, although that was hard at first when he saw pictures of her everywhere about his workrooms and in his clothes. Imagining pictures that his mind formed all the time.

He wondered if Charlotte was having similar fantasies about Tony. Actual images of the two together were scarce; they had disappeared to Tony's estates in Canada and Australia and were not seen.

Then suddenly, almost with an audible click

Sophia's image disappeared from around the place as Charlotte's came in. It was as if Charlotte had exorcised her.

Or perhaps it had something to do with the re-decoration: doors were removed, windows flung open and a colour scheme of white and apricot established.

In this ambience they had their own fitting rooms and offices, but shared other resources. They had their own appointment-books and their own customers, but they bought fabrics and supplies as a team. Thus overheads and expenses were down and profits up.

Charlotte's customers poured joyfully up the staircase to what became known as 'Butterfly at Redmond & Bruce.'

For a time she had regular meetings with Charles Scrope, always carefully formal and businesslike on her part. Then, at the beginning of the summer, he announced he was going to America for some months on business for the Beauclerc estate. 'I shall be coming and going, but basically I shall be away. I've set your affairs in pretty good order. You are on your own now.'

Rumours drifted back to Charlotte and Diana that he was going to marry a girl who was daughter to one of the Queen's ladies-in-waiting. Diana, who knew the girl, expressed her doubts. 'Don't believe it,' she said squarely. 'He won't and she won't, the Mama may be pushing it, that's all.'

James recognised quite soon that Charlotte was an innovator. As such he mentally saluted a talent superior to his own. He had a vague sense of unease about this, but he also enjoyed it.

Within a few months of Charlotte coming into Redmond & Bruce, the lease of James' own small house in Chelsea had ended, and he had rented another near to where Charlotte lived, overlooking the river. It was handy to be able to pop round to see her when a problem arose. Number 20 Little Cheyne Row, was his address.

'Little' was the operative word, had been Charlotte's comment when she first saw his new house. It was the tiniest house she had ever seen and would not have suited her style at all, but it was right for James. In it he had the Staffordshire figures he collected, together with the early Victorian furniture which he enjoyed. 'Nothing later than the Great Exhibition is a sound rule,' he told Charlotte. 'After that it gets too fancy, and heavy. Before that you are usually safe.'

Charlotte found the idea of 'safe' antiques amusing; she found James amusing, too.

She helped him to redecorate his house, doing some of the papering herself. In return he escorted her to a meeting of The Incorporated Society of London Fashion

Houses, made up of the dozen or so most distinguished couture firms in London, of which, by virtue of her share of Redmond & Bruce, she was now a member.

The party which followed was covered by all the leading fashion magazines.

As she looked around the room Charlotte realised how shrewd Charles had been to make her buy into Redmond & Bruce. With that one step she had moved several rungs up the fashion ladder. She might have done it on her own, but it would have taken much longer.

And time, Charlotte sometimes thought, was perhaps what she did not have. Or not so much as other people thought...

James caught the dark reflection on her face. 'Are you all right, Charlotte?'

'Fine. Just fine.' She was at once assertively bright. 'But they are quite alarming this lot in their own way, aren't they?'

'Some more than others. I've grown up with them so it's hard for me to see them clearly. Old Mother De Lys is about the most formidable. She trained under Chanel. It was a hard school. Monty's not bad.' Monty was the nickname of an eminent male dress maker. He was of Scottish birth, and markedly unmilitary, which provoked his cynical world to call him jokingly after a famous general. 'He employs the last full time embroiderer in London, and for her he would fight to the death, so don't try to lure her away. But I don't imagine you would.'

'No. My designs don't need embroidery. I'm not saying they won't, things change, but at the moment I like things plain. Though I can see a future for pleats,' she said earnestly. 'And even frills, but not embroidery.'

'Well, don't tell Monty so, his clients love it.' He was laughing at her. 'Frills, indeed.'

'Oh, they are several seasons off, but wait and see.'

'Don't you ever stop working?'

'Is that what it seems like?'

'Yes.' James hesitated. 'You're so young, you've come so far, you're going right to the top. You know that, I expect.'

'That's a big compliment you've paid me, James.'

'I'm ambitious as well. I like my work, but I do other things. I paint, I cook, I've got a boat on the Thames. But you … I'm not probing, Charlotte, but what do you do?'

'I have *had* other things in my life.'

'Yes. We both have. We've never talked of Tony and Sophia. One day we ought to. But not now.'

'There's nothing to say about me and Tony,' Charlotte snapped. 'It's all been said.'

Suddenly emotion was flaring between them, a profoundly complex emotion made of many strands, twisted together like a plait. And, most awkward of all, a sharp attraction to each other. Charlotte fought against that attraction; James sensed the fight.

81

A great feeling of tenderness towards her crept over him. 'Come on, let's get away from here. Come back to Little Cheyne Row and I will cook you dinner.'

Living on his own from an early age, James had taught himself to cook from books. 'If you can read, you can cook,' he had told Charlotte. By now he had a good repertoire of dishes, mostly rich and expensive.

Diana had arranged for one of the colour supplements to do a feature on James in his kitchen; it would be appearing any Sunday now. With her own hands Charlotte had made him a blue and black striped apron to wear.

'I'm not sure if I feel strong enough for your cooking tonight,' she joked, warily.

'That's exactly why you need it. Come on, Charlotte.'

They made their way out of the party.

'You know, we nearly quarreled back there.' James smiled.

Charlotte laughed. 'It's got to happen one day. We are bound to quarrel.'

'You know I'm going to hate it,' said James earnestly.

'Oh James, you are nice. I think you are the nicest man I know.'

'That's better, now.' He helped her on with her cloak, a loose wrap of cashmere in off-white.

It was like putting on a warm fur coat, being with James, thought Charlotte. He made her feel relaxed and comfortable. Happy. Tony and Jehan had never made her feel happy in this simple way.

The silly throb of pain at the memory of Tony which James had read in her face faded away. What was past was done with; she had to look to the future now.

Charlotte drove them to Little Cheyne Row in her tiny Fiat. One of the things that James was not good at was driving.

Once in his house, James took off his coat, gave Charlotte a drink and settled happily into his cooking. 'Watch me and you'll learn how.'

Charlotte was not good at cooking. It was astonishing how those hands, so skilful when fitting a sleeve or settling a cuff, became clumsy when cutting up onions.

Charlotte obligingly watched while sipping her drink. 'Nice wine, James.'

'*Nice*, woman? What a word to use of a first-rate hock!'

'Oh, is that what it is?'

Tony had kept a good cellar, and Jehan had just drunk anything he could get, and the stronger the better, but neither of them had seen wine as a gloss on the pleasures of life in the manner James did. When one drank wine with James it was an occasion.

Charlotte played a game of being more ignorant than she truly was because he enjoyed it so. She did play up to him a bit, it gave them both so much pleasure.

83

'Show me the bottle,' she said meekly. 'Oh yes, brown. Hock bottles are always brown. That's right, isn't it? And Moselle's green.'

'You're learning. It is not, however, the essential element of a hock to be in a brown bottle. You are supposed to recognise the taste.' He waved a cooking fork. 'By the colour, the aroma, the life in it. That is how you know a hock.' He put fork down. 'Hand me the chopped parsley.'

She passed the dish across. 'Why are you beating it into the butter?'

'To make green butter to eat with our steak.' He gave her a sharp look. 'You know that. Don't pretend to be more ignorant than you are.'

'No, James.' She was meek, amused.

It was comfortable and homely in the kitchen with James, and then eating their meal in front of a fire. She felt utterly relaxed. How easy life could be sometimes.

For a while they discussed work: both were plotting the spring 1969 collection, which they would launch this coming September, as usual, six months ahead.

Then a peaceful silence fell. James broke it. 'Brandy?'

'Mm—No.' Charlotte shook her head. 'Not for me, thanks.'

'I think I'll have some.' He got up and poured a good measure into a crystal goblet. He threw a log on the fire before coming back

84

to sit beside her.

'You were right to make me keep the fire-grate in this room.'

'Oh, it's right for this sort of house. Totally wrong to get rid of it.' Charlotte watched the flames leap.

'You've done a lot of things right for me, Charlotte,' James said. 'I know that's not how I sounded just at the very beginning ... I had a bad time after Sophia left me. I expect you guessed. I couldn't work. I had a major crisis of confidence. Thought I'd have to give work up altogether.'

Charlotte nodded her head.

'I'd have killed Sophia if I'd had a chance. Tony too, I expect.'

'Oh come on.' She wondered if it was the brandy talking. 'But you didn't.'

'Didn't get the chance.'

'If you'd really wanted to then you would have made the chance.'

'Well—I nearly did. Make that chance, I mean. I thought I'd lost everything, you see: the woman I loved; my own power to create. And she never told me you know. Never said a thing. Just cleared off.'

It all came pouring out, as if it was something he had to clear out of his mind. How he had watched Sophia's flat, how he had tried to follow her, but had failed. Gone again the next day, prepared to wait, only to find she had left. Moved away. 'Mercifully. Thank

85

goodness. I see that now. Did you want to kill Tony?'

'Once. Not now though,' she replied.

'Oh Charlotte, I do love you.'

'Come on, now'.

'Yes, really, I think I do.'

'Like brother and sister, eh?'

'I'm not sure yet.' He was staring at her with a puzzled frown.

'Well...' Charlotte's voice had slipped several octaves with her surprise. She was lucky in that, unlike most women her voice went down, not up, with emotion.

James was amused. 'You growled that out like a friendly tigress. Seriously, you got me back on course, Charlotte. I'm designing better than ever now. I can't forget it. Means a lot to me.'

It was true, and there was a certain irony in that Charlotte's long term plans demanded the suppression of his couture world, and she was uneasily aware of this. She ought to tell him soon.

'So are you, for that matter. Going great guns. It's amazing how well our styles fit together, considering they are so different,' he remarked.

'We aren't in the big league yet.'

'It'll come,' said James confidently.

'Yes, I think it will. But it may have to change,' observed Charlotte cautiously.

'You have your ambitions; I have mine, but

together we are a team. We won't change it, we can't.' He finished the brandy, and stood up. 'Come on. I'll see you to your car. Tomorrow's a working day.'

'OK', said Charlotte yawning.

* * *

As she drove the short journey home, Charlotte thought about what James had said. He was very proud of what he had achieved. He would not like it if Redmond & Bruce changed in the way she and Charles envisaged. Perhaps it would not be necessary; perhaps they could stay as they were; only bigger and better. Charles might not be right.

* * *

Next morning, she was eating her breakfast of yoghurt and coffee when the telephone rang. There were only three people who rang her at this hour: Diana, James and, when he was around, Charles Scrope.

This time it was James. 'I know you will think I am mad, but it's about yesterday evening. How are you, by the way? Sleep well?'

'Very well, and I am now drinking my breakfast coffee. What is it?'

'I'm wondering about our conversation. We do agree about the future of Redmond & Bruce, I hope? I caught an undertone of doubt in your voice. I wouldn't like that, Charlotte. We need each other's support.'

'I am totally, absolutely behind Redmond & Bruce.'

'No reservations?'

'None.'

'Oh good.' He sounded relieved. 'I've been having nightmares all night. 'Bye, then. See you at work.'

Charlotte picked up her coffee. You told a sort of lie there, she thought.

It was an odd little conversation to start the day with. She went back to her coffee.

The lie inside her lived on. Then the telephone rang again. This time she was definitely reluctant to answer it. 'Hello?'

'Charlotte?'

'Charles! Where are you speaking from? I didn't know you were in London.'

'Fleetingly. But I must see you. And there is something you must see. Lunch?'

'Lunch would be lovely, but I am pretty busy today.' Charlotte had reached out a hand for her diary, and was flipping over the pages.

'You mustn't be too busy for this.'

Charlotte could have read him the list of her customers that day, but she never wanted to boast with Charles. Rather the impulse was to underplay it. This gave her the feeling, which she felt she wanted with him, of having strength in reserve.

'There is a garment factory out in South

London, in Greenwich, that I want you to go and look at. They are thinking of selling. It might be just what you want,' Charles told her.

'So soon?' She was horrified. Especially after what she had just said to James. 'I thought we said a bit longer.'

'Events don't wait on you. This place is coming up for sale. You ought to consider it. In any event, you have to start looking somewhere some time.'

In the end, she agreed to a flying visit to Greenwich. Charles had set up the engagement, so she kept it.

Charlotte drove herself out, threading her way expertly through the South London streets. Greenwich, she thought, it would be Greenwich of all places, but at least it meant she knew the way.

She glanced at the address, just scribbled on a piece of paper.

"Esther Angel, Angel Modes, Ltd., Malplaquet Road, S.E."

Malplaquet Road must be down by the river somewhere. She could almost predict the grubby grey bricks and the aged pavements. A slight rain was falling, making the road greasy. Angel Modes was housed in a small, two-floored factory.

She was expected, and shown in at once by a doorman. 'Mrs Angel is waiting for you.' So there really was an Angel on the premises?

Esther Angel was elderly and white-haired.

'You want to look around? Well, this is a nice place, if I do say so myself, and a better set of girls working for us you couldn't hope to have.'

The girls, as Charlotte had known they would be, were middle-aged ladies, some fully as old as Mrs Angel herself. They were working away energetically at their sewing machines, lined up in neat rows. There was a fair buzz of conversation going on as well. The room represented the other end of the scale in the fashion world from her own couture workroom. There was a slightly sweet smell hanging in the air from the fabrics mixed with oil from the machines.

Charlotte turned to Mrs Angel. 'Who does the cutting?'

'I do. There's no one can get more out of a length than I do. Except my late husband,' she added thoughtfully. 'That's why I am considering selling, because he's gone. At a price, mind you.'

Charlotte nodded; she understood.

'I know what I've got. This is a good outfit. Who will do your cutting?'

'I will,' said Charlotte.

'You know, eh? It is a special thing. A proper art.' Esther Angel looked at Charlotte sceptically. 'So young you are, too.'

The tour continued. Charlotte could see that everything, although on a small scale, was efficient and in good order. The machinery was well maintained, while the workrooms were freshly decorated. Charles had chosen well. Or rather, one of his assistants had made a good choice! Charlotte did not suppose he himself had seen the place. But he would know to a penny the price to offer. By the look of her Mrs Angel knew, too.

In the next room several long tables were spread with lengths of fabric. Mrs Angel fingered the silk. 'Feel the silk. Good quality.' She put her head on one side, looking at Charlotte speculatively. 'How many dresses now do you think you could get out of it.'

'Show me the pattern you are using.'

Charlotte studied it, made a calculation, and produced a figure.

'Just what I say myself,' said Mrs Angel, receiving the pattern back. She sounded half disappointed. 'It should be more, but I can't see how.'

'The sleeves are the difficulty. But if you tried cutting the cuffs and sleeve in one it might work better. Personally, I don't like the cuffs. Throw them out.'

There was a pause while Mrs Angel considered. Then she laughed. 'You know your business. I tell you: the cuffs are already gone.'

Across the room, Charlotte caught the eye of a tiny, dark-eyed girl. For a moment they stared at each other, then Charlotte turned away. Nothing there, she thought, nothing and no one I know in the whole place. I've never seen anyone here in my life before. Just my imagination. No one here knows anything about me.

*　　　*　　　*

Charlotte was late that week for her visit to the Adelina, her dear old Addie. A part of her hated going, but she never defaulted. She had no illusions: she knew she went there for her own sake as much as to bring any pleasure and comfort she could to the small patients.

What they gave her she found hard to put into words, but basically it was the assurance that life was worth having whatever the disability.

There had been many lunches, and dinners too, with Charles, since that first meal they had shared. She understood him so much better, now. Still, a meeting with him was always something of an occasion, one for which she prepared herself.

They met in the restaurant in the roof of a smart, new hotel in Knightsbridge. Not usually the sort of hotel Charles patronised, he must be wanting to be unobserved by the outer circle of his friends.

He began, as usual, with a battery of questions about Diana and James. Questions which she always answered fully, although suspecting he always had information of his own and only wanted to know what she had to say.

'Diana? Oh, she's in fine form. And making money, of course. Things are easier on that front. I think in the end I may even unhook her from her sisters.'

They were agreed on the subject of Diana's sisters, and about the fate they deserved: oblivion.

'I hear she has quarrelled with Virginia.' He was ordering the meal. 'The lobster's good here. Chablis to drink?'

'Lobster would be lovely. Those two quarrel and make up, quarrel and make up, all the time. I think they enjoy it. Well, Virginia does; not so sure about Diana.'

Charles looked at her, half amused. 'And James?' he prodded. 'How's he finding things?'

'He's hit a winning streak with his new little day dresses and jackets. I almost envy him them. He doesn't know about my visit to Greenwich. I haven't told him.'

'Much wiser not.'

'I feel disloyal.' She drained her Chablis with a kind of angry despair, which Charles observed.

It told him something about Charlotte, and a great deal about her relations with James. He was not a man who needed things underlined for him.

'No need. What did you think of the place?'

'Pretty good. Very good, in fact. Ideal, if I wanted it.'

'You *will* want it.'

'Perhaps. I'm not as sure as I was. James and I are riding in tandem at the moment and doing splendidly. Maybe we should leave it that way.'

'I'm giving you good advice.'

'I'm sure you are. For you.'

'For *you.*'

'For me, then, but perhaps not for James. As I've said: I feel rotten about it.'

'You didn't say it, but I could see you meant it.' He spoke almost tenderly, as if he liked her for the feelings. 'Well, the decision doesn't have to be taken now. You have time.'

'You mean we won't buy the place?'

'I mean I already have. I'm holding it for you. Mrs Angel will carry on as manageress. She's quite willing to do that. She just wants her capital out now her husband is dead.'

'You're pushing me.'

'No. Honestly not. The place is just there ready and waiting for you when you want it. And if you never want it, then it is a very good investment in itself. A splendid site for development.'

Charlotte laughed. Suddenly she felt it was impossible to beat this man, and it really didn't matter if she couldn't.

He was busy ordering a certain pudding from the waiter, throwing the comment over his shoulder that it was the best thing they did here.

Charlotte took in his appearance with pleasure.

He reached across the table to rest his hand gently on hers. Charlotte looked down at it. It was a nice hand, tanned and neat of nail.

It was idle to pretend that his interest in the success of her firm did not reflect an interest in her as a woman. What she should be to him and he to her was implicit in their every meeting.

'Well, Charlotte?'

Charlotte hesitated. 'What, about...' she fumbled for the right words, 'that is, I heard—' She stopped dead.

'You mean Jocelyn, I suppose.'

'I never heard the name mentioned. Just a story going around that you were going to marry.' Diana had said it would not happen, but Diana did not always get things right.

Charles said: 'When I marry, it will be announced in a proper fashion, not handed around in a rumour like a bad coin. So, Charlotte, where do we go from here?'

She wasn't sure exactly what he was offering. Not marriage, she thought, but it didn't much matter anyway, for the answer was the same.

She laid her spare hand gently on top of his. 'No, not now. Perhaps not ever, but anyway, not now. For the first time in my adult life I am free of emotional tie-ups. My career is going well and I'm happy. I want to stay that way.'

He accepted the decision gracefully, but without giving ground. She knew he would try again.

*　　*　　*

The rest of the day passed peacefully. She did not see James, nor did she tell him about her visit to the factory. She had pushed the idea to the back of her mind while she concentrated on work. He too was doing the same, they passed on the stairs and that was that.

*　　*　　*

On the next day Charlotte had a routine meeting in her office with Diana to discuss publicity for the next collection. Diana was late, and when she came, was distinctly edgy and out of temper. A quarrel with Virginia again was on the cards.

Diana shot through their business together as if she couldn't be rid of it fast enough. She looked rotten.

Silently Charlotte got up, poured some coffee from the pot standing on her work table and pushed it across to Diana. 'Unless you'd rather have brandy.'

'God, no.' Diana shuddered. As she reached out for the coffee, Charlotte saw a thick bruise on her arm.

'Diana!'

Diana covered it up quickly. 'Only my idiot sister. Forget it. You didn't see it. I've already had Virginia on at me.'

'Poor Diana.' Charlotte gently touched the bruised arm.

Diana jerked away. 'Don't touch me.' She sprang up and moved to the other side of the room. Her back to Charlotte.

Charlotte sat rigid in shocked silence.

Diana spoke as if the words were wrenched out of her. 'I love you, Charlotte. In love with you, if you can take that idea. So please don't touch me unless it means something.'

'Nothing,' said Charlotte sadly. 'Nothing ever.' She repeated the word. 'Ever. Ever.' It was like a knell. Life did play cat-and-mouse with you, she thought. There I am, twenty-seven years old, and I still don't know how to handle my emotions.

Probably Diana felt the same because she controlled herself, and departed, saying she'd have to work on the material Charlotte had given her and would telephone about it. 'Forget my hysteria,' she said as she left. 'Blows up occasionally. Pretend it didn't happen.' She smiled miserably. 'Joke, of course. You can't forget.'

I wonder what I answered? thought Charlotte when Diana had gone. It seemed just a few silly words like "sorry" and "thank you," but it must have been right because it sent Diana away smiling. I didn't handle that so badly.

It was hard to work after Diana had gone.

Charlotte drank the coffee that Diana had not touched, swallowing an aspirin with it. A headache was hanging over her with the threat of worse to come. She might feel sick if she didn't loosen up soon.

The headache slowed her down, making her feel stupid at a time when she wished to be particularly bright. The afternoon appointment was an important one: the first fitting of the English correspondent of *American Vogue*, a lady of power. Mrs Alice Connaught was a French woman married to an Englishman who had worked for years in Washington. She knew everyone and most of them feared her.

She was also bird-thin, difficult to fit, with an elegant ugliness almost better than beauty. She had chosen three dresses, which were now prepared in a toile, ready to fit. When this thin, cotton proto-type of the garment hung exactly as Charlotte (and her exacting client) desired, then the real dress would be made.

Val came in to the office to announce Mrs Connaught's arrival. Behind her came a girl from the work-room with the three toiles over her arm.

'She's waiting,' she announced bluntly; there was no finesse to Val, never would be.

'I'm coming, I'm coming.'

'Now don't get flustered.'

'I've got to get this right. I know why she's here. It's to see what I've got, what I am, and

98

she'll pass judgement.' Charlotte could feel her hands beginning to tremble. It was a bad sign, for her, ushering in what she thought of as one of her 'black times.'

'Take the toiles in to her,' she said, her voice sharper than she meant it to be. 'And get her started. Put her in the day dress with pleats. I'll be along.'

She went into her private bathroom next to her office where she leant against the basin, taking in deep breaths. Presently, the waves of shaking that had begun to build up, ebbed away, but her hands still trembled.

She drank some water, then took a pill-box from her pocket. A pretty pill-box, it was fashioned of gold and enamel, made in Bilston. Diana had pills for many occasions; Charlotte had only one, a pale blue lozenge with a division down the middle.

She broke the tablet in two, swallowed one half, the prescribed dose, then went to face Mrs Connaught.

*   *   *

The headache was still there, banging away, but the shake in her hands was less, although her right hand seemed to have developed a life of its own.

Mrs Connaught noticed the tremor, observing it with an alert brown gaze like a bird, but she said nothing, merely moving herself nearer to the mirror which covered one wall. 'The bodice is fine. Great. But the collar?' She put her head on one side. 'It hasn't come out quite right, has it.?'

The toile was fine cotton; the dress would be silk. Charlotte pointed this out. 'It'll fall better in silk.'

'A bit more shape here, though, I think?' A small, firm finger indicated what Mrs Connaught wanted. 'Not floppy, eh? No flop, please.'

'The silk will pleat like this.' Charlotte picked up a small piece of the yellow silk she would be using. 'See? Firmer. The silk holds the pleat very well.'

Eventually this toile was pinned up to everyone's satisfaction. The second dress was easy, but with the third they ran into trouble.

The dress was destined to be made up in a rose-printed chiffon by Celia Birtwhistle, a ravishing design. Mrs Connaught had chosen the dress from a sketch shown her by Charlotte.

It was a short ball dress, floating from the shoulders. Mrs Connaught said at once that it looked "heavy." No greater word of condemnation could pass her lips at the moment.

Charlotte came forward to explain: 'I'll just pin this tuck in the shoulder-yoke and you'll see.' Her hand shot the box of pins down Mrs Connaught's neck line. 'Oh, I'm so sorry!'

Slowly, deliberately, Mrs Connaught removed the toile. 'Let's forget it for now, dear. Perhaps let's forget this dress. I don't see a future for it, somehow. But I'll be in tomorrow. Let's try again then. I'd *like* to take the three dresses. If I can...'

Charlotte understood the significance of what she said: she knew all about Mrs Connaught's "rule of three," as did everyone else in their world: Mrs Connaught had to accept *three* good dresses from a designer before she took them seriously. Anything less did not count. Anyone could score once. What she was looking for was a sustained talent.

Three dresses, at least, for three seasons was the rule. Charlotte felt she was about to fall at the first fence. 'Tomorrow,' she said miserably. She consulted her appointments book. 'In the morning?'

*   *   *

Damn Diana, she thought, damn everything. 'I'll be working late tonight,' she told Lotty. 'Get me some sandwiches in, please, and leave some coffee made.'

Usually she enjoyed a session of late-night work. She liked the feeling of the hours stretching ahead of her without interruption. In these conditions her imagination was liberated so that her thoughts roamed freely, plucking ideas out of the air.

101

A picture, a piece of music, even the view from her window (not that there was much of one) could inspire her. Sometimes a force outside her seemed to take over and move her forward. Inspiration, a divine afflatus, a breath from the gods the ancients had called this vital force; but to Charlotte it was happiness.

No magic tonight. She picked up swathes of silk, then threw them aside. She drew sketches, then rejected them as hopeless.

For an hour she draped lengths of chiffon over a dressmaker's dummy, but nothing good came of it.

There were many different ways of working. Charlotte had various techniques for getting ideas to flow, such as hanging silks around the room to see how the colours flowed, suggesting shape and form, or stripping off her clothes and shaping the silk directly onto her body. Flesh and silk together often produced a flash from her mind as if the body itself was speaking.

But tonight nothing worked. Printed silks, chiffons and even velvets were thrown around the room but no original ideas came.

In the workroom was a blue and white dress which had been rejected as a failure, but Charlotte had always felt there was more in the basic idea behind it than she had been able to bring out. The blue and white silk was flowery, beautiful. Charlotte had ordered two rolls: one with white flowers on blue, and the other of blue flowers on white, so she had plenty of silk to play with.

The dress had been dropped into a corner, where it was lying in a forlorn, crumpled heap. Charlotte picked it up, planning a sharp word for the work-room forewoman about untidiness. She pressed the dress with a warm iron to remove the creases and then hung it on a dummy.

She stood back, assessing it. Yes, there had been a good idea in the free fall of material from the gathered shoulders, but it hadn't quite come off.

She walked the length of the room to study the image in the looking-glass on the wall. Sometimes you got a completely different notion of a dress by seeing it back to front. This time the trick worked and a little frisson of excitement ran through her.

The length was wrong. Wrong for the shoulder line, wrong for the fullness from the shoulders. It was *too* long, and thus looked a pretty maternity dress which was definitely not what she had in mind.

Charlotte swung round, picked up her big cutting-out scissors, then sheared a dramatic six inches off the dress.

Suddenly, she had an exciting visual object. A very short, blue and white dress swinging free.

She got her sandwiches and sat on the floor as she ate them, keeping her eyes on the dress.

103

She poured herself some coffee, still watching her creation as if it might move away.

Then she stood up. 'No, damn it. I've boobed again. She'll never wear it. As a dress it may be great, but not for that lady. Not with those legs.'

She started to walk up and down the workroom, scissors still in her hand, the length of material she had cut off, hanging around her neck like a scarf.

Like a guardsman, Charlotte marched straight up to the mirror and tied the silk round her head like a turban. It looked marvellous on her, but did nothing for her spirits. 'I think I'll scream.'

She had never screamed aloud before. To shatter the silence of a room with her own voice had never seemed a possible thing to do. Any pain she had had to endure she had suffered in silence.

Now she looked at her face in the mirror, opened her mouth and propelled a noise into the air. The first scream was difficult, but it got easier. The third scream was good and loud.

She stepped back, satisfied, and a little surprised to see everything still in one piece, with the glass unshattered.

From the door James said: 'What the hell is going on?'

'I'm screaming.'

'I heard that. But why? I thought you were being raped, at least.'

'I'm in trouble. And I'm not as nice as you are, James. Trouble does not improve my soul.'

'You mean your temper. That's only because you have a sense of sin.' He walked over to the dress she had been working on. 'Show me what the trouble is.' He held up the short skirt, studying the material and the way it hung. 'So what is it?'

'What do you mean about sin?'

'Oh Charlotte, fancy asking me to explain. It's just a thing I said. Just as I might say you have shiny dark hair and brown eyes. All the same, it's true. I spoke without thinking, but I meant it. It's what gives you your strength.'

'I'm as weak as a reed.'

'Oh no.' He laughed. 'Strong. But there's something inside you that sometimes shows in your face. I would call you a happy person who sometimes loses the trick of it.'

'And is that a sense of sin?'

'It's one way of it, at all events.' He was half joking but sometimes he had seen a strange expression on her face, of which he thought she was unconscious, as if a lucid, wary, anxious animal was looking out through his friend Charlotte's eyes. He was an imaginative man; his mother was from the Western Highlands, and saw ghosts. James' father had feared the couture world, fleeing from it to join the army, but coming back to Redmond & Bruce after the war. He died of drink. His wife never saw his ghost, although revenants from the seventeenth and earlier centuries were common with her. James on the other hand, felt his father's ghost about him all the time, and wondered his mother did not sense it, too.

Charlotte said, 'You shouldn't read too much into faces, especially mine. Don't you know I pull faces just to keep people wondering?'

'What's the trouble then?'

Charlotte told him.

'Let's work on it together and see what we can do. I had a session with Alice Connaught once, but she decided I had nothing to offer her and she never came back. Bought two dresses and that was that. She pays her bills, though, I will say that for her.'

'I want more than money from her,' wailed Charlotte.

'Don't we all? An elusive lady.'

'You sound as if you like her.'

'I do. I admire her. And you'd better do the same if you want to make clothes for her. If you don't like her, not at all, then you won't succeed. But above all, don't be neutral. Better to dislike her. That works sometimes. But if you have no feeling at all it's hopeless.'

Charlotte stared at him. 'I believe that may have been the trouble. I was so intent on the dresses themselves I hardly noticed her. The other two dresses got by, but I wanted one out and out winner. You can't always hope for a three out of three, but I do need one now.' With conviction, she added, 'There *ought* to be one too. If there's anything in me at all, I ought to be able to pull this off.'

Charlotte studied her blue and white creation. 'It's just so ordinary. The proportions are right now, although it's very short even for this season.'

'Have you got any more of the blue and white silk?'

'Oh yes.' She went to fetch a bolt of the silk from the stock-room. 'I ordered a lot. Too much probably.'

'No, it's charming. Not pretty-pretty, yet very feminine. I mean, it could look formal.'

'True.' Charlotte was holding a length of the silk against her, studying it in the mirror. 'I'm not usually dead like this, you know. I usually have ideas.'

'I wonder if a long tight skirt beneath the short dress would work?'

'Turning it into a sort of tunic?' Charlotte twirled round, displaying her image. 'Making the dress into a tunic?' She hummed a tune under her breath as she experimented. 'A silver belt?—A bit 1930's, I think. No, it wouldn't do. It would make her look elegant, but old. She won't like that. The wrong image. Especially for *now*. We're all young. Not old and elegant.'

'She *is* old and elegant.'

'Middle-aged. Don't be hard, James. And it would be the wrong sort of elegance. Not right for here and now. It ought to be more flip.'

107

'More what?'

'Free. Loose. Vibrant. Not so ladylike. She doesn't want to look ladylike. She wants to look like a lady who could be very sexy if she chose.'

'That's asking a lot of a dress.'

'It's what all my clients want.' Even if they did not say so explicitly. It was the difference between James' clients and her own.

'Since you've got it all so clear, then ask yourself why you aren't succeeding with this dress.'

Charlotte looked at herself in the mirror. 'My lipstick has run and I'm in a rotten mood.'

'Any special reason?' He shook his head. 'Don't say if you'd rather not.'

'It was Diana if you must know. She made a kind of scene. I expect you know how things are with her.'

'I wasn't sure if you did.'

'Well, I do now. It sort of burst out of her. So at last she confirmed the rumour I had heard. A rumour I desperately hoped wasn't true. Another sad case of unrequited love. Poor Diana.'

'Oh dear.' His voice was sympathetic.

Charlotte went on: 'We'll go on being friends, of course.'

James laughed. What a child she was. Always ready to kiss and make up. Friends indeed. Poor Diana it was. 'And that is behind your bad mood? It affects your creativity?'

'On that dress, yes.' She stared from the dress to James. 'There's a block. Why?'

'I think you are finding out.'

'Yes.' The excitement was rising inside her. 'When I cut that dress I was heading a certain way. But something blocked me. Stopped me bringing my thoughts to their logical conclusion.'

'So?'

'I was going to put trousers underneath, not a skirt. A perfect silhouette, right in mood. But that was an ambivalent projection. Trousers. Men. A double sex. Diana's image blotted it out. Until now.'

'You are too intelligent, Charlotte.' James went across to hold the material up beneath the floating dress. 'Let's see what we can do.'

Laughing, amused with each other, and happy, they worked together at cutting, pinning and tacking. The time went fast.

'Let's blur the image even more,' suggested James. 'Not tight trousers but very full.'

'Like a pretty sailor?'

Thus transformed the dress, now a loose tunic, drifted in a cloud of blue and white above the trousers. Charlotte had reversed the material, so that where the top was blue flowers on a white ground, the trousers were blue with white flowers.

Charlotte had an idea. She pleated the trousers at the ankle. Pinning the material tightly at one side, so that they pouched over the foot.

She turned and raised an eyebrow. 'What do you think?'

'Shorten the trouser leg so that the fullness just falls over the ankle and doesn't touch the instep. That's right, blouse it, as it were. Fine. I call that good.' He looked up at her. The shining cap of dark hair was still tied up with the blue and white silk, she was flushed and pretty. 'And sew up a turban to go with the tunic and trousers, like the one you have on and you'll have a trio.'

'The rule of three?'

'Exactly.'

'And you can call the whole set Topkapi.'

'What's that?'

'The old palace of the sultans in Istanbul.'

They were laughing and relaxed with each other.

'Oh, I am glad it was you that helped me,' said Charlotte. 'Glad it was no one but you.'

'I don't think I could ever want to work with anyone but you now,' James answered.

They were hugging each other and laughing. This man makes me happy, Charlotte thought. The first ever. With Jehan it had been like having an illness, and one from which she was glad to have recovered, although nervous of a relapse. Tony had been a rest-cure after Jehan, but something of an illusion. Now you see him, now you don't. Neither of them had given to her this sense of happiness.

110

This tranquil state lasted into the next day and beyond. She was able to tell James that the rule of three had operated, ensuring that she had triumphed with Mrs Connaught.

She took James out to lunch to celebrate. Then he took her out to dinner to celebrate her buying him lunch. The next day they bought a picnic lunch at Fortnums to eat in Green Park, and then in the evening went to Covent Garden.

Every day Charlotte felt closer to James. The relationship between them began to take on a different shape. She was nervous of using the word love, but something very close to it was growing between them, a feeling that had in it deep affection, humour, shared interests and trust.

Charlotte did not see so much of Diana as she had done. Diana was busy moving into new offices in a narrow alley off Piccadilly, and setting up her own small staff. One ambition had been thus fulfilled. For the moment, life was a roundabout, on which Diana travelled, round and round, hoisting on board the smart and new, then throwing them off as expendable when they showed wear.

Business meetings, sometimes diguised as friendly luncheons, still took place however, at irregular intervals. They *were* friends even yet, but friends whose relationship was changing from one shape to another. Charlotte hoped it would be a good shape but she was far from sure. Once or twice at their meetings it appeared that Diana had been crying, but Charlotte said nothing.

She relied on Diana for news, of which Diana always had some to spread.

One day in September, at lunch at a new restaurant she was promoting, Diana said she had heard that Jehan was heading homeward.

'Oh God.'

'Don't worry; he won't trouble you. He's said to have a mortal illness. No one knows what it is yet. He's coming home to consult some special doctor. Or die. It's not sure which yet.'

'Don't you believe it. In no time at all the doctor will be the one with the dread illness and Jehan will be off and away. That's how he operates. I ought to know.'

'Only Jehan causes you to make such black jokes.'

'So tell me some more news.'

'Sophia Beauclerc is coming back to London also. No one knows why. Everyone thought they were perfectly happy commuting between the island in the Caribbean and the ranch in Canada with the occasional stop-off in New York, her spiritual home, anyway.'

'Perhaps she's ill, too?'

'No chance. As strong as a horse that girl. No, what we all wonder is why she's left Tony behind. Probably nothing in it. But I wouldn't take my eyes off him myself.'

'I'm not interested in talk about Tony.'

'No? I am. She's not very bright, you know.'

They finished their lunch in more or less silence. Charlotte thought the food not very good.

'Does James know that Charles has bought that factory in South London for you?'

'It's not for me. It's an investment.'

'So he doesn't know. You ought to tell him. And *you* are Charles's investment, by the way. But you know that.'

Diana stood up. Charlotte reached out for her handbag. 'No, we don't pay for the lunch. It's one of the perks of my promotion job. I don't think it will last very long, do you?'

* * *

Early in the next week Charlotte had arranged to go to the theatre for a first night with James, with supper afterwards. It was to be her treat. They had arranged the outing in high spirits because both of them wanted to see the play whose leading actress had been dressed by James.

He didn't come into work that day, but sent a message saying he had a migraine.

'He has too many migraines.' Charlotte was fussing to Val. 'I ought to go and see him.' But she knew that with such an attack one wants

113

nothing but a dark room and stillness. 'I'll send some flowers. No, not flowers the scent would make him feel sick. I'll leave him alone to get better and go to the theatre by myself. Then I can tell him all about it.'

She went to the first night, enjoying it more than she expected, storing up little jokes to pass on to James when he was better: 'The set was horrid: like mouldy Bath-buns, but your dresses *shone*. She's put on a lot of weight, though. Pounds, I'd say.' And, 'I sat next to Barny Hepplewhite in the stalls, your empty seat so pathetic between us, and he was taking nips of brandy from a flask all the way through. Afterwards, he asked me to supper with him. Not likely.'

After the theatre she took herself out to a meal. Not to the Savoy where she had planned to take James, but to Mr Chow's. She felt like Chinese food. Besides, they had promised themselves they would try it. Now she would have been there first, and it would amuse James.

It was very crowded but she got a small table in a corner, her view of the room blocked by a huge and noisy party. She didn't mind, enjoying her own quiet, solitary meal.

When the party moved away, she saw James sitting at a table across the room. He was with Sophia. He was leaning towards her and their hands were touching. His head was very close to Sophia's.

They left before she did. Whether James had seen her or not, she could not tell.

* * *

The following day, a Wednesday, black Wednesday for ever more, Charlotte took herself into the work-room used by James. He was at his drawing-board. He worked from sketches much more than Charlotte, who preferred the stimulus of the actual fabric. She was undecided whether to say she had seen him with Sophia or not.

'How's your headache?'

He barely looked up. 'There never was a headache. That was just an excuse.'

At least he was being honest.

'I had to think things through before I could speak to you again.'

He was on the attack, aggressive as she had never seen him before.

'I know about the factory in South London. I know what plans you have. Thanks for not telling me.'

Charlotte wanted to shout at him: And what about Sophia then?

But pride froze her into silence. 'You would have been told,' she said stiffly. 'When there was anything to tell. There isn't yet. But I'm sorry. If you feel I've let you down, I apologise. I should have told you.'

She stared at him, hopefully. Now, you

115

explain, she was thinking. Tell me about Sophia. Say it meant nothing, nothing at all.

But James spoke not a word on this subject. Sophia's name was not mentioned. They had quite a long conversation about the factory at Greenwich. She couldn't make out how hostile he was to the idea. On the whole, not so hostile as she had expected. 'Bring him round,' Charles had said. She thought she could do it. They talked of other things, but about Sophia he said nothing.

When she got back to her room, she looked through the newspapers while she drank some coffee. There was an item in the William Hickey column about Sophia being in London. Nothing about Tony.

She's married to Tony, but she's going to keep up with James as well. Ah well, they're that sort of people, after all. Always were. I'm not, I know that now. I didn't think James was, but apparently I was wrong.

She folded up the newspapers as carefully and neatly as if part of her life was tidied away with. She was facing the desolate conviction that she was not the sort of woman that a man loved seriously. Or for very long.

CHAPTER SIX

At the beginning of the Sixties Charlotte had felt she was living at a wonderful time. She had been very young.

In the middle of the period she had started to feel a little inner doubt as to whether she was doing such great things after all, or if indeed anyone else was.

By the end of the decade Charlotte had mentally wiped the slate clean of the Sixties Dream. The years had not been what she had hoped; she was a realist about them, if about nothing else.

The years meant different things to different people, but she herself would have figured in everyone's list. If she had thought about it she would have known that her position was stronger at the end of the period than at the beginning. *She* had *grown* in stature. She herself was one of the faces of the decade. Charlotte saw the period in terms of faces. Faces, and clothes.

Charlotte thought of this period—the final year of the Sixties beckoning—as the time of betrayal. She was betrayed, and she did a bit in that line herself. Certainly James Bruce would have said so, as he saw the way Redmond & Bruce developed. Carved up, he called it. He never said it aloud, but Charlotte saw it in his eyes.

To the world, he seemed to assent what took place as a natural, indeed desirable, business progression. But Charlotte knew that "progress" was not how James saw what happened to his beloved couture house. To him it must inevitably have seemed a deterioration, a reversal of everything that he stood for.

So, it was treachery time. Perhaps it was the fault of the times themselves, those years, which promised so much and delivered so little.

But relationships like that between Charlotte and James, especially when they are also professional ones, do not fall apart at a touch. It takes time.

They met. She accused him of dissimulation over Sophia; he ignored the accusation and countered with an attack on her for lying over the factory at Greenwich.

'There was no lying,' she said angrily. Val came through the door of the office under the impression she was being summoned, then retreated hastily, fully aware that she was not. 'Not on my part.' But had there not been?

'And none on mine,' James declared angrily, back at her.

The row spread tension all over Redmond & Bruce. People took sides. Diana was equivocal: she was too fond of both of them, she said.

Meanwhile the apricot and white salon echoed to the silent quarrel between the

118

two principals.

In one of the strange line-crossings that life presents, it was a woman she had only met once before, and not liked, who cleared her mind for her: Phoebe, Diana's sister, the drunken one. Even meeting the woman was a freak chance.

Charlotte had gone back to her own apartment after a long, weary, hostile day at Redmond & Bruce.

The telephone did not ring, there was no post, as far as she could see, and no one in her entire world wanted her. She moped round her sitting-room, newly re-decorated in an even cleaner, sparser style than before in navy-blue and neutral tweed.

She desired to be loved. Suddenly it was clear in her mind. She faced the fact that the minutes and hours were ticking away as steadily for her as for the decade. She had to run with it, or get left behind.

She brushed her hair, telephoned Diana to see if they could eat together, got no answer and took herself to the Terraza Paduano for a meal. She liked Italian food, and it was the new smart place. A place to see what was being worn. She ought to eat there and keep an eye on the competition.

She disliked eating out alone, but James had not completed her cookery training and it did not look now as though he would do.

Across the room she saw Diana's unmistakable back; there was no missing the set of her shoulders and the shape of her head.

Her hair, that fine, soft hair, looked more untidy than usual, from which Charlotte deducted some emotional crisis, for Diana had been very much on the fidget lately. She too was alone.

Charlotte went across and tapped her on the shoulder. 'Hello! I was hoping to see you somewhere around. You don't usually dine alone.'

'No, but I drink alone.' She turned round. It wasn't Diana, but her sister, the drunken Phoebe.

'I thought you were Diana.'

'People do. Did even more when I was younger. Sit down. Have a drink. Join me for dinner.'

Charlotte found herself settling into a chair. There was something compelling about these sisters; one found oneself doing what they asked. I must learn the trick, she told herself, but perhaps it had to be inherited.

'Actually I'm not drinking so much tonight. For me, I am tolerably sober. And, I owe you an apology. I behaved badly to you when we last met.'

Charlotte made a demurring noise about not needing an apology. She was almost surprised the woman remembered, so drunk she had been.

'Oh go on. Take it. I don't make many, believe me. Life wouldn't be worth living if I did,' she joked.

As the ice was broken, Charlotte found herself learning how Phoebe had become the way she was.

'My husband taught me to drink. He had a gift for it, a great knack. I should think he taught scores of people. A privilege to be taught by a master.'

Phoebe had been brought up in the Forties; flowered and married in the Fifties; divorced and drunk in the Sixties. The Seventies would probably see the end of her.

There but for the grace of God go I, thought Charlotte. She has emptied herself for a love betrayed, and that is just what I must not do. It nearly happened to me with Tony.

'What about your ex-husband?' she asked.

'He can't stand me now. But we have the children and occasionally he approves my taste in port.'

'You don't look like a port drinker.'

'Ah, I drink to suit all tastes, all moods.'

Obligingness had been bred in her, nourished by youthful training. It was just what women were encouraged in and what ruined them.

It was not what Charlotte wanted for herself. But she knew herself and understood aloneness was not for her either. Not for anyone, probably, why should it be?

Phoebe said: 'I expect you are thinking I would have been better off without my husband? You are quite wrong. I should have been much worse. And so would most women.'

After which, to the surprise of both, the two women settled down to a companionable dinner. They were both in agreement in disliking garlic and in loving Diana. On parting:

'You do have the most lovely clothes,' said Phoebe wistfully. 'I wish I could afford such.'

'Lay off the gin for three months and I will give you a wardrobe.'

'You'd do that for Diana's sake?'

'I'd do it for you,' said Charlotte.

*   *   *

Charlotte's first act next morning was to summon Val with her note-book for instructions. Val was used to Charlotte's way of giving thumb-nail sketches, with measurements, of future clients. 'Bring in some samples of next season's wools and silks. I'd like to select colours.'

When she had taken down the details, Charlotte said: 'It's in performance of a promise to a reforming drunk. She stops drinking, I do a mini-wardrobe.'

Val raised a sceptical eyebrow. 'Do I know the lady?'

'You could put a name to her, I daresay.'

'Thought as much. Do you think she will

give it up?'

Charlotte considered. 'No. Truthfully, I don't think so. But a promise is a promise.'

Charlotte looked at her diary for the day, saw she had an interval of twenty minutes just before lunch and selected it as the time to talk to James. Talk there had to be. They couldn't go on like this.

She ran up the stairs wondering exactly what she was going to say. All the present happiness of her life was built between these apricot and white walls; now it seemed in jeopardy.

She had not made an appointment to see James. She would just take her luck.

Charlotte paused outside his door, her hand on the door knob. All around her came the sounds of quiet activity. She could just pick up the murmur from the work-rooms, backed by the subdued rhythmic roll of the sewing-machines. From below came the bell-like tones of Eileen, the chief vendeuse. This was a happy, prosperous enterprise, she wanted it to go on. But going on meant changes. Five years time, ten years time, where would they all be?

She tapped on James' door, then went in before he could answer.

He was there, on his own, standing with his back to her, looking out of the window. He was wearing the loose white jacket, like a doctor's, which he wore when he had been doing a fitting.

'Come in, Charlotte. I know it's you.' He did

123

not turn round. 'I know your knock.'

He did not say he could also smell her scent, but he could. It was deliciously like her.

'Well, look at me,' she pleaded. No doubt she was wrong to let her personal feelings creep into business relationships. It was a hang-over from the bad, old fashioned ways still inside her, that she must eliminate. She must not mind about Sophia.

'I don't mind any more about Sophia,' she said.

'Thank you.' He had turned round. The gentle pleasant look he had used to give her was gone. He looked almost a stranger.

I'm not sure if I like this man, she thought.

'You really have got a cheek sometimes, Charlotte. Sophia is my business, not yours. And it *was* business.'

'All right.' She only half believed him. 'We have to work together, so let's get on terms again.'

'I won't take the easy way out. I won't go off in a huff. You won't get me out of Redmond & Bruce that way. You won't get rid of me so smartly.'

'I don't *want* to get rid of you!'

James shrugged. He had his own opinion. 'I have one claim-hold you may have forgotten: the actual freehold of this property belongs to me. When you and Charles Scrope bought the majority share, you bought the lease, but *not* the freehold.'

Charlotte waited. There was more to come.

'Study the small print. You will see it also gives me a right to work here if I so desire. Payment is not mentioned. I could do it and starve. But I'd do it if I have to. I'd hang on.'

'I *don't* want you *out*! I want to work *with* you, James. I admire your work.'

'Thanks again.'

'I shan't try to break the small print of the lease. Nor will Charles. And I won't probe into you and Sophia. It's not my affair as you say.'

James made a gesture with his hand, as if to stop her, but she pressed on. 'But the working together is different. We have to see things the same way.'

'Your way.'

'No. We'd talk things over. We'd come to an agreement.'

James threw open his arms, it seemed in despair. 'You'd always win me over. You're doing it now.'

Charlotte turned away. Perversely, a part of her didn't want James to capitulate so easily. Perhaps I should draw away from him, not let myself become any fonder. He would be my child not my partner.

Anyway, what was on offer for her? It seemed there would always be Sophia in James' life. Sophia who appeared to have a knack of hanging on to the affections of those who loved her, which Charlotte herself did not possess.

125

Perhaps it was her body language. It might be that Sophia sent out all the right signals to retain love while Charlotte sent out the wrong ones.

When she tried to get a picture of Sophia in focus it was hard. She recalled a tall, lithe figure with a mane of hair which just, but magnificently, missed being sandy and became tawny, matched with the only topaz-coloured eyes in a human face she had ever seen.

She remembered a genuine flair for wearing grand clothes casually, and for showing leisure clothes as if they had grown on her. An ideal model, in fact, but what, if anything much, was inside, Charlotte could not tell. She wanted there to be nothing. She wanted to call her a doll, and to be able to tag the word empty on to her as well. Yet, at the same time, she had the uneasy feeling that the essential Sophia might have more stuff in her.

'My horoscope for today said to watch out for trouble this morning,' said James gloomily, breaking into Charlotte's dark thoughts. 'Do not press your luck, it said.'

'Do you read your horoscope every day?' she asked.

'You bet.'

'And you believe it?'

'It's like the weather forecast, isn't it? You get what's coming to you, anyway. But yes, if it's a good forecast, then it cheers me up. Artistic, creative people are like that.'

Charlotte smiled: artistic baby. Let him have his Sophia if that was the toy he wanted. As for Tony, being in his own terrible way, an adult person, he could look out for himself.

The telephone rang on James' desk. He picked it up. 'Oh, Val? Yes, she's here.' He handed it over to Charlotte. 'For you.'

Val's voice was telling her that Charles Scrope's secretary was on the line for her. Charlotte took the call. She confirmed with Charles' secretary that she would be delighted to meet him for lunch one day that week. And added that she was now ready for a visit to the Stock Exchange. He would know what that meant...

As Charlotte put the telephone back, her hand touched James'. Afterwards, long afterwards, Charlotte wondered what would have happened if the pressure had been prolonged. At the time all she thought absently was how warm and agreeable his hand felt.

But James simply moved his hand away; his stars had given him the wrong messages that day.

* * *

The visit to the Stock Exchange was, as both Charlotte and Charles had known it would be, a signal. And once the signal was given, events moved quickly.

Charlotte had been sought by two men:

127

James and Charles.

In spite of Sophia she knew that James would have laid a claim to her if she had responded. But Sophia, or whatever she stood for, had weighed in there with her sudden appearance.

Money and position didn't come into it, in spite of what Charles said. She would be a richer woman with him than with James, but this did not count. She would go on with her work in any case, making her own money. She took that for granted.

If Charles was pointing out aspects of herself that she had not known, (and was still not quite sure about), then she was discovering things about him.

She was finding that underneath he was not at all what she had expected. She had thought him smooth, easy, completely the ruler of his world. That's what he looked like on the outside.

Inside, as she now saw with surprise, he was rougher and more thrusting, less poised, less self-confident than she had imagined. It was almost as if he was struggling up from the working classes, a man with his way to make in the world, not the safe inhabitant of the sheltered life that had been his. He was more tense and infinitely more self-critical than she had believed possible.

Tony had genuinely been what he appeared to be, but Charles was not. He was humbler, nicer, but also tougher and more aggressive. Charlotte was unprepared for the inner turmoil she now sensed. Not sure if I could cope with it, she thought.

The visit to the Stock Exchange, going solemnly round the public rooms, and then leaning over the balcony to stare at the great, round, thronged room below was more interesting than she had expected. 'How long has it been here?'

'On this site, since 1801. We are about to rebuild. The New Stock Exchange should be ready in the early Seventies. It's time.'

It was the time for building everywhere. On all sides new office-blocks, new hotels were rising, changing for ever the profile of London against the sky. But after all, the city Wordsworth wrote about had not been the London that Shakespeare saw, nor Shakespeare's London that of Chaucer.

'You'll like this sort of thing.' He waved his hand over the Stock Exchange indicating, Charlotte supposed, the span of its whole world.

'I will?'

'Yes. You're not a bit what you think you are. What you thought you were with Tony.'

There, he had said the name aloud. He was very jealous of the memory, and they both knew it. The strong undercurrent between them made her more uncomfortable: it was electric.

'You like an ordered, structured life. You'll fit into formality. I know you will. You were made for it.' He sounded as though he meant it.

Without a word being spoken by them it seemed to be assumed that their lives would be joined. Somehow Charlotte felt this was a dividing line in her life. A watershed, was the term often used.

It was then that Charles asked her to marry him.

Charlotte did not want to decide in a hurry. 'Marriage! Let's leave things for a bit?' But she was only playing, she knew she would say yes, eventually.

'Not for long,' said Charles.

'You almost take it for granted.'

'Almost, but not quite. Charlotte, I will never take you for granted.'

It was the sort of thing that lovers said to each other. She hoped it was true. If so, it was unusual for her in her experience of men.

*　　*　　*

As the weeks passed she relaxed, letting her affections flower. She was amazed to find how gay and cheerful she felt. Loving Charles was making her life-picture brighter and more vigorous. She felt full of energy and hope.

Charles began to introduce her to his friends. Here too she had some surprises. She had imagined that his circle would be much the same as Tony's, and, perhaps, had been dreading meeting them on that account. But they were different.

Not all were the successful, smart people whom she would once have supposed to be his friends.

He took her to meet a young don at Oxford, a shy, awkward young man, but who talked easily to Charles. They lunched in rooms overlooking the Magdalen Park, and although the food was not as good as it had once been, so the young don said, explaining, 'we are all so poor now, even the rich colleges', the wine was delicious and the view elegiac.

That was a happy day. Next Charles took her to see someone he called one of his best friends.

She didn't know what to expect. Certainly not the lame, elderly woman lying on a sofa listening to Schubert. They both liked Schubert, it appeared, sometimes playing it together as a duet on the grand piano in the corner of the lofty Kensington room.

'I didn't know you played the piano,' Charlotte said.

'I don't really. Not seriously. Miss Bates helps me out.' And he gave the elder woman an amused affectionate smile.

They had tea with Miss Bates, china tea and coconut cake to eat. It was a cosy warm occasion.

Afterwards Charles explained that she had

been his nursery-governess, and they had always "kept up". Charlotte suspected that he made her a pension, but she knew better than to ask.

She realised that Charles was quietly letting her into a part of his life he wanted her to know. It was not his whole life; she realised that even then. He was not totally open; she saw that at the time.

For instance, he never suggested they visit the house in Norfolk. She would have been interested. But he never even mentioned it.

'It's been shut up for years,' he said, when she raised it.

They were in the Crush Bar at Covent Garden, in the spring of 1969, drinking champagne and eating smoked salmon sandwiches. They had come to see "The Rosenkavalier". They were on their own; Charles had said you must either be in a great party to hear Rosenkavalier, or, be with someone you loved. As with visiting Venice, Venice was exactly the same he said.

Charlotte began to see what a structured life meant. It demanded a nice sense of timing and occasion. Certainly it was different from life with Tony. But then Tony was himself an important part of the structure, in which both men lived where as Charles, somehow, was not.

'What have you done today?' One of the nicest things about Charles was that he was

132

always interested in her work.

Charlotte considered. 'Had a conference with Diana about an afternoon luncheon-and-TV spot in Leeds in about two months time. Just right for the new autumn/winter collection. Worked on ideas for that collection. Not going well, I may say. I don't think I'm concentrating.'

Charles laughed and sought her hand. She continued: 'Saw several clients ... You're right by the way. I'm bursting out of the couture mould.'

'Seen James Bruce?'

'Not today. Why?'

Charles looked across the crowded bar. 'I have felt I'm on a kind of see-saw—when I go up, he goes down.'

'Oh, that's rubbish,' said Charlotte, uneasily. It had a grain of truth. Charles was perceptive.

'Also, I've heard he's trying to raise money to go independent. I don't think he'll succeed, though.'

'You mean you will stop him?'

'Nothing like that. Just that I don't believe his heart is in it. Or so my informant believes. He'll stay.'

'Your informant: Diana,' said Charlotte with conviction.

'Not exactly.'

'One of her sisters then.'

'Say, a friend of a friend ...'

Virginia, thought Charlotte.

'We've had a bit of a quarrel, but yes, like you, I believe James will stay where his heart is.'

'And you? Where is your heart, Charlotte? If you have one. But I know you have. I always hated Tony for having a lien on it.'

'Lien?' mocked Charlotte. 'What sort of talk is that? Stock-broker's talk, banker's talk?'

'Now I'm making a call, it's settlement day.'

'That *is* banker's talk. Am I at a premium price?'

'To me, yes, always.'

'Well, I'm willing to settle.'

A bell sounded. People started to put down their drinks. Charles finished his. 'We have to go in. I don't want to miss that wonderful moment when the house lights go down. And don't think I'm changing the subject. I'm not. I want to enjoy that moment with you.'

'Thank you.' Her voice was husky.

'Come on.' He put his arm under her elbow. 'If it wasn't so crowded here, I would kiss you. I will anyway.' He kissed her lightly on the lips. 'Lovely scent you're wearing. Do I know it?'

'No, it's a new one I'm trying out.'

'Keep it. Will it be for you?'

'Yes.' It had been made by a new enterprising little firm just starting up. They wanted Charlotte's custom. The origins of the scent were totally synthetic, but the smell was fresh and sweet with an undertone of spice. She

134

was wearing one of her own dresses, a white crepe tipped with silver.

They settled in their seats. Their near neighbours on either side were two large groups, busy gossiping amongst each other, so that Charles and Charlotte were effectively as alone as if no one else sat in the row.

Charles looked searchingly into her eyes. 'Are you happy, Charlotte?'

For a second she hesitated, then she said: 'I can see you mean to make the most of your victory. To make me go down on my knees and admit that I am wildly happy. I can't quite do that at the Garden . . .'

She hesitated again, then continued, 'I care for you deeply. I care immensely. I think I have for along time, but I did not want to admit it. I don't know why. Yes, I do. It had to do with Tony. But now I admit my feelings, they are very strong. Very strong.' She reached out and took his hand. 'I only wonder why every other woman does not feel as strongly as I do.' She gave him a sidelong look. 'I expect they do really.'

Charles laughed. If it was a laugh of triumph, then it was nicely disguised. It sounded like happiness. 'What a joy you are.'

'I'm so glad to feel as I do. So very, very glad.'

The house lights went down, the audience hushed, while the first bold vibrant notes of the overture called across the darkened space.

Charlotte felt a thrill of pleasure. This is one of the happiest moments of my life, she told herself, and one she must enjoy to the full. Take it, hold it, treasure this moment.

She pushed her back against the seat so that she could sense the hardness through the plush upholstery, and let her feet move delicately in their silver sandals, wanting to feel her body wholly alive and sentient. She looked around, seeking memories to anchor the second.

The woman in front had on a three strand pearl necklace with a diamond clasp. Her diamond and pearl ear-rings swung continually as she slightly moved her head. They must be very light and delicate. She had fair hair piled on top of her head. Not a beauty, but elegant.

A row ahead was a man with the ugliest profile she had ever seen. An ex-prize boxer could not have had a more smashed-in nose. But he was looking down at the woman beside him with such affection that she thought he must be very lovable.

She looked up at the boxes. Three children lined one box. Two girls and a boy; they were staring down at the lower auditorium with smiles of pleasure as if this was part of the treat. They were beautifully dressed, the girls in matching blue and white silk dresses, the boy in a white shirt with a blue silk tie. Not English, Charlotte thought, too carefully matched and dressed as a set for English style. Possibly American.

The music hinted at the waltz theme, floated it out in an arc across the audience, then moved on to suggest the motif of the silver rose.

What Charlotte did not know was that she herself was being studied; the observer was observed. Scattered among the audience were a handful of women who were very aware of Charlotte. They had watched her arrival, observed her with Charles, seen him bend towards her, and taken in her eager, happy response.

She's enchanting to look at, damn her, thought one woman, the occupant of a seat in the Grand Circle. She could see the top of Charlotte's head. And the dress, of course, is exquisite. I might go to her myself. After all, it's been some years since Charles and I ... I suppose I'm over it. As far as one ever is with him. Damn him, too. She turned to her companion. 'Sorry if I'm fidgetting, darling.'

While across the aisle from Charlotte, staring at her so burningly that she might have felt the heat, was a much younger woman.

'So that's her. I suppose I might have known she'd look like that—so poised, so well groomed. She looks *free*, somehow. Well, she's got some news coming to her: that's over.'

Another woman, who had brushed against Charlotte as they came in thought, Of course, she dresses to suit herself ... I wish I could afford her prices. I'm glad I've seen her with him. Perhaps that will convince Irene. If I tell her. Perhaps I shouldn't. The truth is not always what you want from your best friend ... But I think I *will* go to her for a dress.

Three sharp witnesses; two new customers.

In her seat, Charlotte relaxed and gave herself over to the delight of the music. She had her moment of joy encapsulated within her. Nothing now could take it away from her.

Or so she supposed. In spite of her experiences she had not then learnt of the existence of retrospective pain.

* * *

After the evening at Covent Garden, came the plans for the wedding. It seemed a natural progression of events.

Also, they talked. They talked of where they should live in London, how they should live, in what manner and in what sort of house. The house in Norfolk was taken for granted. It would be visited at weekends and on certain ritual holiday occasions. 'Badly in need of re-decoration,' Charles had commented briefly. 'Leave that to you. You're the professional.'

They talked about their friends, their work, their hopes and their ambitions. The best thing, Charlotte told herself, is that we've talked so much to each other. I know so many things about Charles.

But what did they not talk about? Some

things went so deep one did not know they were unuttered.

Charlotte had grown up in an age which encouraged her to believe that she had a right, duty even, to have her own life, her own career, and a right to have it in her own way. One stumbled, fell about, got into trouble, as with Tony, but the basic right to happiness and success on one's own terms remained.

Charles was older than she was, and, his upbringing had been quite different. He had been brought up to expect more "structure" to life. What he meant by "structure" was formal rules for a way of life that had a predestined shape that seemed inevitable to him. In a life, certain events happened at certain times and in a certain order. Marriage was such an event which was a structure within a structure, following its own shape. From it flowered family life with children.

Charlotte thought life and marriage could be shaped spontaneously, Charles believed you fitted yourself to a framework already laid down.

Both believed in their own separate truth so deeply that it never seemed necessary to explain it to the other: it was what was, one had no need to speak of a self-evident truth.

* * *

'Where would you like to be married?' asked

Charles, in the course of one of their conversations.

Charlotte said she did not mind as long as she could have time to design and make her own dress.

'And how long will that take?'

'Oh, I could do it in a week. But two would be better! Tell me what sort of wedding we are to have, and I will know what sort of dress to design.'

'We haven't a lot of choice,' said Charles cheerfully. 'If in London, and I take it you wish for London? it has to be in one of two or three churches. It will be a pretty dull ceremony as you aren't one of us, but that doesn't matter.' Charles, so she thought, took a detached, matter of fact view of this question, seeming to regard his religion as something he had been born with, like his colour and nationality, rather than chosen.

'I suppose I could join up.'

'Please don't. Fortunately you haven't been divorced. That would slow things up.'

Whatever had happened to her, divorce had not been part of it.

'Who do you want to ask? Draw up a list. Family and friends.'

'I've no family,' responded Charlotte instantly.

'None at all? Most people have some.'

'Not me. An orphan.'

Charles considered. The Scropes were a

large kin group, but Charles had no close relatives living. 'We'll keep it very quiet and small then. I believe I'd prefer that. Then I need not ask my own family.'

'I shall have a dress like a silver lily,' she said. 'And I shall build the bodice so that it takes the weight of the dress and the material can be projected for the breasts.'

She pictured herself, like a shining lily, coming down the aisle.

*   *   *

When she was alone, at last, that night, Charlotte drew breath to contemplate what she had done. She was amazed at the speed with which it had all happened.

She felt dazed, yet excited. Light as a bird, as if she could fly, yet with an inner tremor. Was she right to marry Charles?

The real question was should she marry anyone? Or, to put another way, was Charlotte, nicknamed Butterfly, a girl who should marry at all? Wasn't it a full time job being Butterfly? How could she take on being a wife as well?

There were too many questions with no easy answers, but over-riding all was her passionate desire to marry Charles. It was what she wanted to do. Suddenly it was so clear in her mind that she wanted to shout it aloud. 'I love him! I love him!'

She thought she could make him a good wife; she knew she meant to try. She surprised herself at her straightforward, old-fashioned reaction.

After all, wasn't she the generation that was going to live without bonds? Marriage was out, free association was in. But now all those conventional feelings were stirring inside her. I'm the late twentieth century, but here I am, she thought. Is it possible those responses are built into women?

Yet if she asked herself what was her most unexpected emotion she would have to answer it was pride that someone like Charles should want her for his wife.

She lay, curled up in bed, contemplating her future. She felt secure at last. Triumphantly happy, with an inner conviction that if they were, somehow, ship-wrecked, in a life-boat together, without food or clothing, they would make it to safety, because they were together and had each other. There would be difficulties; her work, his career, but they would survive.

The sum of the two of us together will be greater than each of us alone, she assessed. I suppose that's what marriage is.

As she fell asleep, she thought: I never believed it could happen to me.

*   *   *

142

Next day Charlotte saw Diana and told her. She knew she had to speak to someone, and there was no one else. Behind her stretched an empty path which she had swept clean. She had carefully cut all links to her childhood past while retaining buried inner pictures.

So Diana it was. Charlotte asked her to come round before work. They talked over coffee in her kitchen where the sunlight shone on the Thames, and glinted back into the room.

Diana listened with silent concentration. 'I'm not surprised. I saw it coming. And marriage, actually marriage? Will that work for you, Charlotte?'

'I love him passionately. I have never felt like this before. It's as if I had never loved anyone else. Perhaps I never did in this way. He has such power and imagination. I feel as if I am completely bemused, physically and emotionally.'

'I shouldn't let him know that if I were you. He'll walk all over you.'

'I'm afraid he does know. Last night, at Covent Garden, I told him.'

There was a certain defensiveness in Charlotte's voice. 'He could already tell how I felt, though, I'm almost sure. It's a very intense feeling, Diana. Quite different from what I felt for Tony or Jehan. Although God knows Jehan had a powerful influence on me. But this is different.'

'And it's going to be a real marriage?' asked Diana gravely. 'Are you sure?'

'Yes. That's what makes it so different from those other affairs. They belonged to a paste-board world. Cardboard, a pretend life, and it *wasn't* real. Whatever there is between Charles and me, it is *absolutely* real.' Charlotte's voice trembled slightly with earnestness.

Diana drank some coffee silently.

'And I rather resent you saying he will walk all over me. He's not like that.'

'Don't you believe it. All men are.'

'No. I have come across one that I believe is *not* like that,' said Charlotte deliberately.

'But you don't know for sure! Oh Charles will give you champagne, and a sable coat, and servants, if that's what you want.' Goodness knows what else, thought Diana. 'But what about all the other things? Children, your career? Have you thought it all through?'

'He is the greatest possible promoter of me,' said Charlotte. 'He knows what my work means to me. I think it's part of what he loves in me.'

'I'd call Charles a pretty complicated person,' Diana finished, wearily. Now I've warned her, she told herself. Charles *is* all she says, but a lot more besides...

For a minute they both sat in silence. Then Diana made an announcement. 'Now I have something to tell *you*. It's great, something you haven't expected.'

144

Charlotte looked expectant.

'Get out the champagne, love. You're going to get the Fashion Designer of the Year Award. I've been tipped in advance. Of course, I've been pushing you, but I wasn't sure it would come off. Well, it has. Congratulations, friend.'

For a moment Charlotte sat quite still, then she jumped up and let out a loud whoop of joy. The two women hugged each other. 'Oh God, how gorgeous. Everything at once. It's marvellous. Oh, I'm so happy. Aren't I lucky?'

So Butterfly still lives, thought Diana. For a while it had looked as if she had been submerged beneath a flood of love and marriage. But no, she was there, co-existing, ready to muddle things up for the wife. Charles was marrying not one woman but two. 'Yes, darling. Very lucky,' she said.

'Oh, I must ring Charles and tell him. He'll be thrilled.'

'They want as much biographical detail as I can supply. Let me have something, Charlotte.'

'Oh, you know the outline: the School of Design, followed by St Martin's. Paris of course. And mention Rome, Milan, if you want to, although I wasn't there long.' Most of this was true; a little invented.

'Personal details?'

'There are none. It's been all work. Leave out the childhood stuff. It's of no consequence.'

145

Diana said, 'You're a strange one, Charlotte. You know all about my family, my past, and I know next to nothing about yours.'

'You know about Tony and Jehan. You know as much as I do about my future.'

'But nothing about where you came from.'

Charlotte shrugged. 'Well, I'm not half-Japanese. Except when it suits me to be,' she joked. 'As for the rest, it's too dull to talk about. I was born, educated and brought up in the usual way. That's all. I never talk about it because it does not interest me. Frankly it would not interest you if you knew all about it. You are only interested because you don't.'

She got up, tidied away the coffee-pot and cream. 'I am what you see. No need to go beyond that.'

'You can't keep secrets in our world; you know that. If you're keeping one, then sooner or later it's going to come out.' And you might mind it a lot more than if you let me handle it now, Diana added silently.

Charlotte had her back to Diana. 'No secrets,' she said. 'No secrets at all.'

There was a lot left unsaid between them at that precise moment, but something of the unspoken dialogue got across, so that both women stared at each other angrily. The difference between them, however, was that Diana thought uneasily: I must do something about the child, while Charlotte drew an effacing veil over that which she did not desire to think about as if it was not there at all.

Then Charlotte smiled. 'I'll tell you something that won't be news to you. It's going to take some courage telling James. I am not sure he will welcome either the award or the wedding.'

CHAPTER SEVEN

James was predictably stiff and formal about her engagement to Charles. He let Charlotte know that it was a shock, and an unwelcome one. His fury he kept to himself.

'That puts you squarely on the other side,' he said.

'What other side?'

They were talking in his designing room at Redmond & Bruce, a room more or less untouched by Charlotte's re-decorations.

'The side of mass production and big money-making as opposed to excellence.'

'You know as well as I do that if we don't make money we go out of business. Excellence has to sit on top of a pyramid of that money-making mass production you despise. And the mass production can be excellent, too.' Nor did she intend her designs to be so massively copied either. She would use discretion.

'And usually is not. Oh, you and I will never

147

agree. Have your wedding, get it over, and we will see how things shake down.'

'I suppose I can ask you to the wedding?' said Charlotte stiffly. 'You will come?'

'Oh I'll come. The firm must show its public face. Mustn't let my anger hang out, must I?'

*　*　*

Telling Diana of the score later on, Charlotte confessed that she had been shocked at his manner. 'It's usually *me* that behaves badly. James has such good manners as a rule. I can't understand it.'

'He's in love with you.'

'You've got that wrong. It's Sophia he loves. Oh, he finds me attractive. I admit that. But she's got the love.'

'I think *not*,' said Diana thoughtfully.

'Charles says I've handled James badly, and I suppose I have. Charles is delighted about the Designer Award. Of course, it means the wedding won't be as quiet as we wanted, but it doesn't really matter.'

'Did Charles say that?'

'Not exactly, but he's proud of me, Diana de Marche, you carping, sceptical thing.'

Diana laughed.

Charlotte reflected that if she could not manage James, she *could* manage Diana. She didn't know for sure if she had yet engineered that new type of friendship between woman and woman that she aimed at, but she was working on it.

What are the obligations of friendship between women? To be gentle, she thought. To be honest, but not so honest that it hurt. The trouble is she thought with wry self-humour, is that human nature *will* get in the way.

In the period that followed the silver lily got under way, although not without struggles. Building the structure of the dress proved difficult. Charlotte confided to Diana it was like the Sydney Opera House, then known to be in technical trouble, but it was achieved at last.

For the Designer Award dinner she had produced a soft, floating dress like cobwebs in moonlight which had been greatly influenced by a Callot model of 1922, now in a museum.

A third dress, a printed evening dress of white silk with a large geometric pattern in black was her own private celebration of her technical skills. It was so cut that it had but one seam, and swept off the shoulder, leaving the right arm bare, in assymetric folds. It was both brilliant and original. The black and white faille dress was also immensely becoming to the wearer.

Charlotte had a feeling of entering into a period of great creativity. It was a blessed feeling which she attributed to having got her personal life settled.

Once we get the actual wedding over, she

thought, it would be full steam ahead. The details of the wedding ceremony had been settled: the church, a very conventional choice, was the Brompton Oratory, to be followed by a reception at Claridges. Privately, Charlotte decided she would give another party later, in her own house. Then they would go away for a few days, returning to a newly-purchased house near Hyde Park. They would be back in time for the Designer Awards presentation.

In the preparation for the Award ceremony she was getting publicity both in the daily press and the fashion magazines. *Vogue* had scheduled a feature on her for which David Bailey was doing the photography.

Under his skilful lens, Charlotte knew she had never looked better. The photo-session was in her own workroom.

'You've got lovely hair, darling,' he said, lighting it from above so that it gleamed. 'Always get them to light you from up here, when being shot, love. Your hair pays for lighting.'

*   *   *

Three days before the wedding, which made it the first Monday in July, 1969, Diana telephoned with some arrangement about making a film of the ceremony and reception. 'Just for the record. I think you ought.'

Charlotte was alone, in her kitchen, drinking

her breakfast coffee; she was happy, relaxed.

'I can't agree without asking Charles. I expect he'll say, yes. He's punch drunk at the moment, poor darling. Saying yes to everything, except when he says no. So a provisional, yes.'

'OK. I just want it to go smoothly. I don't know about you, Charlotte, but I'm getting distinctly jittery about this wedding.'

'I'm not. Why shouldn't it go smoothly?'

'Oh I don't know.'

'Diana, is there something you aren't telling me?'

'No ... Well, yes. Perhaps there is. I've heard that Jehan is planning to attend.'

'But we haven't asked him!'

'That won't stop him if he wants to come.'

'Keep him out!' Charlotte's voice was rising. 'That's what the ushers are for. Tell him he can't come in. That the police will be called it he comes anywhere near!'

She put the receiver down to Diana's wails that that would look lovely in the papers, her hand shaking.

Oh, Charlotte had been relieved when, a couple of months ago, Diana had confirmed Jehan was over his health scare. But why did he have to stay here in England to haunt her? Her lovely peace was broken.

* * *

The beautiful silver lily dress was completed in time, and was judged a great success. Charlotte felt a moment of triumph as she entered the church wearing it. The organist had refused to play "Aquarius", pretending that he had never heard of it. So Wagner it was.

Her joy lasted for about two minutes as she walked down the aisle on the arm of an elderly friend of Charles, whose qualifications for the task were that he had met Charlotte twice, and that he was the right height!

As they passed the great stands of golden and white flowers that flanked the front row of seats, a face turned to look at her.

It was Jehan. He grinned, a great, splitting smile that might have been friendly and might not, then spun round to face the altar.

Charlotte drew in her breath. He meant to make trouble, she was sure of it. From that moment on she was just waiting for the explosion.

She gazed up at Charles when she reached his side, trying to communicate her fears, but he only smiled at her.

The service seemed to take place in an area about a foot above her silver flowered cap where the air was sweet and warm. She joined in, made the correct responses, but inside she was waiting for Jehan to make his move.

Any moment now, he would stand up and shout. Or else stride up the aisle, and hit her. Then it would depend entirely on his mood whether he dragged her after him or not. Charles might, or might not, drag her back.

"Bride torn in two by rivals." Either way, she would not be married. Any madness seemed possible.

But suddenly, she *was* married, she was walking down the aisle on Charles' arm, and Jehan's face was serious, but not violent. He looked at her, then looked away.

Charlotte felt weak with relief. She sank into the car taking them to Claridges, glad to sit down. Charles appeared to have noticed nothing.

He kissed her in that moment they had alone before their first guests arrived.

'My love,' she said. 'I do adore you.'

He released her. 'Now go and repair your lipstick. Then when you come back you shall have some champagne.'

Diana appeared on the late side, impatiently awaited by Charlotte. 'How did *he* get there?' she whispered. 'How?'

Diana shrugged. 'He just came.'

'Why didn't you throw him out?'

'That *would* have looked good tomorrow in the *Daily Mirror* and the *Sun*.'

'Is he coming on here?'

'I think *not*,' said Diana, 'that's why I am late. He was thinking of it, but I persuaded him not to.'

'Thank you. How?'

Again Diana shrugged. 'Oh, he can be very

153

reasonable sometimes.' She did not add that it was her belief that Jehan had plans of his own. He had given way too easily.

'He won't...' Charlotte hesitated. 'Sort of turn up *later*?'

'He couldn't. Even I don't know where you are going.'

'We're going to Venice. Cipriano's. I've always fancied staying there.'

Jehan had said once that if she ever married he would appear at the door of her honeymoon bedroom and bang on it and shout: 'She is mine!' Perhaps he would do it. 'He couldn't find *out*, could he?' she whispered urgently to Diana.

'I don't think so. Honestly. Don't worry.'

'But *you* still look worried. Diana, is there anything else?'

'Whatever it is, and there may be nothing, it's nothing to do with you,' said Diana wearily.

Charles broke in: 'What are you two whispering about?'

'Nothing. Just checking,' said Diana. 'We have details to fill in.' She gave Charles a gentle peck on the cheek. 'Lucky fella. You know that? Bye—See you later. I'll help you change, Charlotte.'

Charlotte meditated telling Charles, but she was interrupted by the arrival of the girls from her work-room accompanied by the quiet presence of James. He shook their hands, murmured the appropriate words of congratulation before moving on. You could rely on his good manners, she thought.

He was soon gone, but the girls wanted to kiss her and Charles, admire her appearance, giggle about the wedding, and be praised in their turn for the technical skill with which they had produced her dress.

Gradually the tension about Jehan ebbed away, and she relaxed. She was married, it had happened. There were moments when she could hardly believe she had let it happen, but here it was. She was Mrs Charles Scrope.

Charlotte Chaudin was gone, temporarily mislaid inside this married stranger. But Charlotte Scrope was still Butterfly.

Other people, of course, had seen Jehan, and were ready to comment on it. Tub, Thomas Underwood Bristow, did so, to Alan Stephens: 'You saw who was in church, I suppose?'

'Yes. Couldn't miss the way he came in. When I saw that familiar figure marching up the aisle I didn't know what to think. Haven't had such a shock since I went to the Eden-Churchill wedding and saw-'

Tub broke in: 'Were you really at that?' Most people thought Alan was a liar, but he did sometimes tell the truth. There was a strain of melancholy in him that surfaced in his lies.

'Certainly. And I'll tell you why—oh, champagne. I was in love with one of the guests and she smuggled me in. We couldn't bear to be

155

parted even for a minute.'

'Who was it?'

'I have a little difficulty now in remembering her name ... I know I was terribly melancholy when we parted. Thought I'd kill myself. Didn't, of course.' But he might do so one day he thought. Not for a woman, of course but out of a general despair.

'What do you think Jehan was up to?'

Alan raised an eyebrow. 'Up to?'

'He's up to something.'

'Very likely.'

'And who are you with now?'

Alan looked shy. 'Sylvia Nye. I'm madly in love with her. Beautiful, isn't she?' He waved to Sylvia across the room; she was talking to Diana.

Tub's eyes followed his wave. 'You'll remember her name all right.'

'Do you know,' said Alan thoughtfully, 'I think I will.'

Peter Bohun had greeted the bride and groom and was now making his way towards Diana. He too had seen Sylvia Nye. 'Lovely creature Sylvia is, but she's beginning to drink. Wouldn't touch her with a barge pole.' Then with characteristic modesty, he had added: 'But anyway a girl like her wouldn't be interested in an old bore like me.' As always he underestimated the power of the Bohun name with its once legendary possessions. The wealth was now almost dissipated, but they

156

still owned a great many beautiful objects.

Sylvia Nye was admiring Charlotte's dress and getting ready to talk to Tub, that old gossip, who was crossing the room towards her.

The conversation and the interest circled around Charles and Charlotte, but amongst this knowledgeable group of people who knew everything before it happened, a new story was surfacing.

It was such an exciting, big story that it was diverting attention even from the wedding.

'When it surfaces it's going to be the biggest scandal of the decade,' said Sylvia Nye. 'But there's only the tip of the ice-berg breaking the surface at the moment. Goodness knows what is underneath, but a hell of a lot I'd say. The stories that are coming out ... Well!'

'So say. You know you are dying to,' said Tub.

'It is titillating,' admitted Sylvia, deliciously enjoying her moment. 'So many hints of sex, drugs, spies, and it's just beginning to unfold. There's a lot more to come.'

'Names?'

Sylvia nodded vigorously. 'A few are coming up.'

'Anyone we know?'

'Of course. Bound to be. It's that sort of case. Goodness knows who will be dragged in before it's finished.' She sounded pretty pleased at the idea.

157

'Who for a start?'

'At the moment the names range from Teddy Clarkeson, the MP, to Francesca Köhl who will service anyone for the appropriate sum. Any service, anytime, anyhow.'

'You're drunk, Sylvia.'

'Oh, the littlest bit. Just the right amount for this sort of wedding. And my information is dead correct.'

'Anyone here likely to be involved?'

Sylvia let her eyes roam over the room. 'I think so. Oh, I do think so.' She sounded gleeful.

The stone had been dropped and the first ripples were showing in the pool.

Nothing so far had appeared in the press, but soon hints and conjectures would start, and the stories would proliferate. Fact and invention would merge, so that it would be exceedingly difficult ever after to establish what really happened.

'Teddy is a surprise,' said Tub.

'Oh no: he has always been infinitely corruptible. And there is some sort of body servant involved. Name and exact profession as yet unknown.' Sylvia's voice slowed happily. 'I intend to enjoy every minute of it.'

'You're so sharp you'll cut yourself.' Tub was mildly reproving. People who live in glass houses, he thought.

'Who was this body servant? I think you do know. Or guess.'

'The name Lance Potter was mentioned.'

'Lance Potter. Good Lord, Lance Potter!' Tub gave a little whistle. *He* knew Lance Potter.

He moved away from Sylvia fast. In his opinion it was no longer a question of people in glass houses but of touching pitch. Tub liked aphorisms. He felt safe among them in a world which offered so many dangers. Instinctively he recognised this as a dangerous moment for a person like him.

Sylvia moved around the room spreading her fables. Little rustles of laughter followed her progress, but for some people scratches of anxiety like splinters of ice picked away at the mirth.

It reached Charlotte. 'Who's Lance Potter?' she asked Charles. 'I've heard the name but I can't place it.'

Diana said: 'An amateur film-maker, among other things.'

Charles looked round the room. 'Shall we go?'

'Suits me,' said Charlotte with relief. After a bit, and with enough tension, silver lilies felt like hot kettles.

At that moment Jehan entered the room, with a tall, curvaceous red-haired girl on his arm. He didn't look defiant, or angry or arrogant, but interested and serious, just as he had in church.

'I think I should like to hit him,' said

159

Charles. Charlotte was surprised at the anger in him.

She put out a restraining arm. 'No, you can't do that. And who's the woman?'

Diana appeared at her elbow. 'Francesca something. You wouldn't know her.'

'Why has he brought her?'

'I don't know,' said Diana thoughtfully. 'Just for the hell of it, perhaps.' She wondered if she should hint to Charlotte that Jehan was the hand stirring up the scandal: he had friends he knew how to use in the press. Sheer malice, she thought.

'Let's go now,' said Charles. 'At once.' He took Charlotte's hand, and pushing past a surprised waiter, proffering champagne, he hurried her through the doors at the back and out.

'What's that scent you are wearing?'

'Oh, it's—' she began.

'You smell like a Parisian whorehouse.'

Charlotte started to explain that it was a very expensive French scent, given in a magnum bottle by the makers. Then she realised he meant it as a compliment!

How extraordinary it was that even the most sweet-mannered of men could sometimes fall into such errors of taste. But she saw suddenly that he was excited, nervous and a little drunk. Deeply touched, she said: 'Dearest darling: you mustn't be shy.'

It was heaven that he should be shy, totally

surprising also; it made her feel very erotic. 'Darling idiot. I've got a large bottle of it. We'll share it. I'll pour it all over you.'

No honeymoon that got off to such a start could fail to be a success, she thought.

*   *   *

Venice, when they got there, was a delight. But it took them three days to get out of Paris where they were to have stayed overnight at the Ritz. As it turned out, it was two days before they emerged from the suite, and three days before Charlotte saw a daylight view of the Place Vendome from the taxi as they left.

She had a moment to look around as Charles dashed across to Van Cleef et Arpels to return with a shining bauble for her throat. 'You must wear it every time we make love.'

'Darling I will wear it all the time,' she said. Her memories of Venice, apart from the diamond (which bruised her badly) was the loveable comfort of Cipriano's; the brooding presence of the Great Madonna in the church at Torcello; the sound of lapping water and strident nasal voices shouting at each other as the Venetians went about their business. It was the sour-sweet smell of ancient water and aged drains; it was the marvellous golden light falling from sky to lagoons then back again from the canals to the buildings.

She took Charles to the Fortuny Museum

and he took her to laugh at Carpaccio and be silenced by Bellini.

Venice was happiness and laughter.

*   *   *

'Did you never ask a single question about Jocelyn?' Diana queried incredulously, when they met, on Charlotte and Charles' return. 'Not ever, in the privacy of the marriage bed?'

'Never,' Charlotte had answered. 'There, least of all. I didn't want to know.'

But Charlotte had learned other things on honeymoon: that Charles was fussy about his food, taking the quality and presentation of it seriously. Fortunately at Cipriano's there were no problems, but she saw trouble ahead if she was cook!

In turn, he had learned that Charlotte was a poor sleeper, a person for whom sleep had to be wooed each night. She was also enthusiastic about keeping her body fit, exercising and swimming every day. If he thought she was a shade obsessive about this, he did not say so. 'You have a very beautiful body, darling girl. Lovely in bed, and glorious for love-making,' he assured her. They were in bed at the time. 'Don't go and get too muscular on me.'

'I don't do it for muscle. Just so everything is working as it should.'

'It does. It is. It will. Let me show you how well it does.' He stroked her breasts gently.

'What a beauty you are, darling.'

'You too,' said Charlotte shyly. It was a surprise to her that she found her husband so beautiful. Jehan and Tony had been attractive to her, but she had never really thought of their bodies as beautiful. Charles' spare elegance of bone fascinated her. 'You ought to be drawn,' she said.

'We both ought to be. We could be. Shall I get us done? There's a very good man in Florence.'

Charlotte buried her face in his shoulder. 'Perhaps one day when I'm braver.'

In fact, she was a little shocked at the idea of being drawn, nude in bed, with her husband.

And what did one do with the picture when one had it? Hang it in your drawing-room for all to see? In your bedroom? In the lavatory? Or keep it secret and look at it alone? No, surely not that. Better never to have it at all if that was all one did.

It was a point at which she should have started asking questions, but she didn't, and then love-making proceeded, putting all other thoughts out of her mind, until dusk fell on the room and the noise of the lagoon floated through the window.

Over dinner that night, sipping her wine, and eating grilled fish, she thought of it again. 'If we had such a picture, you know, that one of *us*, what would we do with it?'

'Well, most people have them set into a panel

163

in the ceiling. No, you idiot, of course, I didn't mean that. It's a joke, stop looking so shocked. If there was such a picture I should treasure it, of course,' and he smiled, touching her hand.

But he hadn't answered her question.

'We might go to Florence sometime. You ought to see it. And I would buy you some clothes. One can't shop in Venice. It's too provincial.'

Charlotte thought she would always buy her own clothes, choosing them to her style. Florence might suit her, and might not. She would see. She was not a doll to be dressed.

In spite of his concentration on her, which was quite equal to her concentration on him, Charlotte observed that he kept in touch with his London office, making a daily telephone call.

Once Charlotte had observed this freedom, she allowed herself some of the same, and telephoned her own office, always speaking to Val. James was either not available, or 'too busy just now to come to the phone.' It was clear that he was not going to sink back easily into friendliness. This was the one sadness in her life just then, because she valued James so much.

Paris was a different matter, the calls there were not so enjoyable, but she had been in the habit of making them regularly and did not want to stop making them, even on her honeymoon.

164

Once or twice, after she and Charles had made love, Charlotte found herself wondering about this artist in Florence, and if he really existed. The other thing she wondered was if, granted his existence, Charles had made use of his services before. But it would be bad manners to ask.

'I can draw,' she said suddenly, in an interval between love-making. 'I could draw us.'

'You could hardly draw yourself in situ.' Charles stroked her arm lazily.

'Imagination. I know what I look like. I could imagine. Would you like me to do it?'

'I'd treasure it.' He was serious and grave.

'I'll start tonight.'

They bought drawing materials from the little shop by the Academia Gallery. It stayed open late. Charlotte chose materials carefully, selecting a fine small canvas. She was running no risks with that ceiling!

'I'm no Bellini,' she said, settling herself down with her equipment by the bed. 'But I'm quite a good draughtsman. Get undressed.'

'Is that an order?' He sounded amused.

'Yes,' and she slid a silk dressing-gown over her shoulders.

'You are so practical sometimes.'

'Keep quiet while I draw. And stay in one position.' Charles laughed.

She drew swiftly, using light quick strokes of a thin stick of charcoal, blowing on it to remove the excess. 'Sometimes, when one is

165

drawing people one sees things in them that one didn't see before.'

'And what do you see in me?' Charles queried.

'I don't know yet. I haven't decided.'

After a while she said, 'Now I am drawing myself.'

Charles gave her a few minutes before coming over to look. 'It's good. Very good.'

'I had some training.'

'Why didn't you go on? Seriously, as an artist?'

Charlotte hesitated. She could have said that she wanted to design clothes, which was true. 'I was afraid my hand and eye would not hold steady,' she said eventually. This was true also.

Inside she thought: Why don't you tell him everything now? This is your chance. He is your husband, he loves you. But she couldn't do it.

*   *   *

When they left, after paying the bill, Charles said, 'What were you calling Paris about?'

Panic shot across Charlotte, but she said: 'Oh, just business. Fabrics. Sorry to let it obtrude.'

Charles grinned amiably, but he knew Paris well enough to know that factories did not abound in the quarter which she was calling.

Charlotte was looking out of her window at

166

the view of Venice across the room as if it was the last time she would see it.

Charles came across and put his arm round her. 'Thinking?'

'Oh, not about anything specific, darling,' said Charlotte in an abstract voice.

There was an intense, high calibre quality about Charles that seemed to raise him to a level above other people. It was a physical as well as mental force which might be dangerous. To her, and perhaps to him as well.

They flew back to London on a private jet loaned by a friend of Charles. They held hands as the plane landed. Watching Heathrow come into sight, happy to be married, glad to be home, Charlotte felt relief that nothing more had been heard from Jehan.

However, on returning to her office the next day a bombshell from a different source awaited her, in a note from James:

> 'Dear Charlotte,
> I have the offer of a position in New York with Bendels.
> I have decided to go. I have finished all the work I had on hand. My clients I bequeath to you.
> I still retain my financial interest in Redmond & Bruce, but for the moment it's over to you, Butterfly.
> James.

A week later, Charlotte was perched on a stool at the end of a table in her work-rooms, holding up a length of embroidered silk from Lyon; she was on the point of deciding it was too fussy for her purpose, when she was interrupted by Diana de Marche.

'Welcome back! Of course, I mustn't ask how things went, but I can tell anyway. You look so good!'

Charlotte jumped down. 'We had a marvellous time. But I thought I'd see you before this. I've been back a week.'

'You're not my only client now, darling. You see before you a busy woman, nourishing a thriving business.'

But Diana did not look particularly happy. She seemed to have lost weight, and although better groomed than usual (tidiness had never been Diana's strong point), some of her dash was drained away. Charlotte hoped she wasn't going to be one of those people whom success destroyed.

'So what's new?' What she really meant was what is happening in *my* world that will touch me. She wondered if Diana would talk to her.

'Let me do a head count. Jehan is still in London. Tony is back in Europe, he and Sophia are on his estates in Ireland nursing her first pregnancy. James, of course, you know about...'

Charlotte nodded. 'Of course. I found a note waiting for me when I got back. He'd left

168

already. He might have said goodbye.'

'I think he wanted to spare everyone's feelings. No emotion. You know,' Diana suggested.

'He must have been planning it even before my wedding,' Charlotte surmised, sadly.

'I think it really was an unexpected offer,' Diana said. To herself she wondered how much Charles had to do with it. He had ways of oiling wheels.

'I wanted to work with him, damn it! He has talent. He inspired me by contrast. In a strange way, we matched.'

Diana did not answer. In her view Charlotte ought to have guessed James would want out. You couldn't have your cake and eat it as well. Though Charlotte often tried to. She looked marvellous, though. Marriage obviously agreed with her.

Instead she said: 'I have here the arrangements for the Award presentation.' She pushed a sheet of paper towards Charlotte. 'You can see for yourself. It's quite clear. The Award secretary sent it to me, because when she telephoned, Val gave a little scream and said she couldn't decide anything without you. You are going to have to get yourself a better secretary.'

'I like Val.' Charlotte was defensive. 'She knows me and I know her.'

'She's not high-powered enough for you now.'

169

'I'll get round to it.' Charlotte looked about her. 'There'll be changes.'

Butterfly was taking over. She had already made up her mind that now James had gone, the couture side of Redmond & Bruce would be eased out. Current orders would be fulfilled, then she would turn over to small scale, but high quality, ready-to-wear. She would design here, creating the toiles, which would then be made up, under her own supervision at the factory in Greenwich.

'I shall be altering the workrooms here. Modernising them. Here I will design my own simple, elegant, timeless clothes for the sort of people who want to dress my way. Lots of them. More than can afford couture prices.'

Not that her clothes, her "Butterfly" clothes would be cheap; quality always cost.

Suddenly she realised all her plans had been forming quietly inside her, ready to be put into concrete shape at the right time.

Butterfly was coming out of her chrysalis with a vengeance.

'Don't tell them too much at the Award Presentation,' warned Diana. 'They think you are the rising young hope of couture!'

'I won't.'

'Right. Here's the programme. You know what to do. How to present yourself. That's it. Business over.' Diana was studiously light. 'And how are you really?'

Charlotte gave her a huge silent smile.

170

'Thumbs up,' she said. 'The future is mine. Ours.'

Inside "our" and "us" might be a built-in conflict, thought Diana. But she had already observed that her friend, sensitive and perceptive as she was in her art, never noticed things in personal relationships. Or not soon enough.

Should she tell Charlotte of the stories that were going round, naming names which might eventually appear in the law-courts, and certainly in the newspapers? A debate in the House of Commons together with a libel-suit would be the least of it. If the worst happened it might be the Old Bailey for some. Anyway, ruin and social disgrace loomed. Even over her, Diana, whose social rating varied by the month.

But a name even closer to Charlotte might be involved. Should she tell her? Give her one of those early warning signals she did not seem able to provide for herself?

She temporised: 'You'll want capital for all these changes.'

'Charles will back me. He always has,' said his wife confidently.

Silently Diana thought Charles has backed you all the way *so far*. He wanted you; he got you. Will he carry on backing Butterfly? Financially, yes, probably. But emotionally? Or will he withdraw support in the way a man can and a woman never would? Only time will show.

Diana put herself together to depart. Her hair, cut yesterday, refused to lie down so that it rose in a crest on her brow. She could see now that when she had made up her face she had dropped liquid powder on her dark blue shoes. She was all blue and speckle; not one of her most successful attempts. But not everyone's got the trouble I've got, she thought, with gloomy satisfaction.

Charlotte, on the other hand, wore a loose white working smock, and black slippers like ballet-shoes. Her newly washed hair had a glint of red in its darkness. She smelt of stephanotis with a touch of verbena: a new scent.

'How do you do it?' asked Diana, exasperated. 'Always look so perfect.'

'I don't always. Sometimes I look a mess. But I know how to tidy up that mess. And I usually do before the world sees me.' She flipped a quick glance at Diana. 'I could tidy you up if you'd let me. You've slipped while I've been away.'

'I may take you up on that offer. It takes real talent and a bit of luck to make the sort of mess I do!' Diana joked. She had decided not to tell Charlotte of the scandal rising to the surface in which so many familiar names were involved, possibly including Charles, and now, she could hardly get out of the room fast enough.

I am a coward, she told herself, as she drove to her next appointment. I can't raise

172

unpleasant subjects. Besides, it might take ages coming to the boil. Tub said so; he always knows. By that time the marriage will have shaken down. And maybe nothing will ever come at all.

One could always hope.

*   *   *

'Do you know what's up with Miss de Marche?' Charlotte asked Val, not so unobservant of her friends as Diana had supposed.

Val shook her head. 'Afraid not. She's always a bit mad, isn't she?'

'What's wrong with Diana? Any idea?' Charlotte asked her husband.

'No idea,' Charles answered aloofly, as if he didn't want to think about it.

So Charlotte's query went unsatisfied. James being gone, there was no one else she could question about her friend.

*   *   *

The fashion world was in a position to hear all the newest and hottest gossip, but it was so self-centred that nothing really interested it unless its own particular interests were touched. The world outside hardly existed as a real place.

Rumours and jokes and sometimes crossed

173

the invisible barriers the rag-trade erected. Indeed, as a group it specialised in the second and third hand tale, recounting and embellishing a story, rather as a dress might be decorated, but not believing in it.

Little spicy anecdotes were certainly going the rounds at present; names were mentioned but only lightly dwelt upon. Even Charlotte's marriage barely registered except in as far as it might impair her competitiveness.

Woman's Wear Daily reported that a new star had appeared in the fashion sky who would bear watching. *W.W.D.* was watching. The *Tailor and Cutter* commented that it didn't like gimmicks, but this new designer could be commended for technical skill; while *L'Officiel des Modes of Paris* wrote austerely that the "nouvelle vague" of novels and plays had now produced a "nouvelle vogue" in couture and Charlotte was its leader. Only time would show her worth, the editor added sombrely.

*   *   *

It had been decided to jazz up the Designer of the Year Awards party. Hitherto, it had been a dignified stately affair conducted with an air of serious satisfaction. But now it was decided it should be livelier. More in keeping with the new image of fashion.

A rising new pop group was hired to play in the models. While drinks were being handed

174

round, the models would dance to the music, wearing a selection of clothes by important designers.

As they lunched they would be entertained by a showing of Charlotte's latest collection, again to the music of the group. If you wanted to get up from your table and dance, so be it, you would not be discouraged. Many did dance. Age had nothing to do with it. Mademoiselle Violette came over from Paris as an honoured visitor (she was thinking of opening a shop in Bond Street) and danced expertly, even if in a rather tiny way.

Charlotte wished to be introduced to Mademoiselle Violette whom she admired greatly. However, the meeting was only half successful: she would be intruded upon but would not say much. 'You are good at flou, Miss Charlotte. I was good at flou. You are not as good as me.' Then she turned her back, and went back to twisting. It seemed a miracle that her fragile, aged bones could gyrate so.

'Bloody rude,' said Charles, who was with Charlotte, and not at all pleased with the way his wife had been treated.

'With *her* talent, one forgives her everything,' said Charlotte simply. I am lucky to have had her shadow fall upon me, she told herself, lucky that she spoke to me.

Without surprise she observed that Violette was more attracted to Charles than to herself. He was the type she always went for: brisk, sporting and well-bred. They had more than "flou" in common, Charlotte, and Violette.

It aroused questions in Charlotte, though. None of the men Violette had loved had ever done her much good. Would it be the same for her?

She pushed the question to the back of her mind as she received her award, murmuring her thanks. She slipped back into her seat amidst applause. Violette smoked, not clapping.

'Old witch,' said Charles.

'Violette? Forget it. Why do you mind so much? I don't.'

'It's because it's *you* she's being so rude to.'

I love you, he was saying, what happens to you *counts*. Your pain is my pain.

'Oh darling. That's lovely of you,' she said, touched. And then a little voice of doubt entered her thoughts: was it what happened to her, Charlotte, that mattered to him. Or, was it simply a case of: whatever happened to Mrs Charles Scrope reflected on him? Charlotte shivered, and put such uncharitable thoughts away.

She got up, moving around the room to talk to her friends.

In the background the band were still keeping it up.

The lead singer walked to the side of the stage as he sang. A spotlight followed him, lighting up, for a second, a couple seated alone at a table for four. Charlotte had not noticed them before. Whoever notices other people at one's own award presentation? Now she did so, and felt as if she had fallen down two steps fast.

It was Jehan. And with him the red-haired girl he had brought to her wedding.

'Damn. I hoped you wouldn't see,' said Diana, following Charlotte's shocked gaze.

'Why? Why is he here?' she whispered.

'He bought his ticket like everyone else, I guess. And he's entitled. It's his world, too.'

Charlotte looked quickly to where Charles was sitting; he was talking happily away to his neighbour, a large lady who owned a chain of boutiques in New York. Good. She did not want another rush of male protectiveness.

She started to walk towards Jehan. Diana said: 'Don't. Leave it alone.'

'No. I must.' She had to face him out. Otherwise she would go on being frightened of his power over her.

Jehan stood up as she reached the table. 'Hello, darling. You know Francesca? Francesca—Charlotte.'

'Hello. Nice of you to come, Jehan.' Hypocrite, she thought, you hate him for coming. 'But why did you?'

'Nice question, Mrs Scrope. I was asked. I did the hair of three of the ladies who gave you your award, and they said Jehan, you must come and see Charlotte accept.'

She didn't believe a word of it. Jehan had that cocky smile on his face that meant he was pulling a string. Somehow, once again, she was dancing to it.

She began to regret approaching him. Diana had been right.

A hand touched her waist. Charles had come up behind her. 'Come on, Charlotte, we're leaving.'

In clear voice Jehan said: 'Voltaire said: "When a banker jumps out of a window, always follow him. There will be money in it."'

One always had to remember that Jehan, in spite of the way he spoke, was a school-mistress's son and had been exposed to education.

'I'd like to knock you out of the window,' Charles retorted.

Charlotte put her hand on his arm. 'Don't, Charles.' She had the nightmare feeling there was a cycle in her life in which the same scene with Jehan occurred and recurred.

Diana tried to push between the two men. 'Here, none of that, Charles. We don't want any ketchup spilt here.'

But Charles had already punched Jehan, who staggered backwards but did not fall, knocking over a glass of wine.

People at the tables around them were gazing with absorbed attention. Any noise the quartet might be making was masked by the fervour of the band.

No one ever punched Jehan without getting hit back. He took a step backward with a view to taking a hefty swing. His foot skidded in the puddle of wine, while at the same moment, the lead singer moved upstage, the spotlight swinging with him, momentarily resting on Jehan's face, and dazzling him.

Charles gripped Charlotte. 'Come on. We're going. Diana?'

The three of them left the River Room hurriedly.

'I'll kill him one day.' Charles was hailing a taxi. 'I'd enjoy it.'

'Who wouldn't?' said Diana gloomily.

Charles put them in a taxi, then departed himself, back to the City and a meeting.

'It's nice being looked after,' commented Diana. 'I've never known anyone as good at getting a cab as Charles. No taxi-driver would dare to refuse him, I suppose. None of this, "I'm just going off to my bed, guv."'

'Yes, Charles does look after one,' sighed Charlotte.

'So?'

'I'm quite good at looking after myself!' she exclaimed.

'You count your blessings, my girl. I wish I had a Charles.'

'You could get yourself one, darling.'

'No, I could not. They aren't so thick on the ground. Anyway, there are reasons.'

Charlotte was silent. There were reasons,

179

and alas, she was one of them.

'It isn't a disease, you know,' said Diana irritably, answering what had not been said. She took hold of the cab door. 'I get out here. I can walk across to my office. Goodbye, and congratulations on everything.'

She jumped out of the taxi, blew a kiss and was gone, her long legs carrying her quickly along Piccadilly. A bus nearly mowed her down, and she narrowly avoided a van. She wasn't looking where she was going. Tears in her eyes? But Diana never cried.

*   *   *

Val welcomed Charlotte back at the office enthusiastically. 'How was it? Lots of celebs? Who was there?' Charlotte gave Val an edited version of the afternoon, leaving out the Jehan débâcle.

'And I bet Mr Scrope was proud,' Val went on. He is so handsome, she thought to herself. And kindhearted with it. Some people have all the luck; she was quite at one with Diana on that subject. Of course, Charles never looked her way, you couldn't expect it. But had he done so she would not have hesitated to grab, employer's husband or not. She had an instinctive feeling that Charles was capable of looking many ways at once if he chose, and she wondered if Charlotte understood this.

'It will be on TV tonight,' Charlotte told her.

'Diana de Marche fixed it.' She was turning over the messages on her desk, while still thinking of Diana, and beyond Diana, of Charles. Not to mention Jehan and that woman.

Charlotte's mention of Diana reminded Val of what she had found out.

'You asked me about Diana de Marche?'

Charlotte looked up at once. 'Yes?'

'There's a story going round about someone in the Cabinet, I'm not sure who. But he was at Eton and Cambridge. The story is that this fella, very rich and well connected, has been mixing with a Russian spy. They have drinking parties together with tarts at Rockingham Towers.'

Rockingham Towers was the newest, smart hotel, overlooking Hyde Park. It was also a kind of mart for sex. Everyone knew.

'They hold parties at Fenning, too. Lord Belvedere has a cottage there. Lots of people go, apparently.'

'I think I've heard of those parties. Never been asked.'

'No, you wouldn't. Plenty do go. Miss Diana has. Of course, it doesn't *matter*. No one minds these days what goes on where.' Val knew this was not true, but she enjoyed sounding more liberated than she was. She, personally, had so far done very little that she could not have given to her mother in a censored version.

'But it's the Russian connection the police have come in to investigate,' she ended solemnly.

She was treading on thin ice. Any minute a pointed question from Charlotte would force her to say more than she wanted to say. Charlotte had only to ask: 'Anyone else I know involved?' and she would either have to lie, or, to answer...

Charlotte did not ask that question.

That evening, husband and wife dined alone in their new house, and watched the Award Presentation on television. Virginia had set up, and edited the programme, also doing the commentary herself. Charlotte had not seen her for some time, but her voice came across as familiar and warm. Virginia was someone one had to watch, but was probably a force for the good. She had been so to Charlotte, at least. And if she was so for Diana's sake, then so be it.

'She's running pretty close to the wind,' observed Charles, as Virginia appeared on the screen at the end, winding things up. 'Personally, that is.'

'I suppose you mean the Rockingham House parties?'

'You know about those?' Charles asked, in surprise. 'Yes. But she's always had some pretty dicey friends.'

'Diana is one of them,' Charlotte admitted.

'I meant Diana. A truly reckless woman.

Neither of those women have any sense of self-preservation.'

'I thought you were fond of Diana.'

'I am never fond of women like Diana,' Charles retorted. He stood up and turned off the set. 'You looked marvellous. Come to bed darling.'

He put his arms round her; she leant her head on his shoulder. He too had his thoughts. But he didn't voice them.

Instead he made love to her with the intensity that was his substitute for speech. Charlotte responded, moving easily from peak to peak but she was sensitive to emotion, and she thought it was more like a punishment, freely entered into on both sides, but for what sin?

* * *

There was a health club of which both Diana and Charlotte were members.

Another case of wheels within wheels: the money which had set up "Babes" had come from a small syndicate in which both Charles Scrope and Tony Beauclerc had a stake. There were a chain of "Babes" (under a different name) in Canada and the northern United States. The money was small, but the partners involved had found the project amusing.

Diana had been a founder member, then recruited Virginia and Charlotte. She used it

183

intermittently, but Charlotte was a regular attender. She minded about her body, unconsciously testing its worth every session. One day signs of weakness might appear, then panic would set in.

Charlotte went there early next morning, before work, as usual.

Diana was there, as Charlotte had hoped she might be. She was sitting in one corner of the dressing-room, pulling off her tights. Her eyes looked puffy and bruised as if she had been crying. They were the only two in the room.

Diana is a sufferer, thought Charlotte, almost professionally so. I am not. It's funny, Diana is an emancipated woman but she still cries. Yet very few men seek relief from their emotions in tears. Perhaps they should. Not that it seemed to have done Diana much good.

She went straight over. 'Come on now, what is it? What's up? I know there's something.'

'It's Virginia. She's been sacked. Lost her job.'

'Oh, I see ... Because of Rockingham House?' Charlotte asked, tentatively.

Diana turned away. 'That's it. But it's my fault. She's only a victim. Her bosses scent trouble so they are ditching her.'

'Perhaps she's asked for it.'

'Oh, you've never liked her. I know that. I'm not sure I do myself. But she doesn't deserve this. It's my fault. If she hadn't known me she would still have her job.'

'Perhaps you exaggerate.'

'Oh don't you start!'

'I am sorry.' Charlotte sat down beside Diana. 'Is it really so bad?'

'The whole business you mean? Yes. If it comes out, and it may not, my friends know how to hide trouble, it will drag people down. I shall probably be one of them. We've all done things, said things, let loose things that we should not have done. Selfish, mad, bloody. I know that now. I'm sorry for your sake I'm mixed up in it.'

'It can't touch me,' said Charlotte with confidence.

'No? I hope you're right.'

Diana stood up and started to strip. 'I'm going to swim. What about you?'

'Gym first, then swim.' Charlotte looked at her watch. 'I have twenty minutes.' Usually she had thirty, but she had spent ten on Diana.

Diana tied her hair back. 'Oh you, why do you exercise so much?'

'To keep myself well. To see how my body works.' There was complete sincerity in Charlotte's voice. For a moment Diana thought she might have a clue to much that puzzled her about Charlotte. She seemed to have an obsession about her body. Oh well, many women did. Perhaps she was a lapsed anorexic.

'Maybe I'll be able to help with Virginia,' said Charlotte from the edge of the pool. She would need help with her expansion, something could be worked out.

Diana prepared to dive in. 'Oh she'll bob up again,' she said irritably. 'That's not it. It's just bloody she should have to.'

As she left, Diana asked Miranda: 'Does Mrs Scrope come in every day?'

'Very nearly without fail, Miss de Marche. One of our keenest members. *And* she works at it. If only they were all like her.' Miranda was tall, slender, but well muscled, having been a professional gymnast for years. She was extremely glad that the vogue for exercise clubs for women had spread from the States to London. She herself came from Toronto. 'Toronto the Good,' she always called it, hinting that she had helped it to be just a little bit bad.

PART TWO

THE SEVENTIES

CHAPTER EIGHT

Six months later Charlotte was standing in her newly refurbished work-rooms at Butterfly (late Redmond & Bruce), looking about her with pleasure. A new decade had begun, and with it, a new era for Butterfly.

In Greenwich the factory had undergone change; Charlotte had an office there which she visited daily. Soon the production line for her ready-to-wear designs would begin to move.

And she would watch every step. Her clothes must be impeccable.

Diana had mounted an interesting publicity campaign to promote "Butterfly" in which she had no scruples in making use of Charlotte's personal life in articles and interviews.

Charles endured what went with this, as he endured much else.

And Virginia had indeed bounced back: she was the presenter of a new TV show; a combination of news and culture, crisp on the outside and sweet and soft in the middle. It was going to be a big success. Virginia had learnt a lesson and was watching her step.

Temporarily a hat had been put on the threat of open scandal, rather as one puts a cover on a singing canary to quieten it.

There had been a statement in the House of Commons by the Prime Minister saying that all was well, all members of his government (however minor) were men of rectitude and knew no spies, socially or otherwise. (Tory laughter reported *The Times*.)

An injunction preventing publication of an article was slapped on a leading newspaper, while a smart magazine received warning of a libel action.

The canary stopped singing and went quiet.

But it was a persistent bird, and Diana fancied she heard twitterings from beneath the cover.

'And will it be all right now?' questioned Charlotte. 'Will the threat go away now?'

Charlotte was showing Diana around the new workrooms enlarged and re-decorated, but which maintained her apricot and white colour scheme. It looked chic, quiet, and immensely expensive. They had just been photographed for publicity purposes.

Diana nodded, and crossed her fingers.

'With any luck,' she said. But she did not *truly* believe in the luck: to her there was an urgent feeling of foreboding about the business. She was surprised Charlotte did not sense it. But no, Charlotte was deeply involved with being "Butterfly", and, Mrs Scrope. You might have thought that as Mrs Scrope she would have noticed something, but apparently not.

'It's been all quiet for some time now. I haven't heard a rumour for what seems like months.'

It had been a good six months for Charlotte. She had settled happily into her marriage and the new shape of her career. Every day brought hard work, with practical details to be cleared, but she enjoyed it. Behind her she had Charles with his strong business sense, and his grasp of her finances. They both had a busy week, seeing each other only at breakfast and in the evening when they went out a good deal. But at the weekends they went to the Scrope place in Norfolk and were on their own. Charles had a tiny house on the estate, and this was where they stayed.

In a few minutes Charlotte would take Diana out to lunch at Favelli's, the new, smart Italian eating-place, full of green climbing plants and blue waist-coated waiters, where Butterfly maintained an account, and where the table by the middle window was "hers".

At this lunch they would feed and lavishly pour Martinis and wine into the capacious mouth of the Fashion Editor of *Favorite*, currently the voice of chic. From her they would be seeking promotional material about the new "Butterfly". Competition was fierce, and the lady was being difficult.

In the taxi to Favelli's, Charlotte rehearsed what she would say to Della Dean, their guest. 'I shall tell her what plans I've made for the future, expansion and so on. Show her the pictures of the new work-rooms—splendid photographs, by the way, Diana. Did I say thanks? Thanks. Basil did a fine job.

'Then I will describe the collections to be launched as the "Butterfly-Design Ready-to-wear Collection" for next summer. I have the models made up. She can see them if she likes. I'll invite her round to Bond Street.'

'Take a breath,' said Diana.

'I shall offer a unique preview if she'll give us a feature, describing the Bond Street design centre and the new factory. I will tell her we've pre-sold to Harrods and Harvey Nichols. Do you think she will buy it?'

'I've been working on her.'

They were both anxious about the publicity side; they needed all they could get. It was proving hard to come by. Charlotte was moving into a new world where she had to compete with well-established brand-names. She knew this as well as anyone. It had looked so easy from the outside. Now it looked as though she would have to chisel out every step of the way ahead. The ready-to-wear world was bigger and colder than the couture world. Or so it felt.

Their guest had already arrived and was drinking while she waited. She was a large, jolly lady whose fund of good nature never touched her shrewd business sense; she had a soft mouth and a hard head.

As she ate with appetite, she listened to the performance of Charlotte and Diana. They've rehearsed this, she thought, spooning up generous mouthfuls of zabaglione. But they're not doing badly. Only I've heard it all before.

Over coffee, refusing brandy, Della Dean explained her position: 'I can't promise anything. I am sure you wouldn't want me to pretend to anything that I couldn't perform. Oh, I *know* you are *very* talented, darling, and you've got that lovely banker husband behind you. How many peerages in that family? Three, is it? Oh, it was a lovely moment when he took a swing at Jehan. I've longed to do it myself for years. I'm up to his weight too, but his wrists are stronger. Oh, it made my day.'

Diana and Charlotte looked at each other.

'But you're not unique, darling,' went on Della. 'I'm besieged, on all sides.'

Charlotte felt hurt. This was being pulled down to size with a vengeance.

'Not that you're pestering, darling. But there seems to be so many of you couture designers at the moment, opening boutiques; setting up ready-to-wear collections. Some will swim, but most...' she gave a shrug. 'God—life's awful, sometimes.'

Charlotte opened her mouth to protest, but Diana stopped her. She knew her Della. 'Do have some brandy, Del. I think you need it.'

'Well, it's been a bloody week,' conceded Della. 'Come to that, a hell of a month, a hell of a year.'

'It must have been, you poor darling. I heard

you'd divorced,' said Diana. 'Another woman?'

'Oh considerably worse. *Considerably* worse. A succession of little girls.'

The atmosphere at the table at once became radiant with sympathy and understanding.

'Poor love! So how are things now?'

'I miss the bastard,' Della sighed. 'I have to live without him, but it's its not easy.'

'Don't give in,' Charlotte advised.

'Oh, I can't. Not after what he's done. But I've become a compulsive nibbler. Some people starve; I eat. Can I have another petit-four? Thank you. You see what I mean?' She ate a chocolate cake. 'It can't go on. I'm bursting out!'

Charlotte was quick to seize on this: 'Let me make you a dress.'

Della looked doubtful, but was soon brought round by Charlotte's enthusiasm. Soon they were discussing colours, with the odd comment on the rotten husband, and they parted amid promises that she would see what she could do.

'We're in.' Charlotte and Diana agreed as they left.

*　　*　　*

Two days later, they heard, amidst cries of recrimination from Charlotte about the disloyalty of women to women, that they had not "got" *Favorite*, but *had* got, the much less glossy *Strawberry*, newest give-away paper handed out at railway stations and tubes. It was not quite what Charlotte had in mind.

When the interview appeared she read it at the desk in her office with Val and Diana reading it over her shoulder.

'"Harvey Nichol's, Harrods and Bagatelle Group." Well, now to make it come true.'

Val looked at her: 'You mean—not a word of truth? Nothing signed?' With awe she said: 'Wow! That's what I call *confidence*!'

* * *

Charlotte set up her interview with the buyer from Harvey Nicholls with loving care. She had pre-selected the store as being one that would want "her" sort of style. As she wanted their house style. She believed they matched, and the two of them would complement each other 'Butterfly at Harvey Nicholls.' It sounded good.

She had consulted very carefully with Diana, who had done her stuff, getting on good telephonic terms with the other party's secretary, and had picked up some useful details:

'She enjoys a large gin and tonic—ice, no lemon: says the acid rots the teeth—and she smokes a special brand of little cigar.'

'Should I offer the G&T before or after we

talk business?' Charlotte queried.

'Oh, after. This is a tough lady. But make sure you have got in some of her favourite brand.' Diana also reported that Teresa Mountjoy (that was the lady's name), detested pink, but could be turned on by black and grey in combination. And what one must always say to her was that one knew she was buying for a young, self-confident clientele who would spend a couple of hundred pounds on an outfit if the image was right.

'She's a sharp woman,' Diana continued. 'Not the top buyer herself, but it makes no difference: she's the top buyer's right hand; they talk with one tongue and see with the self-same pair of eyes.'

'Right,' Charlotte said. 'Well, I'm ready to see her. Where's her boss?'

'Rome. Seeing the Fortuny lot. It's as well to know.'

Charlotte fluttered nervously up and down the showroom as she waited. She had engaged three models, girls of contrasting types to wear her clothes. They had one thing in common: height, and a gentle, decided way of walking, that Charlotte had taught them to project her clothes. They were the usual three girls whom she had used often before, knowing their little ways to a nicety.

She knew that Martha would frighten them all by not arriving until the last minute, and then turn in an impeccable performance.

She knew that Terry would almost certainly cry with nerves and hunger (she was on a perpetual starvation diet) and that Petronella (nicknamed Pet) would smile through everything.

On their day the girls would boost her sales by twenty per cent, off it, she would feel like murdering them.

Charlotte mentally assessed her designs against "the Fortuny lot" (photographs of which would certainly now be available to her visitor); against Scharrer; against Givenchy; St Laurent; Cardin; and Courreges; all of whom she rated her design peers.

She thought over her rather different designs which were to be offered in the new ready-to-wear collection. True, they would not have that perfect fit and polish that a couture garment had, where every last button and seam was placed exactly right for that particular customer, but then the price was so much less. And even so, the quality and cut was *still* there. It *would* work, she told herself.

The buyer, Teresa Mountjoy, a tall red-haired woman with spectacles, wearing a brief skirt and a long waistcoat, arrived promptly, viewing the parade in circumspect silence.

Afterwards, Charlotte nervously went into her routine, remembering what Diana had said: 'You can see I am aiming at a young, self-confident, free-spending market. A woman—perhaps like yourself—who will

197

spend upwards of two hundred on an outfit if it's *just* right.'

Teresa Mountjoy gave a derisive hoot, suggesting that, if so, it would have to be on her store account and with full discount. But she was gracious enough to add: 'All the same, you've got some stuff here I like.'

Their business was negotiated: An order, incorporating most of the "launch" ready-to-wear collection was put on the table.

'Of course it would have to be our "exclusive",' said Teresa Mountjoy firmly.

Charlotte looked thoughtful. She had every intention of placing garments with Harrods, and their order, if she was in luck, would be at least double.

Bargaining began again in earnest. The models were brought in for a second look, this time off the girl's backs, closely inspected, examined for faults by Teresa, defended by Charlotte.

Finally an arrangement was struck by which a certain group of garments would be exclusive, leaving Charlotte free to negotiate other sales elsewhere.

Both sides were as satisfied as they would ever be.

No one said that for off-the-peg clothes Charlotte's prices were high, because the buyers knew they were handling the most innovative and covetable new ready-to-wear name in years. And this was what their customers would buy.

Two weeks later Charlotte had negotiated a fine order from Harrods. A week after that the small Bagatelle chain of shops put in another order.

Butterfly-Design Ready-to-wear was in business, and Charlotte made good the promise of her interview.

*   *   *

Inevitably part of Charlotte's working life was now concentrated in the factory out at Greenwich. Increasingly her days were spent there.

Mrs Angel had not retired, but remained in Charlotte's team. As she put it herself, her "girls" would work better for her than for an outsider. Her girls, mostly middle-aged comfortable ladies, could be driven by her to extreme precision in the placing of a seam, and in the outlining of a button-hole. Charlotte's button-holes were real, not flat imitations. It was for this sort of quality one paid the "Butterfly" price.

Mrs Angel and Charlotte divided the cutting between them, each respecting the other's skill. But a junior was being trained by them.

This junior was a dark-haired girl called Dorothy Benson. Her mother, Bea, had worked with Mrs Angel for years. It had been on Mrs Angel's advice that Dorothy, a girl of natural, perhaps inherited talent, had trained at the local polytechnic; she had a diploma in Fashion & Design.

Charlotte had noticed Dorothy on her first visit. There had been something familiar about the girl—and her mother—that Charlotte had yet to put her finger on.

Dorothy and her mother always travelled home on the bus together to Woolwich.

One day Dorothy said: 'It *is* her, isn't it?'

Her mother nodded. 'Yes love, and I think she knows it's us. I caught her looking at you one day. But leave her be, poor soul.'

Dorothy nodded, but put her knowledge of Charlotte's past into store, like money in the bank, for future use. She was not so protective of Charlotte as her mother, probably because she had not known Charlotte's own mother. It made a difference.

In fact, on Charlotte's part, no act of recognition had been made, but enough residual worry lingered in her mind to make her ask Mrs Angel about the two women.

'Oh, Dorothy's worked here since she finished at the poly. Her mother has been with me for twenty years.'

Charlotte did not recognise the name, which was not surprising, since Bea had re-married since Charlotte had last seen her father's sister, and Dorothy had also taken on her stepfather's name of Benson.

'Why do you ask?' queried Mrs Angel. 'She's

a good worker. They both are.'

Charlotte shrugged. She could have said that the girl reminded her of a tribe of cousins she once had, and could now only dimly remember. But she had a man-hole over that gulley in her mind which she rarely lifted.

It had its effect, however. Charles felt it. Sometimes she seemed to distance herself. 'Are you sure you are not working too hard?' he asked.

'No! Work never harmed anyone,' Charlotte dismissed.

'There are other things in life,' he said gently. 'Stay where you are. I'll bring you breakfast in bed.'

He propped the pillows behind her head and left her there. 'Fresh orange juice,' he promised. 'I shall squeeze it myself.'

He was too nice to her, Charlotte felt.

When the tray came, she upset the orange juice and spilt coffee with a hand that trembled. She burst into tears. Charles could not console her.

And later that morning, while doing press-ups at Babes, Charlotte collapsed.

Diana had just come in, so she was there when Charlotte came round.

The fitness instructors at Babes were all trained in first-aid, and it was the calm, professional visage of the instructor on duty that Charlotte saw first when she opened her eyes, and then Diana's anxious gaze.

'Sorry.' She smiled faintly, closing her eyes again.

'What's the matter with her?' Diana asked.

'A faint, I think. Nothing more.'

'But what's wrong?'

The instructor shrugged, venturing no further diagnosis. 'You'd better go home and rest,' she said to Charlotte. 'And I'd make an appointment to see your doctor, if I were you.'

Over Charlotte's protests Diana drove her home. 'We can leave your car. I'll come back for it later. Or someone can. Butterfly can cope without you for a while.'

Privately she was alarmed. Charlotte looked as though a skin had been ripped off her, leaving the network of fine blood vessels and nerves only too visible.

Once home, however, Charlotte seemed to become more solid and natural. 'I feel better now. Just a bad morning.'

'You've been over-doing it at Babes. I've watched you. You push yourself. Give it a rest.'

Charlotte smiled. 'Good old protective, Diana.'

'I'm fond of you, damn it! I'll make you some tea. Toast too. You ought to eat something.'

While she was in the kitchen, Diana made two telephone calls: one to Val, another to Charles.

'I'd have made someone a good mother,' she

said, as she came back with a tray.

Charlotte took the cup, held it in both hands, and sipped carefully. She did not spill anything and her hand was steady; she sighed with relief. There couldn't really be much wrong with her, could there?

'So would you, for that matter,' continued Diana, fishing.

Charlotte did not answer. She had been to the Addie early that morning: Maisie was not so well.

'I *am* responsible for a child in fact,' said Diana. It was confession time. 'That's why I'm always so hard up. One of the reasons. I bet you would never have guessed.' She smiled-at Charlotte's look of amazement.

'Not my child,' Diana went on. 'But I've taken him on. Nice kid. Which considering everything is a minor miracle. He's four now. I'll have to be thinking about a proper school soon.'

Charlotte found her voice. 'Whose child is he?'

'My sister's—not Phoebe's—the other one, you haven't met. Think yourself lucky! The awkward little part is that the child might be my brother's too.'

'Oh no.'

'My sister can't be quite sure,' said Diana savagely. 'She'd slept with half the county, as well as her own brother. I was all in favour of abortion when I heard, but she'd left it a bit late

203

by then.'

Diana couldn't look at Charlotte. 'However, the child was born. A boy, as I've said. My sister didn't want to know, and I took him on. It's as simple as that. Whether I am his aunt twice or not I have no idea... I'm glad I've told you. I've wanted to, often.'

'I'm glad too. Thanks, Diana.' She squeezed her friend's hand.

'Telling unburdens the soul.'

'Do you think so?'

Not for you, obviously, observed Diana to herself. Confession time for her, but not for her friend.

'Bye for now. I must go. Look after yourself.'

As she left, Charles came rushing in.

'Darling, you've given us all a fright. I knew you weren't well this morning. I shouldn't have let you go out.'

'I'm all *right*.'

He studied her face. 'You look better than you did ... Darling, are you pregnant?'

Charlotte said, 'No. Nothing like that. Never. Don't talk about it.'

Charles sat on the sofa beside her and put his arm round her. He stroked her hair gently. 'You don't mean that, darling.'

Charlotte nodded her head, violently. 'I do.'

'Darling, would your being pregnant be *so* bad? This isn't because I don't value your career. You know I do. But there are other

204

things: there'll come a time...'

'No, there won't. Never.'

Charles was silent.

'I think it must be just that the Pill I'm on doesn't suit me. It doesn't everyone. That's all there is to it,' she added. 'And we might as well get this straight, as we should have done before: no child.'

Charlotte saw her doctor, started taking a different contraceptive pill, and preserved her own silence, as always, about that side of her life.

Charles knew he was being cowardly in not pursuing the matter. But he, too, kept his own uneasy counsel...

CHAPTER NINE

The plane was circling over London waiting for permission to land. Below was fog, but the passengers were assured it was "thinning".

Charlotte sat hunched in her seat, feeling as if she too was losing substance by the minute. She was not usually a nervous traveller, but today Charles was waiting at Heathrow for her and she was longing to see him.

She was so burdened with good news that she felt the weight of it might cause the aircraft to fall through the skies and crash. One surely could not be so lucky, without Life taking its toll.

I shall never get there to tell him that the Galerie Fontainbleau have bought the Winter '70/71 collection of Butterfly, and optioned the next. I shall never give him the dressing-gown from Charvet's, and he will never see my new hair cut from "Gustav's." Oh damn.

There had been times, some not so far distant, when to crash, to be obliged not to be, would have seemed a good solution, but this was not one of them.

The woman next to her complained: 'I can smell rubber.' She shifted nervously in her seat.

'You can always smell rubber on an aircraft,' replied Charlotte.

The captain started to speak to his passengers; the woman covered her ears with her hands, looking in terrified query at Charlotte.

'It's all right. Uncork yourself. We're landing,' she laughed euphorically.

She hurried through the Customs, letting her handsome Hermes luggage bump along the ground rather than hail for a porter or a trolley.

By the end of her first year of marriage, with a first Butterfly-Design Ready-to-wear collection fluttering to a great success at Harvey Nichols, Charlotte was beginning to know what her husband was: his dimensions and moods. He was not always the aloof, chilly Mandarin figure that he appeared as he moved through his business world. He could be emotional, passionate, sensual, and, was easily bored.

Sometimes, however she felt she lost him. He seemed to disappear behind his own face, as if there was nothing there at all; then he came back and was the most delightful person in London. In England. In the world.

Why did he sometimes withdraw like that? Drink? No. Although that might come; she was a little wary already of the way he could change mood by drinking.

But *something* happened to him so that he retreated into his own private hole.

She spent a long time searching for the way into this hole so that she could join him in it, but she never could.

Forced to stay outside, she hated these times, and him with it, then.

They were forced to be physically apart a good deal, pulled asunder by the demands of their work pattern. Charles went to New York and sometimes to Hong Kong and Australia on his business, while Charlotte went to Paris and Rome on hers.

Their lives did not quite match.

She had rung him twice from her hotel in the Place Vendôme but failed to get an answer; she knew from hotel messages that he had tried to telephone her. This pattern of not always quite meeting must be interrupted, she resolved.

The visit to France had not been totally

pleasurable. Paris, for her, was a kind of code-name for certain duties to be fulfilled. In Paris she had met men and women with whom she had worked at the School of Design. She had some good old friends, useful contacts. Not all her meetings were strictly business for Butterfly; one at least went back to earlier days...

'Hello, Lou-lou. Me again. Yes, Charlotte, Is all well? No, I won't go out. Couldn't bear it. But the bill is paid.'

But some bills are never paid. They come back in again, and again...

She was looking out for Charles, longing to see his face. Instead she heard her voice called.

It was his company chauffeur. 'Mr Scrope's apologies, madam, but when he heard your flight was delayed he said he couldn't make it.'

He handed her a note. In the car she read it:

'Dearest, Sorry I couldn't get there. See you this evening. Look in our bedroom.'

The bedroom was full of golden flowers: jasmine and freesias, and a bottle of champagne in ice, with two glasses, stood on the dressing-table.

Charlotte smiled.

Charles had done this before to welcome her home. She was amused and delighted, but also a little disconcerted by it. To her it seemed like a move towards a fantasy world when their life together ought to be quite real, real and substantial as brown bread, cut in thick slices

208

and serviced on plain white china. Deep down she knew something was wrong. They would meet, kiss, drink the champagne and exchange love, but it was too insubstantial, like the froth on the delicious champagne, not nourishing and sustaining as brown bread would have been.

While she waited for Charles, she wandered around their home. It was early evening, with the mist thickening into a white fog. She had decorated, then furnished their home with loving care. Charles being a wealthy man, she could have chosen to use valuable antique furniture; instead she had utilised only one or two quality pieces, the general opulent effect created more by light and colour. A splendidly baroque gilt mirror hung on one wall, reflecting the living room, which was decorated in a strong Chinese yellow and white, like a sunflower. Their bedroom was amethyst and grey. The rooms were linked by colour. Quilted satin cushions walked white in from the living-room, while a big porcelain vase followed violet back from the bedroom. The staircase and hall were carpeted in grey.

A big sofa-table with lyre legs stood at the bottom of the stairs. It was Charlotte's most valuable acquisition. She patted it with a loving hand as she went past.

She thought, I have been married a year. I have created this home and I run it well. In Norfolk I have learnt how to talk to the farm workers, even if I find Charles' hunting neighbours difficult. In my professional life I am building Butterfly into something big; the signs are good. So why this worried feeling inside?

She was in the kitchen when she heard Charles' key in the front door.

At the same moment the telephone rang. Charlotte stood, undecided, between the two. There was really only one way for her to go: she ran towards Charles.

She saw Charles pick up the receiver, he held out his arm to her, and put it around her, as he answered. 'No, she's not here. Her flight was delayed. She's not back yet.'

Charlotte raised her eyebrows.

'Diana.' He replaced the receiver. 'She wants to talk to you. But I don't want you to talk to her. I want you to talk to *me*.'

In spite of the warmth in his voice, he sounded tired. She thought his face looked drawn.

'Wonder what Diana wants?'

'Oh she's been fussing away all the time you've been in Paris,' Charles dismissed it.

'She could have phoned me in Paris. She had my number.' Diana's "fussing" worried Charlotte. Diana never "fussed" without good cause.

'She probably *did* try to get hold of you in Paris. As did I—but you were never there,' Charles replied.

'I called *you* and you were never here,' Charlotte responded.

'No. I can't stand the house without you in it.'

'Where did you go?'

'Oh here and there.'

She knew that he had many places to hide; men usually did.

'And where were you all the time?' His voice was light, but he wanted an answer.

'I had a lot of business to do,' she said seriously. 'I was out and about. You know how it is.'

'Out of Paris so the Ritz said.' In fact, the Ritz desk had been impeccably discreet, but Charles could read the unspoken code much better than most.

'Are you being suspicious?'

'Should I be?'

'No. It was business. Nothing untoward.'

He kissed her hair. 'I never thought otherwise. Now tell me the good news. I know there is some. I can see it in your face.'

They sat on the bed and drank the champagne, while Charlotte told him about the Fontainbleau, together with the 'tentative' offer from the Bagatelle chain. He was pleased, but it was quiet pleasure.

'You look tired,' she said. 'What's up?'

'Tony's being difficult. Wants to float a loan for some enterprise. He won't get it on the London market. He'll have to go to Germany.'

211

'Why?'

'It's for South Africa,' said Charles briefly.

No further explanation was needed. Sharpeville and apartheid cast their shadow, even over banks. South Africa had become a doubtful credit risk.

'I thought you didn't let him interfere much.'

'I don't. But it is *his* pool and sometimes I can't stop him jumping in,' said Charles briefly. 'This time he might get wet.'

Charlotte produced the dressing-gown from Charvet. 'I thought of buying one from Lanvin; they had some beauties. But this one seemed right for you.' It was yellow and red, glowing with colour.

He was delighted with it. 'I've never had a silk dressing-gown before.'

'Really?' She was surprised. 'I can't believe it.'

'Tony was always the hedonist. And also, my father was a bit of a puritan. Dressing-gowns were wool and the scratchier the better! I suppose I've sort of carried that on in a way. Though I suppose also, that I've always envied Tony's ease with the luxuries and playthings which come his way.'

'You didn't want me just because I was one of Tony's playthings did you? I've always wondered,' she was ashamed to admit.

Charles answered her honestly: 'Perhaps at first. The very first. But soon it was just that I loved you. You do believe that?' Now his voice was gentle.

'Take off the dressing-gown, and I'll show you how I believe it.'

She could be the initiator too. Sometimes both of them preferred it that way.

But it didn't always work. Today it didn't.

In spite of the champagne, the flowers, the silk dressing-gown and the celebration, the willingness and the love, there was no joy for them that day.

Sweating and exhausted Charlotte said: 'What am I doing wrong?'

'It's not you, it's me.' Charles rolled over and buried his face in the pillow.

She reached to take his hand; he pulled it away. She had felt so alive, now she felt dead.

'I'm not going to be beaten,' and she sat up, to give him a sharp slap across the back. It was a hard blow, delivered with more anger than she'd intended. She could see her finger-marks on his shoulder. She saw something else too.

Charles stirred. 'Do that again. Hit me.'

With a violence that surprised her she delivered a stinging blow; her fingers felt numbed. She meant the violence.

From then on it was easy . . .

The champagne and the flowers had been unnecessary.

*　　　*　　　*

'We have to dine with Aunt Helen tonight,

213

remember?' Charles stroked her cheek, admiring her flat neat profile. Not Japanese, more Renoir, he decided. 'Nuisance really. But there it is. She gave us a Dufy for a wedding present and we said we would.'

Charlotte hadn't liked the Dufy, but it was a valuable painting, now hung in Charles' office. 'I'll go and get dressed.'

'What will you wear?' he called after her.

'Does it matter? The green faille with the pointed collar.' She had decided on the flight back from Paris. It had a low cleavage through which the tops of her breasts were just visible. Aunt Helen had been the lady for whom Schiaparelli had designed the famous fish-net dress with the black nipples and she had to be shown her place. Otherwise she was too outrageous. She prided herself on it.

Charlotte went into her little dressing-room, which she had decorated in silver and plum with such loving pride; she sat down in front of her toilet-table, and putting her head in her hand, wept. What she wore for dinner with Aunt Helen seemed of little importance at present.

There was something wrong with her marriage. She could hardly bear to face it.

Across her husband's back was one long wheal which *she* had *not* inflicted.

* * *

214

The dinner at Aunt Helen's was as disastrous as might have been expected on a day clearly starred for trouble.

Helen, still living in the past, could tell them all about what she had said to Harold Nicholson on the day war was declared, could even (and did) let them know whose bed she had been sleeping in (not her husband's, he was away in North Africa) the night the bomb dropped on the Embassy Club.

However, she had forgotten they were coming to dinner, and had retired to bed with a Chinese take-away: 'So handy. I learnt to order on the phone in the States. They do it all the time. Pizzas mostly. You'll find the idea'll spread here.'

However, she nipped out of bed spryly enough and declared she would take them out to dinner at the Dorchester.

'Not too sorry. The sweet and sour has to come all the way from Slough; it got chilled on the way. I have a charming boy who brings it to me. I always ask for Freddy. I daresay he'd come out to dinner with us now if we asked. I was planning to ask him to hang on,' and she gave her famous lewd and wicked smile.

However, all the other invited but forgotten guests began to arrive then, so Lady Helen was forced to improvise a dinner at home.

A delicious meal soon appeared, as if by magic. Charlotte wondered if there was a devoted housekeeper in the background. But no, Charles said, Aunt Helen had sent out to a restaurant around the corner. It was one of her little tricks, 'She's as rich as Croesus, don't you worry, and wicked as an anti-Christ.'

She sat opposite an elderly man to whom she was never introduced except as "Buffer", who proved to be extremely well informed about her affairs and subjected her to a quiet interrogation on her husband, her work, and, surprisingly, Diana. When she complained on the way home to Charles on the ill chance, he said chance had nothing to do with it, and that Aunt Helen arranged things on purpose.

In the car Charlotte soon realised that her husband had taken too much wine and was now drunk. he didn't offer to drive but got into the seat beside the wheel and waited for her to proceed.

Angrily, Charlotte sat behind the wheel and drove them home. Drunkenness always made her fierce. As Charles well knew. It had not stopped him drinking too much lately.

We'll talk when we get home, she thought. I've got to ask him some questions, and then we'll see. If he asks me some back, I will try to answer honestly.

But they did no talking when they got home. Charles stumbled into her amethyst and grey sitting-room, slumped into a chair and fell asleep.

Charlotte looked at him, half compassionate, half angry, then went up stairs to bed.

216

In the morning her first caller was Diana. Charlotte answered the telephone sleepily.

'Must see you.'

'I'm not up yet.' She looked across to the other side of the bed. There was no sign that Charles had slept there. 'What's so urgent? I sent all the important stuff over on the fax. Couldn't the office tell you?'

The days of Val in supreme command were over, although Val herself survived to queen it over a larger, open-plan office with underlings beneath her.

'This isn't business.'

'Drop in to the office this morning. I haven't got my diary. But Val can fix you up with a time.' Charlotte yawned. She was thinking more about Charles than Diana.

'You're not getting this, are you? I want to talk to you because of trouble. And I want to talk privately. Not with Val breathing down my neck.'

'Come round to breakfast then.' God knew if Charles was there or not. Probably he was not, judging by the silence below: Charles up, and around on a normal morning made a certain amount of noise.

Now she was coming awake, she was catching the pain and weariness in Diana's voice. 'Have you had *any* sleep?' she queried.

217

'It doesn't matter.' Diana's voice was brittle. 'I'll be round within the hour.'

'Wait a minute.' Suddenly Charlotte was frightened. 'Your trouble or mine?'

'Ours.' And Diana was gone.

Charlotte got up and went downstairs to look for Charles. He wasn't there. But there was a note on the kitchen table:

"Gone to the office early. Stuff to catch up on. Sorry."

A bleak little note, she thought, offering small comfort.

Charlotte started the coffee, produced some fresh orange juice, then went to take a shower and dress.

She was making toast when Diana arrived. She looked terrible. Not as if she hadn't slept for a night; more as if she hadn't slept for a week.

Charlotte poured some coffee into a mug. 'You've got that jacket buttoned all wrong.' Even in her present anxious state she minded how her clothes were worn. She had designed that jacket for Diana; it deserved better treatment.

Diana took it off. 'Sorry. Buttons don't seem important sometimes. Well, the short answer to the question you have not asked is that the balloon is about to go up, after all.'

'You'd better tell me what you mean because I don't understand you.'

Diana took a deep breath. 'Are you on your own? Where's Charles?'

'Gone to the office early.'

'Oh boy, does he know when to slip the leash. Well, I'm glad he's out of the way.'

The telephone rang. It was Charles. 'Charlotte? You saw my note? I'm in the office. I'll see you later.'

'Yes, all right, darling.' She heard herself speaking quietly, but inside she was screaming: I must see you; I want to talk to you.

Diana said: 'Charles? It's a rotten old world.' She drank some coffee. 'Where were you all the time in Paris? Where were you last night?'

'Dining with Charles' Aunt Helen.'

'That old witch. What did they talk about?'

'You, me, Charles. And the approaching elections.'

'I bet they did. And I don't suppose you even understood what that was all about?'

'I didn't listen particularly.' She had had other worries.

'You should have done. The PM is bound to go. He laughed the scandal every way out of court. He could see the funny side. Now there's a sort of change of wind. Everyone's going to draw their skirts aside. A few public victims will cleanse the scene.'

Charlotte stared. She was silenced for the moment.

'I shall be one of them, I expect,' went on

219

Diana. 'But I won't be alone. Two or three other sacrifices at least will be required. A death or two wouldn't come amiss in some quarters, but I shan't oblige there.'

'You're joking.'

'I promise you I am not. It's going to be nasty for all of us. Not least of all you.' She looked hopefully at Charlotte. Do you know what I am talking about? she was saying mutely. So that it won't have to be me that tells you.

Charlotte still looked blank. Diana saw that she suspected nothing. Abruptly, because if she didn't speak now she never would, she said: 'Has Charles mentioned *anything*?'

Just the sound of his name was enough. No more had to be said. Charlotte put down her coffee, ceased to butter the toast. She had gone white and her hand was shaking.

'I get you. Charles is involved. Deeply, or you wouldn't be telling me. Thanks, Diana.'

Diana muttered something incoherent about hating to do it, then told all, including the part that Jehan had played. Damn him.

*   *   *

I'm glad Charles was not around, thought Charlotte, after Diana had left. We couldn't have had a witness to the scene we are going to have.

Surprised at her own calm, she put on her

make-up, and went off to work.

Everything there was peaceful and normal. No terrible premonitions of trouble to come. Her logo "B", and a painted apricot and white butterfly, swung on its signboard above the door as usual, while inside business went ahead. The days of the private customer, drifting in for her fitting, were over. The only clients now were trade customers, come to see the collection, to view and order in bulk. Though never in too much bulk, because "Butterfly" clothes were special and must not appear prolific. It was a fine balance.

Charlotte sighed and put her head in her hands. She had a terrifying suspicion that she was about to start to lose control of her life. It so happened that she was a person who could not afford to let decay set in—anywhere at all. Even a hardening of the emotions might set off a more general decay. It was the way she feared she was made. She had seen it happen to her mother.

There was so much in the hereditary make-up: Charles and his pride; Charles and his strange way of loving; probably you could trace a similar streak right back through the Scrope family if you knew where to look.

Diana too, without doubt, had cause to blame her forebears. All three of them then, caught in their family web. She hoped the story of Diana's sister's little boy would not come out with all the rest.

221

It was odd how she did not have to look up the number she was dialling. Out it came, as if it had been tucked away in the back of her mind in preparation for this moment. She'd thought of using it before, but had never really been able to justify it—until now.

'Good morning, the Faringdon Agency.'

'Hello. My name is Charlotte Chaudin. Would you be interested in taking on something of a rush job?'

Detective agencies can work fast if they have to.

*　　*　　*

Charlotte and Charles met after a day which had been disagreeable for both of them.

For Charles the morning had been the worst. The telephone calls had started from the Press. Not asking much yet, just probing, softening him up.

He felt as though the wolves were out there in the streets, restless and unfed; baying for blood. When he had a moment to spare from turning a calm, unbroken face towards the world, he wondered who would declare themselves among the attackers.

He had little illusions about what would happen, because he had had months and months to think about it. First, some small victim would be thrown out, people like the young Foreign Office clerk, and then it would

222

be Diana's turn, and finally, would come his moment to be eaten. Tony Beauclerc would come through unscathed because Tony always did.

Where do you take her, when you are about to meet your wife and you want to avoid a searing scene?

Charles, ever the conventional, decided on the very conventional: Covent Garden. This had been a success once. Why not try again? He obtained tickets for "Siegfried". Who could quarrel during Wagner?

They could have smoked salmon and champagne at the back of their box and he would talk to her then. He made it sound delightful on the telephone, when he called Charlotte late that afternoon. Or so he hoped, trying to keep the tension out of his voice.

Charlotte did not know whether to laugh or to cry. She could see what he was up to. 'I don't know if I could bear it,' she whispered. For the Faringdon Agency had wasted no time in their enquiries about Charles. And their preliminary findings, phoned in to her an hour or so ago, had certainly been devastating—though not in the way she had expected. Far, far worse, in fact.

Charlotte perceived that she had given herself away somewhat: through her reaction, she had intimated her knowledge to Charles. The silence at the end of the line was a long one.

'What do you mean by that?' he said, in a

heavy voice. One she had never heard before.

'I'm not going to talk on the telephone. Covent Garden if you like, but I don't undertake to sit through too much Wagner.'

*   *   *

Charlotte took a taxi straight to Covent Garden from her designing room. She carried a brief-case, and wore the plain grey linen suit in which she had gone to work. This was no outing for pleasure. She was already late. Half half on purpose. Anger made her want to torment him.

As soon as she got to the Garden she went to the cloak-room to repair her make-up. For the moment she could delay their meeting in the Crush Bar.

A woman next to her complimented her on her perfume.

'Try some,' offered Charlotte.

'Oh thank you. Well, I will.' Her eyes were bright with pleasure: she was a happy woman. 'This is a celebration evening: it's our silver wedding anniversary,' she confided.

And it'll see the death of *my* marriage, thought Charlotte, bleakly. She had been married less than two years.

For this pleasant-looking woman's sake, Charlotte forced herself to smile back. 'Congratulations!' she said. 'Please, have the scent.' She pushed the spray across. 'A present

224

from me.'

She hurried out before thanks could be offered. She thought the scent would be one she herself could never bear to use again.

She walked straight into the arms of Charles.

A relieved smile spread across his face. I'm going to wipe that smile right off the map, she thought, and wished she did not know.

'I thought for a moment you'd stood me up,' he said.

'No, I'm just late.'

'Never mind, you're here now.' He was drawing her into a corner where there was a seat.

She sat down and let him slip into the seat next to her. She could feel his tension. She herself felt the room darken suddenly; she breathed hard. I mustn't faint. Whatever happens I must hang on. Not faint or cry or shout. She felt sick at what she was about to do, but without doubt she was going to do it.

'You know *something* already. I heard that in your voice, so perhaps I don't need to say much.' Charles could not keep the hope out of his voice.

'Don't tell me anything you don't want to,' she said gravely.

'The worst is that I shall be smeared. There will be publicity. Talk. Unpleasantness all round. Odious for you. I am truly sorry.'

Good manners to the last, she thought, but it no longer matters.

225

In a polite voice she said: 'I have something to read aloud to you. When I have done so perhaps you will tell me in what manner we should continue with our evening.'

Charles stared at her in stiff surprise.

'Jilly Myers: October 1969. We'd been married just a few months then. I was in Milan on business. You phoned every day.'

'Charlotte!'

'Don't interrupt. Anne Beresford: December 1969. An American I understand. Duration of affair very short. I was home in London. We met daily, you and I. You wrote me loving little notes.

'Early 1970: and for all I know, all through the Sixties, Francesca. Although I exempt her, really. A matter of business. Shall I go on?'

She was about to proceed with her reading but he stopped her.

'Where did you get all this?'

'I employed a detective. I seems you have been pitifully remiss at hiding your adulterous tracks Charles. You just carried on as before we were married, didn't you?' Her lips closed.

She felt as if she could never speak another word through that stone, hard mouth which hardly seemed to belong to her. The room was moving all around her, now darkening, now dazzling bright, but she clung on.

She saw that his face had flushed, that, incredibly, there were tears in his eyes. She did not know that she too was crying.

226

'You don't know what love is,' she said, finding, after all that words would force themselves out like blood through the mouth of a wound. 'You never have. Did you really think I would care about all the public scandal business? No Charles, I would have stood by you and gladly. But clearly, I haven't anything to stand by.'

'But you're my wife ... The rest is unimportant. We are married. You must see the difference. Charlotte, I beg of you. Let's put all this behind us. We could go to Norfolk and start a family...'

'Never. Never. I shall never have a child.'

He responded bitterly: 'You say I don't know what love is: I think you don't know what marriage is.'

'I shall divorce you.'

Their two worlds had met, and collided with great force.

And it was Charles' world that was smashed.

*   *   *

Charlotte moved out of their house straight away, settling herself in rooms in Chelsea near Diana.

A new Prime Minister came in, questions were asked and answered in the House of Commons. For Charles the trial by ordeal had begun. Gossip and speculation about him spread.

227

He had been handling two important financial deals involving several million pounds. When confidence in him collapsed as whispers spread, those deals came crashing down. He resigned from the board of William Scrope's. People began to say he had never had financial insight at all really, just luck, and now that had run out.

Charlotte did not start divorce proceedings. Impossible to divorce Charles just at that moment. A dog couldn't do it. But she had decided inside herself.

Diana, unhappy herself, made an effort to reconcile them, but nothing came of it. Charlotte would not meet Charles, not even talk about him much.

'Are you sure, darling, you are doing what is right—best for you, I mean?'

'Quite sure.'

Diana shook her head. 'I don't understand you. It seems to me that you are throwing everything overboard too easily. You do love him, I swear. What else matters?'

'I matter.'

'So?'

'The way I think of myself, myself as a person. My wholeness, integrity, what I am. That matters.'

Diana said slowly: 'I know you value your creativity ... but he supported you there.'

'No, it's not that. We just couldn't be what the other wanted.'

'Well, I know Charles wanted to start a family...'

'I'm not going into that. That's a subject I won't discuss.' Charlotte stiffened at once. 'Oh God, how can I explain this? Not only was Charles constantly unfaithful to me, I think he actually got gratification out of feeling guilty about it; out of being punished. Yes, I mean that literally, Diana, so take that look off your face. I couldn't do that. I couldn't live with it.'

'Poor old Charles.'

'Poor old Charlotte too. You showed me your bundle of pain, Diana. Now I've offered you mine.' Or part of it, she thought, not even to you have I told all. There are some things I prefer to bear alone. Must bear alone. Have always borne alone. Will never tell anyone until it is finally ground out of me by life. If it ever is. But I do pray it will never be. Death would be better.

Diana could read a lot from Charlotte's expression, but not all of that. But something she picked up: 'What a lot you've lost. What a lot we've all lost,' she said sadly.

To Diana, nothing Charlotte had told her seemed so strong as to break a marriage. But her sexual manners were easy. She was a woman who took some things lightly. To her it was not so important.

She wondered if Charlotte knew exactly how much she had lost in Charles.

* * *

Nearly six months later, time had healed nothing for Charlotte. Nor, Diana suspected, for Charles, of whom, she saw a fair bit.

Diana was the perpetual go-between; it was her chosen way of life. Since she could not have perfect love for herself, she tried to get it for her friends. A vicarious living, and she knew it.

The first collection of Butterfly-Design Ready-to-wear had come on the market in a painful but triumphant birth in April of that year. And now, two collections later, buyers reported that her clothes were 'walking' off the racks, no sooner put out than tried on and sold.

Charlotte's triumph was there for all to see. But soon, her pain was to be so too...

* * *

One rainy evening the car which Charles was driving from Norfolk to London crashed into a lorry at a roundabout. The driver reported that Charles "just didn't seem to be looking where he was going."

Charles died instantly; Tony Beauclerc who was travelling with him was unhurt.

Charlotte went through the inquest, followed by the funeral, calmly enough. Afterwards, when Tony Beauclerc had spoken to her, and when Henry Barnard, who had succeeded Charles at William Scrope's had taken her hand to murmur sympathy, Diana saw Charlotte's colour recede, then return in a tiny, concentrated patch of colour on each cheek.

Charlotte turned to her, tears streaming down her face. 'Oh Diana, don't let them come near me again. He was twice the man they are, twice the man.'

Diana held the thin, beloved figure in her arms. 'Poor darling, poor love. I wish I could comfort you.'

For both of them the close of 1970 was the saddest, darkest time. But Diana had the courage to comfort her friend because, in her own life, although she had hardly noticed it yet, a relationship was growing which gave her strength. A tiny little seedling of hope which provided for them both.

CHAPTER TEN

Out of the saddest, darkest times, Charlotte and Diana climbed together; two women on their own.

The collapse of the growing financial empire which Charles had commanded, brought a terrible quandary to Butterfly.

Money, or the lack of it, was the worry.

'Only one problem,' said Charlotte, 'but all the rest follow from it.'

She was under-capitalised; she had built her business on that backing (firmly promised) of Charles' capital. But under the leadership of Henry Barnard, William Scrope's had withdrawn their backing. Moreover, Charles had debts. These debts, as his widow, Charlotte must now pay.

The London house, and the Norfolk place were sold. Charlotte regretted neither. Both homes, especially the Knightsbridge one, had been prepared and lived in with a love that was now painful to look back upon.

Once again, she moved: into a smaller, less expensive flat near Diana, but still overlooking the Thames. Only the Thames remained a constant. That, and her visits, more irregular now, but still taking place, to the Addie to see Sarah and Maisie. They were growing older but otherwise, little changed; not quite young children but not adolescent either. They would not, though, make old bones—as her grandmother had once said of Charlotte herself.

Her present establishment was modest, just two rooms, and a small bathroom, which she had not bothered to re-decorate. All her energies, and Diana's too, were going into saving Butterfly.

Charlotte looked after her appearance since it was, after all, a business asset which she could not afford to let go to waste. But an inner light seemed to have died inside her, so that she no longer felt she looked as good as she once did.

'Already I am becoming a "has-been" in the looks department,' she joked wryly to Diana.

Diana shook her head, but denial wasn't something Charlotte was going to believe.

In fact, she was lovelier than ever because grief had brought a depth and delicacy to her beauty that had not been there before. Many people noticed, but Charlotte herself could not see it.

It was a desperately hard time for her. She slept badly, with nights disturbed by dreams in which Charles was not dead. In such dreams they were usually together at a dinner party strikingly reminiscent of Aunt Helen's awful function. At these dinners she and Charles were separated but facing each other across the table; they could not speak to each other. These dreams were easier to bear than those others, in which Charles was dead and she knew she had murdered him. She felt very guilty, as if she had indeed killed him.

She told Diana of these nightmares, but Diana only said she was always murdering people in her dreams, and very often felt guilty, and Charlotte should not worry, she was in no way unique.

This was not as much a comfort for Charlotte as Diana had plainly expected it to be. Charlotte did not wish to have killed Charles even in her dreams; she was afraid it might be true.

Perhaps he had been thinking about her when the accident happened and when he "didn't seem to be looking where he was going". Or perhaps it had been his last desperate effort to punish himself. If so he was punishing her, too.

Also included in the punishment was the lorry-driver, who had had a nervous breakdown as a consequence. Following on this his marriage had broken up. Charlotte had kept in touch with him out of sympathy, so that she knew that it was not his wife he missed so much as his child. The child was disturbed too, and had run away from home. It was amazing how far the energy released by one act of violence could spread.

Charles had lost his life, she had lost her looks, the lorry-driver had lost his reason (temporarily) and his wife and child, more or less permanently. The most innocent seemed to have suffered the worst.

What Charlotte had to hang on to now was her creative career. Butterfly must live.

*   *   *

Butterfly survived.

For the next year it was all that Charlotte allowed herself to think about.

She had to learn, and did learn, how to arrange her own financial affairs. She was lucky in finding a sympathetic new financial advisor. Lucky also that at that time, interest rates were relatively low. Charlotte could, and did, borrow. She gambled on her talent.

As the weeks passed, a new phenomenon took the place of dreams. She would wake in the small hours, sweating and tense.

This time her fears were harsh and concrete: Had she risked too much money? Could she survive? Or would she go bankrupt? At one point, the threat of bankruptcy seemed very real.

Then an American buyer took all her collection for the following fall, placing a huge order. This was soon followed by two big British orders.

The tension eased. Charlotte found she could smile again.

But, as she soon discovered, one problem soon succeeded another. Success brought with it the question of logistics.

Could the factory out at Greenwich meet the production levels demanded by the large orders? Mrs Angel was still Queen Bee of the South London factory, looking after her workers there like they were her children.

Once or twice, lunching in the small canteen, Charlotte ran her eyes over the assembled faces, searching for those two faces that pricked at her memory.

One Saturday, Charlotte secretly let herself into the factory to study the workers' files; their names, ages and addresses. To her frustration, she found no names she knew.

What a secretive woman I am, she thought, disparagingly, as she replaced the cards in the filing-cabinet, remembering, also, how she had twice now used a private detective. And might need to use again soon . . .

*   *   *

On Monday morning, Mrs Angel knew at once that her files had been disturbed, and guessed who had been through them. She shrugged; she already called her boss "the mystery lady". And why shouldn't she check on her employees as it suited her? She, Mrs Angel, would look around, too. One often saw things on the quiet.

The following week, Charlotte was called to an emergency meeting with Mrs Angel. Diana drove Charlotte out to South London, having offered moral support.

'How is the boy? Your nephew, I mean,' enquired Charlotte, her eyes on the masts of the Cutty Sark.

Diana waited for the traffic-lights to change to green before she answered. 'He's fine,' she said thoughtfully. 'Really well. Thank God, he's clever. And such a sensible child. It will make all the difference to his life. We've always been such a foolish family.'

To Charlotte it seemed, if that were true, that the query of his parentage was settled.

Wasn't it likely that this came from "outside blood"?

Diana had come to the same conclusion. 'No damage from the fucking incest,' she said. She said it quietly, delicately, as if it was a moment of purest pleasure. She would have said it again if Charlotte had not put a gentle hand on hers.

It was not the way Diana usually spoke, but she needed to let out the emotion clammed up there.

Charlotte understood the impulse behind her friend's outburst.

Mrs Angel met them with a cup of strong coffee. 'Have it while it's still hot, dears, and a bit of my chocolate cake to eat with it. You look as though you need it. And you'll need it even more when you hear what I have to say.'

Charlotte took her coffee and sat down at Mrs Angel's desk, which also doubled as her own. 'So?'

'We *nearly* had a strike.'

Charlotte sat up straight. 'A *strike*? That would be murder!' She had deadlines to meet. The whole factory knew it.

'We don't have a strike.' Mrs Angel sounded comfortable, pleased with herself.

'Glad to hear it.'

'No. It's a question of holidays. You've been so busy I don't suppose you've noticed that there are one or two Bank Holidays coming up. Now the factory next door (plastic boxes) is giving a week. Ditto the biscuit factory round

237

the corner. Our girls wanted the same.'

'Why didn't you tell me?'

'I didn't want to worry you, when you already had so much to worry about.'

Mrs Angel put her hands on her broad, black-satined lap. 'So I settled it. I offered a bonus. A percentage on the pieces worked so that we meet our target figure. They accepted. Glad to.'

'It'll cost,' said Charlotte gloomily. She had already agreed prices with her customers.

'A little, a little. But you will have your orders on time. You establish a good record for the future. That is money in the bank to you.'

'True.' But still, no decision should have been made without her.

'Besides, I hear from my cousin that Debenham and Freebody's are opening a new boutique. They are going to want your style; your name has been mentioned. A whole shop within a shop to yourself, maybe.' She put her head on one side, making it not quite statement, not quite a question.

Charlotte laughed. Her anger melting away. She knew already that Mrs Angel followed her own rules. Now she no longer owned the factory, she allied herself with the workers more than Charlotte. This might have been her way of getting them the raise in wages she felt they deserved.

Charlotte knew she was going to have to exercise firmer control over Mrs Angel; she

238

could almost hear Charles' voice in her ear telling her so, but for the moment she could afford to laugh it off.

'Diana,' she said, 'as you are here, fill us in on this new scheme of yours for tele-advertising. Explain it, so I can see if I can afford it.' Charlotte wanted to maintain Mrs Angel's support; keep her feeling involved with Butterfly's development.

'It's like this,' began Diana, drawing a chair up to the desk, and opening a folder.

*   *   *

In the autumn of that year, 1971, Charlotte sat on a chair in the offices of Washington Swains the advertising agency, watching a film showing her own clothes. The video was for in-store viewing in every shop where her designs were being sold.

The video was short, set to run a mere ten minutes, but it was eye-catching, designed to grab the attention of the wandering customer; force her to look at the clothes, and see them at their best; how they *should* be worn, and with what accessories.

A model twisted on her heel, swung a jacket over her shoulder, then strode off with a backwards wave.

The video began again. It was meant to go round and round. The cost, which had terrified Charlotte, had been shared between Butterfly and the accessories firm, producer of the gloves, shoes and handbags. Even so the bill had been high.

'Well, what do you think of it then?' Diana was anxious to know. The suggestion of hiring Washington Swains to make the video for them had been hers.

'I love it. Run it again.'

Charlotte sat in tense silence, anxiously watching how her clothes performed. To her the clothes were the performers, not the models.

'Esther—what do you think?' Charlotte called Mrs Angel Esther now; they had become close business allies and friends. Esther and Diana between them bolstered her up when she showed signs of weakening. Which was quite often. Her creative spirit never gave, but her nerve certainly did.

For the first time, Charlotte was moving almost exclusively in a circle of women at the moment. She was designing for them, working among them, and depending on women for her amusement.

'I won't say I don't miss a man's company,' she had said wryly to Diana. 'But my body doesn't seem to call out for one.'

'That'll come later.'

'I'm too tired most of the time. It's a nice kind of tiredness, though. I don't really mind. I just flop into bed and go out like a light.'

Diana studied her friend and thought she

240

looked better than she had for a long while.

Esther Angel broke in with her response to the television film: 'It's great, fine. It would sell to me, and I'm a toughie. But will it pay for itself?'

'Oh Esther, you cautious old thing. Yes, I believe it will. Anyway, if not this time, then it's an investment in the future.'

Good, thought Diana, she believes in the future. Just once or twice I've wondered.

'The old ways were good enough for me.' Esther could be slow to move. 'You made the clothes and the shops sold them. Now that sounds grudging. I don't mean it to. I think your clothes are so good they should sell themselves.'

'Thanks, Esther,' said Charlotte soberly. 'But these days *no* clothes sell themselves. Competition is that fierce.'

They all knew it.

'That wraps it up then, Miss Chaudin,' said the young executive from Washington Swains who had been waiting on the sidelines.

He led the way out of the darkened office. He had drawn the blinds to get the best possible viewing for his brain-child.

Charlotte and Diana blinked their way into the sunshine. Esther had already disappeared: mysteriously she had a cousin who worked for Washington Swains and who must be talked to before she left.

'You always know where you are with

Esther, don't you? Feet firmly planted on the ground, that's where. She's been a god-send to me this last year,' Charlotte said.

Charles' last and best legacy, she thought. If she had a reservation about Esther it was that she reminded Charlotte of the painful past.

'Let's get a taxi,' she said to Diana. 'I don't think I've got the energy to walk down Piccadilly.'

'If you're not feeling on top form, why not see my doctor? He's into homeopathy. I recommend him.'

It was more a fly cast upon the water, than a serious suggestion from Diana; she wanted to see what Charlotte said. Her friend's obsession with her health and fitness puzzled her.

'I've got my own doctor; I see him regularly. And I'm fine.'

'No more of those faints?' Diana still thought Charlotte looked—not weak exactly, but distant, somehow.

'Not since then. And it was nothing.'

'I still go to Babes,' Diana said. 'Never see *you* there now.'

'Too busy. I still keep up my exercises, though.' She waved a hand. 'Here's a cab. Can I give you a lift?'

'As far as Butterfly. I'll walk from there.'

But at the door of Butterfly Diana hesitated and delayed.

Charlotte realised she wanted to talk. 'Come on up and have a drink. It's time we celebrated something. Not sure what exactly. Survival, perhaps.'

'We've done that all right.'

'Yes. We've come through.' Charlotte spoke with sober, gentle conviction. She wasn't happy, exactly. She was living in a fragile bubble whose security might, at any moment, be pricked, but she had kept Butterfly alive. That must count for something. 'And we've not attenuated, either. No ghosts. What we've got here is a healthy and kicking baby.'

Diana raised her glass. 'To baby. Whose birth has given us some trouble.' She put her glass down. 'Can I talk?' She sounded both excited and nervous.

Charlotte sipped her wine and considered: I hope she's not brewing up a crisis, she thought. 'What is it? Not going to give me notice?'

Diana swung round. 'I'm happy. Haven't you noticed?'

'Yes. I have seen it. I was glad, but I didn't know what to say.'

'You must have wondered why. Who I was seeing. You knew I was seeing someone?'

'I guessed.'

It hadn't been hard to guess: Diana had had telephone calls at which she had laughed, letters she kept tucked in a pocket; she had experimented with new hair styles. She had had frequent engagements to which she had hurried with a cheerful laugh.

There was certainly someone, but whom?

Not Virginia, that was certain. Virginia had taken a year's sabbatical leave from her television company, and gone back to her Oxford college to write a book. A thesis, even, Charlotte had heard.

Virginia would certainly be back. People like Virginia did not disappear from the scene. But for the moment she was gone.

'I must be extraordinarily obtuse,' she said. 'You are my dearest friend; I see you all the time, and yet I have no idea what has been going on with you.'

'It's not your fault,' replied Diana. 'I've taken great care to keep things quiet. I didn't dare not to. I was so frightened that if I talked too much things might go wrong. I didn't dare risk it.'

This room, Charlotte's office, had changed over the last year, reflecting differences in Charlotte herself. She had done nothing to it, the colour scheme of apricot and white remained as before; just the way she lived in it had altered.

At first, had she been able to afford to redecorate she would have done. The room was too vividly reminiscent of those first happy days with Charles. Even before they had married, he had been a hope she had carried in her heart. She saw that now, and was amazed that she could have been so blind to her own feelings at the time. Still, that was her mark. She seemed to keep her eyes permanently blindfolded.

So she had left the room as it was; worked hard in it, not looked at it much, neglected it. And now, papers had silted up the desk and floor. Fashion magazines were spread across a long table. On the wall a cork board was pinned with her designs. It was now a working room, comfortable and homely, a little battered, in need of painting.

But Charlotte was not anxious over the sea-change it had undergone.

The room had seen some tearful anxious conferences in the days after Charles' death, when Diana herself had been under public scrutiny, so it was natural they should talk here.

A wave of affection for Diana swept over her. She went across to put her arm round the other woman's shoulders. They had created a friendship between them. Whether it was an old style or a new style friendship between women did not seem to matter. What they had was real. 'Come on, love, out with it. Who is it? Anyone I know?'

Shyly Diana said: 'No, no one you know. I met him in Norfolk. He has a house near the cottage. He was sweet to the boy. Teaching him to ride. You shall meet him, though. I want you to know him.'

'I'm so glad, Diana.'

'We've been lovers for some time now. I didn't think it could ever happen to me. With a man, I mean. But I like it.'

Charlotte started to laugh. 'Oh Diana. You sound so surprised.'

It was funny, but it was touching too. Diana was so earnest.

'I've been longing to tell you all about it, but it never seemed the right time. But now—well, it's possible we might get married. I'm not saying we will, but we might.'

'I think it's marvellous; I am so happy for you.'

'The thing is,' said Diana simply, 'It was the boy that did it. I have become so fond of him. Proud, too. I began to relax about sex. About men. I don't know why, but loving the boy helped me to love Sam.'

'That's his name?'

'Sam Howden. He's a dog breeder.'

'Now that really does surprise me. You hate dogs.'

'Not pugs. I've got to quite like them. They have such human faces. He also breeds Boxers. They are rather terrible, I must admit. But I expect I'll get used to them. Oh, by the way, as well as breeding dogs he works at Washington Swains. It was one of the reasons I chose them for the promotional video.'

'*Not* Esther Angel's cousin?'

'No. But they know each other.' Diana was on her feet, striding up and down the narrow room. She had recently given up smoking, so she poised a pencil between two fingers, as if she might smoke that if she got desperate enough.

'I'd like to meet Sam soon.'

'You shall. Tomorrow then? Lunch at the new place in Blays Street?'

She's got it all settled, decided Charlotte. She and Sam have talked it over and decided that tomorrow is the day.

A little sadness arrived with the thought: inevitably Diana was moving away from her.

'I shall look forward to it.' She mustn't be selfish, especially towards Diana, who gave so much.

For a little while they discussed Diana's hopes and plans.

'If you do get married, then I shall do your dress, of course. A sort of creamy colour for you, my girl, and a big sweeping hat.'

'I'm taller than Sam.'

'I'll take care of that. In my dress you will look fragile and vulnerable,' promised Charlotte. 'Size won't come into it.'

Diana smiled. 'Tomorrow then?'

'Tomorrow.'

*   *   *

Sam Howden was of middle height, a thick set, sturdy man, with a tanned skin and bright blue eyes. Diana need have no fears that he would mind about being shorter than she was, Charlotte concluded. Sam was totally self-confident. He was also agreeable and unaggressive, or at any rate, had the good manners to seem so. Charlotte liked him at once.

He was waiting for them with a table in the window at the restaurant in Blays Street. He sat them both down, then took Diana's hand in his. He had large, capable hands. Of course, he'd need them for the dogs, thought Charlotte.

'Di's told you about us?'

'Yes. It's the best news I've heard for a long time. I am so glad.'

'Good. That's what I hoped you'd say.' He motioned to the waiter. 'I've ordered a beautiful burgundy. I hope you're a red wine girl?' He was still holding Diana's hand.

'Love it.'

Sam was promptly served. He had the air of a man who expected and received good service.

The wine was beautiful. Charlotte sipped it with pleasure and let Sam order their meal. He would do so in any case. In the nicest possible way, Sam was in the driving seat.

Her eyes met Diana's across the table. Diana looked proud and pleased. She also looked a little shy. That was a very good sign, Charlotte decided. It meant it went deep. And with Sam it would have to be because he was so genuine himself.

Charlotte raised her glass. 'To you both. I'm so pleased for you.' But how much did Sam know about Diana's past, she wondered, worriedly.

Sam released Diana's hand. On his own hand was a heavy gold signet ring worn on the little finger. A faint smell of Floris soap hung around, matching his well-scrubbed look. There was money here, she decided, along with the dog-breeding and Washington Swains. It would be nice for Diana to have some money.

'You are the first to know. Di said you had to be,' Sam said. He was conducting a mild flirtation with her. But on this score Diana had no need to worry, either. Sam would probably be totally faithful to her.

'Let me get a word in, Sam.' Diana leaned forward. 'If it's convenient workwise, we thought we'd get married very quietly, very soon.'

Sam kept quiet. He knew his strength.

'Of course, love,' Charlotte replied. 'I can manage. Have a long honeymoon. You've worked your guts out for me this last year. Now it's your turn.'

'Well, actually, we plan to get married tomorrow. Special licence and all that. Sam's just fixed it.'

'Never been married before,' said Sam. 'But I know what's what. With this one's track record, there can't be any hanging about!' So he *did* know about Diana. Of course. Between Diana and Sam there would be total honesty. Another thing to envy her.

249

'Am I invited?'

'Yes. Just you, and a friend of Sam's as the second witness.'

There was no question of making a special dress now. 'Come along to the work-rooms sometime this afternoon and we'll see what you can find in stock for you to wear,' Charlotte offered.

She walked back towards the office, leaving Diana and Sam still holding hands. Then suddenly, she turned on her heel to make for the bus which she knew would drop her near the Addie. It was a few days in advance of her usual visit but she felt a strong need to go there. The bus was crowded so she had to go upstairs where she sat, watching the London scene. She usually enjoyed watching the crowds in the street. But today the crowds only served to underline her feelings of loneliness.

She was so preoccupied she almost missed her stop.

'Watch it, girlie,' called a taxi driver as she leapt to the kerb.

She passed a newsagents and confectioners. Neither sweets and chocolates nor fizzy drinks were encouraged at the Addie, but today she decided to smuggle in a selection of both, as well as the usual comic.

Usually she went through a couple of wards first, saying hello to some old friends, and greeting new arrivals, but this time she was met by one of the nurses she knew well.

'Alice, nice to see you. This isn't my usual day, I know, but I thought I'd drop in.'

Alice Morrow's face was serious. 'I'm glad you have.' She hesitated. 'Maisie's—not so well.'

'Ah.' Charlotte stood still. She understood the style of the Addie: not so well meant bloody ill. In the case of Maisie, who was very vulnerable in any case, it meant it was touch and go, 'Right. Thanks for telling me.'

Alice Morrow turned to walk with her down the corridor. 'I know you take an interest in Maisie. She's a sad case—inherited syndrome, you know.'

'I do know.'

'Of course there are many inherited conditions. Some don't show up until maturity, but Maisie—well, she was born that way. I think that's the saddest—no life at all.'

Maisie has more life than you know, thought Charlotte. Even the best of nurses did not always get it right.

I am tuned into Maisie, she thought, and I know she has loves and hopes even if she cannot express them.

'You may find Nurse Beryl in there,' said Alice Morrow. All the nurses at the Addie went by their Christian names.

Curtains were drawn around Maisie's bed, while Sarah lay on her bed, face in the pillow. No one else was there.

'I won't disturb them,' whispered Charlotte,

251

even while her heart told her nothing could disturb either child more. Nurse Alice's parting look told her that she knew this look.

Charlotte parted the curtains: Maisie lay curled up, foetus-like, her eyes closed. She touched the child's hand which was very hot.

Better than very cold, she thought, and then: No, the temperature will go up and up, beyond the body's control, and then drop. For that is what death is: the body's systems frantically struggling to keep control, struggling like a cat falling from a tree, burning up energy, then giving up: dead.

She sat holding Maisie's hand, wanting no response, and getting none. She understood; death was such a big positive thing one had to accept it, this she knew now.

Softly she said to Maisie: 'I believe you can hear even if you are very far away. Goodbye, my dear. God bless.'

Sarah's head was still buried in the pillow, but Charlotte came to her bed. She turned, her eyes open. A little smile curved her lips, but no words, nothing.

Charlotte took Sarah's left hand, the only one she could reach, for the other was tucked under the girl's body, in both of hers. There was a response, a pressing of the fingers against her own, and with this she was content.

Charlotte sat there for what seemed a long time, ignoring the nurses who came in and out, until at last Nurse Alice touched her shoulder.

As she rose, Sarah turned her head again into the pillow. Charlotte knew she was willing herself to die, and that when Maisie went so would Sarah.

She knew she had said goodbye. The visits to the Addie would, of course, go on but would not be the same. She had come to love the pair of children, in her seeking to help herself.

As she got outside there came a sad, savage irony: I've been approaching this from the wrong end! Now Maisie and Sarah don't need me, I should visit a home for the old and lost.

*   *   *

It was now almost a year since Charles' death. Charlotte *was* recovering, but there was no one to take his place, and she feared her own future.

With a sigh she turned to her design table. Where work piled high at any rate offered a distraction, after taking the previous day off for Diana and Sam's wedding.

At the end of the day she had to face it: there was a gap in her life. A sense of dissatisfaction, even with Butterfly.

Butterfly was not quite what she wanted. She realised now how Charles had influenced her thinking here, pushing in a direction she might not have taken.

It was good what she had done, but it still did not satisfy. There was something about

Butterfly that was not just how she wanted it. Not exactly right.

As Charles himself, she realised now, had not been exactly right.

Inside Charles was a built-in flaw that she herself had somehow perhaps, accentuated. She was anxious to accept her share of the blame.

Another type of woman might not have brought out the basic masochism in Charles that had so frightened her. She had a strange affect on some men, she realised. Look at Jehan. With her, he became violent. She hadn't heard that he was so extreme with other women.

Her short-comings as a wife (and goodness knows they were real enough) had made everything worse for Charles. She sought no excuses.

But she saw now how dazzled she had been by his flair for being Charles Scrope. He had projected a picture which had attracted her irresistibly. It was unconscious, she was sure. He didn't know he was acting, but acting he was just like the rest of us, she thought, sadly. Inside that ultra-confident figure was someone quite frightened.

I ought to have helped more, she concluded. Instead of that, in a way, I launched a subtle attack.

It was very sad to say aloud: 'I shouldn't have married him.' But to that had to be added:

'Likewise, he should not have married me. I was not, as it turned out, the wife he thought I would be.'

There was one man to whom, as she was now beginning to realise, she might have been a good wife, but that was all in the past now. Too late to go back.

Charlotte finished her work, tidied herself and left the office. She was the last one to leave. All around was quiet and darkness.

One ghost walked, or rather ran up and down these stairs. The figure of a man with crisp hair, and bright blue eyes.

Sometimes Charlotte almost saw this ghost, through a half-opened door, at the corner of the stairs, or caught a whiff of the mixture of soap and Turkish tobacco that she associated with him. Not Charles, but James Bruce.

CHAPTER ELEVEN

Charlotte locked the big front door behind her. Tomorrow she would be out all day at the Greenwich factory.

Outside in the street, she stood for a moment to have a look at Butterfly Design Ltd.

To satisfy the commercialism of the day she had converted the big downstairs bay into a shop window. It had taken the architect some pains to create this effect while not transgressing the rules laid upon the owner of a listed building. The facade of the house had to be preserved intact. The clever fellow had achieved it by building a kind of stage-set behind the two windows and lighting both so that Charlotte's clothing stood out boldly. Each window had one outfit in the foreground and others arranged as a backdrop, behind.

In the darkening evening her window was eye-catching. Charlotte felt like a cat watching a particularly promising nest of birds.

Two women stopped to look at her window. They were at the end of a long, shopping day, weighed down by bags from Marks and Spencer, Selfridges, and Fenwicks, but there was still some fight left in them.

Charlotte lingered, to observe them studying her display, longing to know what they would say.

'What do you make of 'em, eh?' asked one of the other.

'Outlandish, Kath.'

'Oh, Brenda, no. Some are lovely. Look at that dress on the right.'

Charlotte listened, fascinated. Clever of Kath to have picked out the dress on the right. It was the best in the window.

Nor was the word 'outlandish' entirely out of court either. Her dresses in the window were in the extreme of fashion, because they represented the 'cutting edge'—derived from street fashion—always the forerunner of the catwalks. What you had here was the quintessence of the mode, distilled on purpose to knock the eye out.

'I think it's wicked to spend that sort of money on clothes.'

Charlotte surprised herself by breaking in. 'You pay for excellence. That's what costs. That dress was cut by hand, not by a machine. Every stitch of the finishing was put in by hand. And it was designed by a master.' Might as well blow her own trumpet.

Brenda looked at her in surprise. 'How do you know so much?'

'I work there.'

'Sweated labour, is it? What do they pay you?'

'I think the clothes are lovely,' said Kath.

Her eyes and Charlotte's met in sympathy; they understood each other.

Charlotte decided to walk home; she trudged through the streets, somehow uplifted by the brush with the two women. She had defended her side and given a more balanced perspective, she hoped.

All the same it would be nice to be able to offer something to women in Kath's clothing price range. Someone like Kath ought to be able to buy well-designed clothes.

Oh, it was true chain-store clothes were much better than they had been. But the need to play safe often made them painfully dull. Average. They were designed for the average market. In other works, for no one in particular.

She hoped she could do something for people like Kath. Somewhere, somehow, she might do.

She suddenly felt more cheerful.

*   *   *

However, Charlotte's spirits were not high as she got back to her flat to prepare an evening meal.

Her flat was the most undecorated, ordinary living place she had had since she had set out on her own, leaving her family behind.

Always before, she had taken trouble to make the place where she lived her own. From the one-room student pad to the elegant house overlooking the Thames of Tony's days, she made them her own with her colours, pictures and pieces of furniture. Not this time, though, and the reason was that the place was unloved, and it was unloved because Charlotte did not love herself. The flat was orphaned, a deprived child.

When Charlotte really noticed her flat, as she did that evening after her meal, she felt as though she had reverted in time to her childhood.

Then, she had lived in an uncared-for room and felt uncared for herself. It was terrible being unloved, because it made you unloving back. Not that she had been an abused child, exactly; known roughness or cruelty, but she had sometimes known hunger and neglect. A neglect born of circumstances beyond her mother's control.

No one had been surprised when her father went off and left her mother, it had always been on the cards that he would.

Charlotte had been old enough then, just, to become the bread-winner, and it was then she had sometimes gone hungry. During this lean time she had ceased menstruation to become virtually sexless.

Of course, the hormones had bounced back later she reflected, so that one of her mother's sisters had said she ought to be exorcised, which she seemed to think of as a form of spaying for sexually over-active girls. Not true. Charlotte then had lived chastely, only, apparently, sending out signals of promise. Other aunts had been kinder. They were all good with their needle, making themselves pretty clothes. It was during this period that she had come back to the district lived in by her father's family to find work and assistance. This period had not lasted long: she had found her father's family no help. She got a scholarship to the local polytechnic, had then got another to work on design in Paris, and from then on, had been Butterfly.

Quite often she was asked about details of her early life. She was always either evasive or a downright liar. She was her own creation now.

* * *

'Khaki, pink, violet, yellow,' said Charlotte aloud. 'Colours for Summer '72?'

She was sitting at her drawing-board, a palette of clear colours spread before her. A clutch of patterns of silk, with some thin cottons, were pinned to the board so that she could study them.

In her mind she saw a bevy of loose, gentle, casual dresses, but her fingers, usually so docile to her commands, refused to carry out their part of the job and produce the drawings she desired.

Until the dress was on the board, sketched in full details, it had not begun to be born. Usually it came easily. Today, the designs defied her, remaining tantalisingly elusive.

Something was blocking her. She had to accept it. Progress was nil.

Angry she threw charcoal aside (she liked the free flow of a charcoal stick) and moved away from the drawing-board. Sometimes it was her practise to work with swathes of material. Perhaps this time, it would be the way.

'Probably that damned injection.' She touched her left arm gently.

A projected trip to Hong Kong to see suppliers there had made a visit to the doctor for a series of immunisations a necessity. Her arm and her mind were mind were still bruised from the encounter.

She hated her visits to the doctor, although he was a nice man to whom she might, under different conditions have felt a friendliness. She disliked all doctors. They told one unpleasant truths.

Not that this one ever said much; he was a taciturn man. Twice a year she went in for a check-up, reminding herself each time that she was a private patient and could have what she paid for. She knew Dr McClintock had her written down as a neurotic, and resented it.

He had a heavy hand with a needle too. She had winced as the jab went in. He had seen that too. 'Relax,' he'd said.

Then he had reminded her that this appointment was also for what he called (sub-ironically?) 'one of her check-ups'. Perhaps she was too sensitive to overtones. Or in this case, undertones.

He had gone on to say, thoughtfully, that he always took her blood-pressure twice, for a reason. Experience with her had shown him that her blood pressure was always abnormally high at the beginning of their session, then it dropped to normal by the time of the second test.

When she had been given the all-clear, he had said, still thoughtful, that the test had made him wonder if she had something that worried her, and would she like to let him into her confidence?

Charlotte now draped a swathe of crocus yellow cotton over her shoulder and stared at herself. I didn't say a thing to him, she remarked silently to her image; didn't answer. Pretended I hadn't heard.

Dr McClintock knew better than that, of course. No doubt it was all written down in his folder labelled: '*C. Chaudin (Scrope)*'. She had been his patient well before her marriage. He must have his own ideas. A professional opinion, professionally reserved. Doctors sometimes didn't tell one the truth until it was too late.

The yellow, now joined by a violet silk-cashmere mixture, was giving her some rather exciting ideas about the mixing of natural fabrics.

The ghost was back on the stairs; the image of James, running down, past the work-rooms to the room where Charlotte worked.

Charlotte put down the materials and listened. It was late afternoon. Everyone else had been gone for a solid hour.

She went to the door. Her heart was thumping. There *were* footsteps.

They were coming down.

She opened the door. A figure rounded a bend in the stairs and took the last two steps in a familiar leap.

It *was* James.

*   *   *

She could hardly believe he was here. It was
marvellous, a mini-miracle.

'James—it's you! *Really* you. What are you
doing here? I can't take it in.'

'You don't deserve me to come and see you,'
he said lovingly, severely. 'You never wrote a
word to me.'

'I know, I know. Some letters just don't get
written.'

'But still...'

'It wasn't sloth. More a sort of fear.'

'Of me? Oh come on, Charlotte!'

'You did rather storm off.'

'Did I?' His voice was gentle. 'I thought I
had quietly withdrawn.'

'It's so marvellous to see you. How long are
you back for? Is it just a visit?'

'Let me come in and I'll tell you.'

'It's just so wonderful that you should
suddenly be *here*!' she exclaimed again.

'Yes.'

They stood staring at each other in happy
amity.

'Oh, I am glad to see you,' said Charlotte
again, unable to hide her happiness. She felt as
if life had given her a new chance. Not exactly a
second one, but a complete turning over on to a
fresh page.

How ridiculous, she thought, that this rush
of feeling should all come about because a

263

slight, curly-haired man stood there looking at her with a smile.

She recovered herself: 'Come on into my room. I was working late.' She turned back, he followed. 'To tell you the truth, I thought you were a ghost. Your own ghost. I've heard your feet on the stairs a lot lately.'

'Truly?'

'Well, there was something.' She was opening the refrigerator where she kept drinks. In it were a couple of bottles of champagne. In her job there were often occasions to offer a buyer or, indeed, a seller, champagne. Sometimes their nerves needed a rally from the shock of the price!

'Telepathy, precognition or just mice?' She poured the champagne carefully, and handed James a glass.

'Charlotte, it's marvellous to have you welcome me. I didn't count on it. I hoped, but wondered.'

In fact, James had been very doubtful of his reception. He had no reason to believe Charlotte would be delighted to see him, and some reason to believe she would turn away angrily. Or at best, meet him with a cold face. This was the reason for his unannounced arrival.

This visit now to Butterfly had been to reconnoitre. See how things stood. Something about the place, some sense of the atmosphere might tell him how Charlotte was. At the very least, he would have been where she often was: he cared that much for her.

'How did you get in?'

'I still have my key.' He had let himself in, meaning to go up to his old office and look around. 'You've changed things, but not that much.'

'How long have you been in London?'

He was silent for a minute. Then: 'Two days,' he admitted.

'Two days without telling me? How could you?'

'I wasn't sure whether you would want to see me. I was just going to have a quiet look round here, then make up my mind.'

Fate had made it up for both of them, almost throwing them in each others arms.

James shook his head, as if shaking off a mist from around it. 'Suddenly it's all cleared up. The question is answered. You want to see me; I want to see you.'

Charlotte poured them some more champagne. She realised she had given herself away almost completely to James; but she did not care. She had surprised herself by the warmth of her pleasure. Her emotions would need some thinking over. But not now. Other questions first.

'You haven't told me why you are home. Or for how long.'

'Let me come back with a question. Are you happy with Butterfly just the way it is?' If she was, then he would go away, never to come back.

Charlotte put down her drink. 'That's a funny question. And an unexpected one too, if I may say so.'

'But is it? Answer, please, Charlotte.'

'Butterfly is what I've made it.' Not quite true; rather what she had made it under Charles' influence. Now her own personality was floating free and she was beginning to wonder. Left to herself, would she have created something other. She was still fumbling with this notion. There seemed a lot of new ideas to think about at the moment.

'I'm making money,' she said defensively.

'And an international name in the ready-to-wear world. That I know. I salute it.' He lifted his glass.

'Thanks.' The dry little word popped out, immediately regretted. 'Well, thanks.'

James waited. The Charlotte he remembered was totally honest, and would, if he gave her time, come out with a true opinion.

'Well, if you want to know, I've been starting to think that perhaps I've lost something. The kind of excellence I valued. The feeling that sometimes, just sometimes, I produced something peerless. I don't get that now. You can't with the market I work for. What I produce is good. I'm not kicking myself. But that diamond-hard glitter of the very, very best is gone.' She looked at him and shook her

266

head. 'And I only just started to realise it minutes before you came back. You certainly arrived at the right time.'

Timing is everything, James accepted, but so is a bit of luck. And then he made an amendment in his own favour: he knew his Charlotte; they moved to the same beat. Perhaps telepathy had operated to a degree.

He had read reports of her collections; had seen photographs of some of the clothes, while actually inspecting those that had arrived in New York. In design they were good, very good indeed. He did not underrate the talent behind them. But he knew Charlotte would be missing the fineness of couture.

He had felt a moment of triumph when she more or less said so.

'What I'd like to do, if the idea appeals, is to start up the couture side of Butterfly.'

'Revive Redmond & Bruce?'

'No. A new start. I think you need what I've got to offer.'

Charlotte sat down; suddenly her knees felt weak. 'It needs thinking about.' But she knew she had already taken the decision: she wanted James here. 'Where are you staying?'

'I shall be back in my old flat. My tenant is on the way out.' He had spent two nights in a hotel at Heathrow. Two restless, noisy, worried nights that he now wanted to put behind him. London life must begin again.

'I'm just round the corner then. I've moved

into a flat in Oakley Street.'

'I take it the answer is yes, then? You do want me back.'

'I do need time ... But yes, yes, of course, it's yes.' There were tears in her eyes. 'I believe I've missed you very much.'

'As a person or a colleague? That's a joke,' he added hastily, seeing the tears run down her cheeks. 'Here, steady on.' He produced a large white handkerchief. 'Let me mop you up.'

'That's silk,' said Charlotte. 'Silk never mops one up. One needs cotton or linen for that. It's all right. I've got myself together now. You were a shock. And anyway, I think it was the injection I had for going to Hong Kong. Emotion is the kick-back.

'Silk, though.' She was examining the handkerchief and identifying the distinguished label on one corner. 'You must have been a success in New York to shop where that handkerchief came from,' she said, half-jokingly.

'Yes. I'm not leaving because I was a failure. Rather I am bringing my success back home. Like a prize. For you, if you want it.'

'Oh James, you are a darling. And you have darling ways of saying things.'

They finished up the champagne, now mostly flat, and agreed to have dinner together. But not before Charlotte had shown James the current work in hand, and he had made one or two suggestions.

This was how they would work together, she thought: prop and cop, like a card game, with both of them winners.

James saw Charlotte back to her flat (get her out of that dump soon, he decided), before driving back to his restless hotel where he must spend one more night.

I am the only man who really understands this woman, he told himself, the rest saw vitality and warmth and love that they wanted and just *grabbed*.

He thought of all this as he paced the night in his lonely, noisy room. What would he, could he, make of his life back in London? With whom and for whom would it be lived? One had to consider the other party, especially when that other party was Charlotte. In his view, she had been kicked around enough.

I won't grab, he instructed himself, but I do want her, and I don't want to share. He knew his own nature: that though he would not grab, he wanted sole possession.

*   *   *

Charlotte had too had plenty to think about. She sat up in bed, looking around her. She forced herself to think about it: it kept the surface of her mind occupied.

It's a hole, this place, she concluded. No wonder I've felt miserable in it. I won't stay.

She settled back on her pillows, pushed the

button on her radio, so that she got a soft, background noise, and considered her situation.

I haven't 'got over' Charles, to use that horrid truism. I have simply grown on and over and around what he was in my life, as if I was a tree with another dead tree in its roots. He's still there and always will be. He and Tony are built into my life. Part of its archaeology. Just as Jehan is still there, a watcher in the undergrowth.

But I have changed. I believe I'm more tolerant than I was, more willing to forgive. I understand Charles better than I did, understand better what drove him on. I can forgive all that, and move on, now.

She turned off the radio; the noise was getting through to her and annoying her. It was a talk-in on sexual hang-ups which did not suit her mood. What things people talked about to each other on the airwaves in the middle of the night!

In some ways she was the same old Charlotte, hanging on to the same old reserves, the same old secrets. Nothing had changed there. Never would probably, the age of miracles being past.

She went to sleep, still sitting up with the light on and awoke to sunlight.

Sunlight, and coffee and a morning of fresh beginnings.

Charlotte ate a large breakfast: a muffin,

thick with melted butter and marmalade and hang the calories. She knew that new beginnings took strength and energy.

* * *

In fact, it took six months from the first cry of joy on Charlotte's part that evening of James' return, to the moment in June 1972, when Diana could show her the publicity hand-out she had prepared for all the newspapers, to announce the fact that James Bruce was bringing couture back to Butterfly.

'There's tremendous interest,' Diana said. 'Your friends are divided between those who say you will live to regret it, and those who say it's great news. But one and all are deeply envious at heart. They think you two have timed it "just right".'

'Hope so. People are coming in to enquire and book appointments.' A first collection of James' clothes would be shown that week.

A big party would launch it. After that anyone could drop in and look. They planned to be informal. There were to be no terrifying vendeuse blocking the way, no charm about getting in to view. The sort of customer they were aiming at wouldn't stand for it, preferring a casual, spontaneous, buy-as-the-mood-strikes-one approach to their clothes.

James had veered between optimism and despair about what he was producing, but finally ended up euphorically happy. 'I know it's good, girls,' he had said to them both.

It had been agreed that he should concentrate on coats, day dresses and suits, since tailoring and the plain line were his strengths, just as Charlotte's was 'flou'.

This first collection was entirely James' but it had been agreed that Charlotte would filter in some of her 'flou' as time went on. It would be a two-way process: a few of his coats and dresses would eventually find their way out to the ready-to-wear factory in South London, to be copied.

New machines were being installed at that very moment. Esther Angel was smiling: she had joyfully engaged new workers, thus extending her empire at no personal cost. She had long since invested her profit from the original sale of the factory into blue-chip shares, and was enjoying herself with a free spirit.

In the fashion world James' return had brought about much gossip and speculation. He was known to have been a 'hot' property in New York, so he had not come back because of failure there.

On the other hand, was his proffered explanation that he 'hankered' for London, the real reason? A lot of people said quietly to each other that he had come back because of Sophia. Others said no, it must be Charlotte.

A few, on the outskirts of the affair said: Are

you sure he's not queer, dear, after all he's never married? As James said when he heard this himself (some friends always tell you) one can't deny this sort of thing; whatever one answers, one always loses.

Diana kept in the background during this time. She could see her part in shaping the pattern of the gossip; she did not wish to embarrass further either Charlotte or her own husband, although she knew both to be robust souls. But she had another reason to seek a quiet life: she was in the first stages of an uncomfortable pregnancy. She looked radiant but felt ghastly. However, she managed to turn up for their bi-weekly meeting with Charlotte, wearing an air of conscious bravery.

* * *

It was a late Friday afternoon, with the weekend coming up. James was expected, but had not yet arrived. Diana and Charlotte were on their own in Charlotte's office, Diana bearing a full folder of papers that Charlotte must study before Monday.

Charlotte had not yet changed address, and still lived in Oakley Street. There had been too much else to think about, she excused herself, she'd been too busy. But every weekend she and James looked at properties to which she might, possibly, move.

'I shall probably be sick over the next person

who tells me how pregnancy suits me,' Diana said to Charlotte. 'Doctors are such liars. They tell one how natural it all is, and how splendid it is for one to have all those lovely hormones released. What they don't tell you is how lousy one will feel.'

'How's Sam?'

She was delighted for her friend, if that was what Diana wanted, but pregnancy was a subject she would not dwell upon.

'Happy. He'll make a lovely father.'

'Yes, Diana,' said Charlotte docilely. 'I shall miss you.'

'I shall go into semi-retirement. But I have worked ahead, on all the promotions for the new-style Butterfly. In *Vogue* and *Harper's* we are simply referring to James as *at* Butterfly. That leaves it comfortably vague.'

'It's all tied up. We have a proper agreement.'

'I know. But he might want to create more of a separate identity for himself later on. You never know. Anyway, if you remember, when we talked it over, this was how James himself wanted it put.'

'He didn't mind if he was never named at all, but, of course, we couldn't allow that. He's a *name*. He's bringing in a lot of custom. The order book looks good. We shall break even quite soon.'

One legacy from Charles that she had not lost was that she now knew how to read her accounts, thus being able to visualise where she would be financially, six months ahead. He had trained her to be a good businesswoman.

She had been lucky in that she had never been burdened with bad debts. Her customers had always paid up. She, in her turn, settled her bills with wholesalers in good time, allowing herself a little leeway, but not too much.

Thus, if there ever came a time when she needed credit for longer, it would be there for her. She also maintained easy relations with her bank manager. Even in the dark time after Charles' death, he had stood by her. Indeed, his support had been one of the factors that had helped her through.

Survival is having friends, she thought. And being on good terms with your bank manager.

She accepted the folder from Diana, added it to the other work on her desk, and offered coffee. Which Diana, shudderingly, refused. 'Sam's doing all the cooking. I can't go near the smell of frying. Fortunately, he loves it.'

'What about the dogs?' Charlotte was unable to resist this slight tease. One didn't hear much about the dogs lately.

'I can't stand the smell of them, either. But Sam's cutting back. He knows I don't really go for dogs, and he doesn't mind.'

Sam and Diana had obviously reached that stage in their marriage when both party's true feelings could be safely revealed and with no hard feelings.

Charlotte envied them. She had never quite got there herself.

'That's James now,' she said, her ears ever quick. She would know that step anywhere. 'We're going to look at a house in Basil Street for me. Too grand, I fear, but fun to look at.'

James appeared, and informed Diana that Sam was waiting outside. 'Parked on a double yellow, darling. Charlotte, I'm ready for you.'

The business side of things had soon been settled between these two; the personal relationships had moved more slowly.

This had been Charlotte's doing. She had hurried into marriage with Charles; now she wanted to take her time. I want my own space to move in, she told herself. I am better on my own. I think I prefer it. Certainly I'm not going to rush into anything.

One thing had soon been arranged by them: That first evening of James' return, before they had said goodbye, James had said: 'About Sophia—'

Charlotte had stopped him. 'Don't go on. No more about Sophia.'

'Charlotte, let me explain. Please,' she said. 'When we met after her wedding it was simply that she wanted advice about her clothes. I was over her long before. There was nothing in it.'

The subject was thus closed, never to be re-opened between them.

Sophia might, probably would, swim into their world again, but they could afford to ignore her, now. Sophia was no longer able to be a barrier between them. Oddly, Charlotte felt secure with James in that way now. While he loved her, *if* he loved her, there would be no more Sophias. She could trust James.

*   *   *

'It's a lovely house,' she said thirty minutes later, looking out at the small walled garden. 'Queen Anne, isn't it?' It was unusual for Chelsea where so much is early nineteenth century or late eighteenth. The pretty, double-fronted house was unique, as Charlotte recognised. Domestic, elegant, prim, it fronted straight on to the narrow street, without a blink. An upright, happy house which had always been well treated.

'Lovely,' she repeated. 'But too big for one person. Even if I could afford it.'

'For one, yes, but not for two.' James moved back from the window towards the fireplace. 'I didn't bring you here just for you to look at it. I was thinking of myself.'

'Are you going to buy it?'

'Why not?'

'If you can afford it.' Charlotte nodded. 'It's still big.' Six bedrooms, a drawing-room on an upper floor with a library next to it, a large dining-room on the street level, and a huge basement.

'Not if we shared. Why not, Charlotte? Why

277

don't *we* live here?'

The slow progression of the months since his return had been leading up to this moment. Neither of them had hurried it, but they had both known this encounter lay ahead of them. They were too grown up to play games, to pretend they did not understand what was happening to them. They had grown together in fondness again as they had worked side by side for the success of Butterfly.

The spark of physical attraction which had always been there was now tacitly acknowledged by both of them.

But Charlotte held back, because she was frightened; she was enjoying the lull in her life. She was tasting a kind of independence she had never known before. At the moment, it seemed worth hanging on to. She might change her mind, but that was how she felt now.

'Live together? Run the house on equal terms?' She didn't ask if they would share a bed. If they moved into that house then they would certainly do so. She admitted to herself that nothing would keep her out of James' bed. She longed for him to make love to her, but, at the same time, she dreaded the emotional dependence that she knew must follow.

She suspected that James understood quite a lot of the emotions she was feeling. She guessed he knew almost as much about what was in her mind as she did herself.

James did know. He had spent weeks

searching for just the right house to show as an offering to Charlotte. A house in which he could stand and say: This is for us. Won't you join me?

It had to be a special house. Not a crazy house, not necessarily a smart one, but a good, beautiful house that had been a happy home for generations. Charlotte would feel the atmosphere and respond. Such houses can anchor people. They hook people. He wanted Charlotte hooked. But nicely; she had to be happy.

This was the house. As soon as he had seen it, he had asked the estate agent who was selling it and had arranged for flowers to be put into the main rooms. The agent, bemused but grateful, had consented not to be present, as James showed her around. Charlotte leaned forward to smell the flowers on the windowsill. Their scent was calming, soothing.

'I'm better on my own,' she said. 'Sad but true. Something I've learnt. I don't think I'll join in. Lovely house, James, but it's all yours.'

James looked at her. 'I don't want to hurt you, Charlotte, but I don't think you ought to go on living the way you do. It's not good for you.'

'I'm living the only way I know how, now.'

James looked at her with sympathy. No one ought to look as weary as Charlotte did at that moment. Beautiful but fine-drawn, as if she didn't eat enough or sleep quietly. Diana reported she had given up Babes, so it wasn't over-exercising.

'Are you happy, Charlotte?'

'Happy? That's asking a bit too much. But I am satisfied. And hopeful.'

'What are your hopes?'

Charlotte looked into the fire. 'That things won't turn out too badly.'

'You're too young to think like that.' He was shocked.

'It's the best I can do at the moment,' she replied. 'I don't believe anyone is too young. I've had a lot happen to me.'

'That isn't all, though is it? There's something else that you never quite say.'

'Oh we all have our secrets,' said Charlotte lightly.

'I don't.'

'I believe you, James. And I envy you for it.'

'Only because I don't want to. Anyone can have secrets. It gets to be a way of life.'

Charlotte stood up. 'Let's look over the house again. It interests me,' she said.

It's hard enough as it is being a working woman with a creative career, why should I complicate it still further for myself by falling in love with James? Because that is what is going to happen if I once give in. So ran her thoughts.

For him, it's all right. James will keep it all together. He got over Sophia with no visible signs of disintegration. Yet he had loved her, no doubt about it.

'I'll think about sharing the house,' she said, as she moved towards the door. 'It might work.' There would be some comfort in it, after all. James was a comforting person.

'That's not what I want. I don't want to share in that kind of way. I'm asking you to marry me.'

There was a loaded silence. Then Charlotte said, 'Oh, James. That means a lot to me. But, no. I've had one marriage, and think perhaps that will do. It's something I don't have the knack of—a happy marriage.'

'Charlotte, listen to me.'

'Try and find someone who has it—the knack, I mean. The most surprising people have. Look at Diana.'

'Charlotte, it's *you* I want. And not just sharing a house, or sharing a bed, but marrying.'

'No. Thank you, James dear. But no.'

'I shall buy the house anyway,' said James.

He became devoted to his house, spending long hours in it working away to get it exactly as he wanted it. He loved that house.

*   *   *

Charlotte went back to her lonely set of rooms. She belonged to herself and no one else. She had her work.

Skirts were getting longer, jackets shorter,

281

and shoe heels correspondingly higher. In all these innovations Charlotte was a leader. Charlotte was beginning to look older, her halo of dark hair somehow accentuating the hollows about her eyes; the slight downward tug of lines about her mouth. But James thought she looked more beautiful than ever.

Diana's child was born, and was a boy, whom they called Samuel, nicknamed Weller. He lay quietly in his crib, looked surprised to be with his parents, but comfortable, as if certain he had done them a favour.

Diana returned to work quite soon, but had frequent days off. Sam was proving an admirable father, the dogs having trained him nicely. Between them they were managing without a nanny or an au pair.

No one knew yet whether the dogs would like the new little stranger, although it was a vital question. Their numbers had not been greatly reduced after all, but Sam had given up breeding pugs to concentrate on Boxers who were said to be 'better with children'.

Charlotte was a reluctant godparent. She was definitely not 'better with children', but she held the child carefully in her arms at the christening, said his name very loudly when asked by the clergyman, then handed him over to the godfather who was James. James was better, but not good. The baby cried.

Sam rescued his son. 'You're not handling him very well,' he said severely, looking around as if for a collar and lead.

Characteristically, champagne was not served at Samuel Weller's christening, but whisky, vodka and strong gin were.

Diana who had previously been attractive but unkempt, had now become pretty in a more conventional way, and today, looked amazingly well-groomed. Charlotte, who had been fond of the old, wild Diana, missed her. She supposed Diana was happy, but she had preferred the former untidy character.

'This is a special effort,' whispered Diana, guessing the significance of her appraising look. 'You should see my closet shelves. More of a tip than a dump. And I have a run in my tights if you could see it.'

She was a woman sensitive to the needs of her friends, and she knew that for Charlotte she must never change.

Reassured, Charlotte enjoyed the rest of the function, and accepted an invitation to go out to dinner with a cousin of Diana's who was in the Guards.

James saw, heard, and did not like it. He was jealous, no other word for it. And he suspected Charlotte knew it.

*   *   *

Charlotte enjoyed her evening out with cousin Nicholas, a pleasingly amorous young man. Over the pre-dinner sherry at Langan's she considered accepting his advances, while drinking the good hock that went with the fish. She was almost sure she would, but with the coffee and brandy she was surprised to hear herself issuing a masked but definite refusal.

She didn't know whether to be shocked or pleased with herself. James would be pleased. At a remote distance, it was all his fault, of course.

*　　*　　*

There was an anxious business meeting out at Greenwich, with James, Mrs Angel and, by courtesy of both the Sams: Diana.

Like the rest of the the business world, the rag trade was shivering, alternately freezing and overheating with the fever of Seventies inflation.

One of James' best friends in New York had been a Harvard trainee economist. 'Watch where the lights keep going on and off,' he had said. James was watching which shops and businesses changed hands most frequently.

And the lights were going on and off in boutiques up and down the King's Road, Sloane Avenue and Knightsbridge.

At first Charlotte did not take in the significance, but then the bankruptcies and the voluntary liquidations began to appear.

The truth was brought home to her most sharply when she saw the clothes of a famous competitor laid out like a jumble sale in the window of his once pretty shop. *'Forced sale owing to closure,'* said a nasty notice, not even printed or typed, but scribbled out in ink. Charlotte felt quite sick. 'I felt ill,' she went back and told James.

For a while, however, her own world seemed to remain secure. She and James had their steady customers, their order books were filled well ahead. So the down beat, when it came, was all the more sudden and terrifying.

Orders, firm orders, were cancelled. Others, hoped for, anticipated, taken for granted, did not materialise. Those which did come through were cut down, drastically.

As a crisis it seemed to happen quickly. One moment Butterfly was in good shape; the next, they were seen to be struggling.

The money seemed to drain away. Now debts, almost overnight, seemed to grow into a mountain. Her bank began to make warning sounds.

It was only a warning, but Charlotte took fright. Uncharacteristically for her, she hid the warning, told no one, took no action. She felt deeply ashamed, as if she had failed everyone: James, Diana, Mrs Angel, the workers at Butterfly and out at the factory in Greenwich, they were all her victims. She hid herself as far as she was able, pretending she was too tired to be sociable.

Then, one morning, alone in her office, she

took a telephone call from her bank which, although it conveyed the worst possible news, brought her to her senses.

She stopped hiding, came right out into the open, and on the telephone, summoned Mrs Angle and Diana to a meeting that afternoon. James had only to walk down the stairs. Of them all he was the most prepared. Mrs Angel had had her own quick thoughts, but not dwelt on them. Personally, she was in the clear; her own finances were not involved.

Briefly and quickly Charlotte informed them that the bank would not extend her overdraft; that she had several very bad debts owing to her, and that in consequence she would not be able to pay her own bills. She could see little ahead but a winding-up of the business. Butterfly was all but dead.

They listened to her quietly. Diana showed open incredulity and dismay, but Mrs Angel pursed her lips and nodded. She was thinking of her girls, debating whether she should buy the factory back, and deciding, almost instantly, that she could afford to wait till prices dropped to rock bottom.

James said: 'Exactly how much do you need?'

Charlotte told him how much she owed the bank. The bridging payment they had suggested wasn't an enormous sum, but if you hadn't got it, then it was enough.

James said: 'I can get it for you.'

'You can, James? How?'

'I can sell the house. Prices have risen quite staggeringly. Especially for that sort of house. And I have no mortgage to pay. All my savings went into the house. I would guess it's worth what the bank wants from you.'

'But James—you love that house. I couldn't let you do it.'

James got up from the chair where he was sitting. He was calm and quiet. 'I loved that house as a home for us. That was why I bought it, and that was why I've been working on it. But it means precious little to me in itself. Don't you see that?'

'Oh, James, I can't let you.'

He smiled at her and took both her hands in his. 'It'd be a pleasure, love. It was always for you, anyway.'

*   *   *

So, a year after he bought it, James sold the house in Chelsea. It was bought by a rich Lebanese family who seemed convinced that one day they would need a foreign refuge from their own country.

Butterfly was saved.

*   *   *

A month later, Charlotte asked James if he would marry her. It was her way of paying him back: Taking the risk on him he wanted her to take. Perhaps she expected him to say no. He did not. Maybe he knew Charlotte and her needs better than she did herself.

They were married quietly a few weeks later, in August 1973. No one was told until they received invitations to a party. 'I thought you'd guess,' said Charlotte to a surprised Diana.

*   *   *

Six months later, in February 1974, Charlotte turned her gaze upon herself and realised she was exceedingly happy. In giving happiness to James she had received it back.

It was now ten years since Charlotte had created Butterfly. And life was good.

CHAPTER TWELVE

Both now married women, Diana and Charlotte found common ground once again in domestic problems.

'I feel much more married this time round,' said Charlotte. 'I can see now I was only playing at it with Charles. For instance, now I have to think about cooking and cleaning. I never seemed to have to do that with Charles.'

'You were richer then,' pointed out Diana. 'Or thought you were. Or lived that way.'

'True. Now I am managing with a budget like everyone else. If I don't do the dusting, no one else does.'

'Do you like it?'

'Not much,' said Charlotte frankly. 'Who does?'

'Oh I think some women do get a kick out of cleaning a house and baking a cake. Baking a cake is supposed to be a substitute for having a baby, did you know that?'

Charlotte was silent.

'Well, I can tell you,' went on Diana, 'that it's nothing like it at all. Until you've had a baby you don't *know*.'

Charlotte still kept silent. People always seemed to be talking to her about babies these days.

'It's not much use relying on Sam too much with Weller now he's walking and talking. He tries, he's an animal lover and all that, but he really doesn't have the knack with animals that talk. Funny isn't it? Even I am better, and frankly I'm terrified. Still, we take turns. Sam takes Weller into work twice a week. His secretary doesn't like it, much!'

'Is Sam jealous of Weller?'

'No.' Diana was surprised. 'He's not a jealous person. I believe he prefers me to Weller. But it's so different.' She thought about it, then said: 'What's all this about? You feeling jealous?'

'No. Not with James. One couldn't

somehow. He gives total security.'

But he was jealous of her. He didn't want to show it; he tried, because he was a generous person, to control it, but she sensed it. Without wanting to, he watched. She could feel the weight of his observation upon her.

She understood why it was happening. It was all her fault. Not because she would be unfaithful in any ordinary sense. Nor, so she supposed, did James really expect it of her.

No, it was her fault because she was not a transparent person, there was an opacity inside her, hard to see through. James felt this barrier.

This was the only blemish on their happiness, and it was not discussed between them. James was struggling with an emotion he was ashamed of, which he did not want to admit.

'Diana,' Charlotte asked. 'Can I ask you a horrible question? What would you do if you lost Weller—if he died?'

'Charlotte! Don't say such things!' Diana looked as if she would like to run home and snatch up Weller. 'I think I'd die too.'

'Ah, then, you do love him.'

'Of course! I'd be absolutely devastated if anything happened to him.'

'More than if you lost Sam?'

'But I'm not going to lose Sam,' said Diana alertly. 'Not unless you know something I don't.'

Charlotte laughed. 'Of course not! Sorry.

I'm being morbid. Let's change the subject:
How's your awful sister?'

'Her ladyship? Being an exemplary wife,
mother and aunt at the moment. On and off,'
Diana said disparagingly.

Charlotte knew that Diana's sister's child,
the little boy, now fast growing up, lived with
her and Sam, treated as an equal by both of
them.

*   *   *

James had given Charlotte happiness, only to
lose a little of his own.

He had never expected to be jealous of her
after marriage. Naively he had thought that the
tumult she aroused in him would subside.
Instead, it seemed to increase.

Intimacy with Charlotte sometimes seemed
like one step forward, then a dancing step
back. She eluded him.

He tried to control the jealousy, asked no
questions (or as few as possible), and was
convinced his wife had no idea. It was not a
retrospective jealousy: he did not concern
himself with Jehan, or Tony, or Charles, as if
he knew his enemy lay in the future.

But strong emotions invade the
neighbouring tissue as through osmosis:
Charlotte knew. She responded by keeping
him in touch with all she did.

She moved around a great deal more than he

did. In their new organisation she was the person out in front, the person who was photographed, interviewed and courted. Of this James was not in the least envious. Professional rivalry, except in the very best sense, did not exist between them.

In any case, James had his own fame. He had always had admirers of his pure, classic line. He was the 'best tailor' in England. As soon as he was re-launched in the new set-up of Butterfly his loyal band of followers reassembled.

He and Charlotte lived "over the shop" using the very top floor of the house that was the home of Butterfly. They lived simply and economically, pouring all their spare cash back into the business. It suited them both to live like this: James because he had never lived any other way, and Charlotte because she wanted to feel her life with James in no manner resembled her life with Charles. This is James' marriage, she said and I want it to be good.

To herself she called it James' Time.

James' *Working* Time, he might have called it himself had he known its secret name. He had never laboured so hard, and with such concentration before.

Men are not usually much changed by marriage, while women often are, but James *had* changed. He was more solid. The old James had been almost boyish. Now, after New York and the marriage to Charlotte he was as buoyant and light of step as before, but most definitely, a mature man. He still ran up and down the stairs whistling, his hair curled as crisply as ever, but there was an unconscious air of authority that he had never had before.

Charlotte was the sun in his world, the ground on which he trod. When she came into a room he was instantly aware of her with joy. He had only to hear her foot on the stair to feel happy. When she was away from him he felt uneasy.

He had never expected such totality of feeling for his wife. Charlotte did not dominate and did not expect obedience from him. It was just that she pervaded all his life. He might have wondered if this would decrease after marriage, instead it grew stronger.

He and Sam struck up an unlikely friendship. Sam was his first customer when Butterfly began to design for men. Sam wore clothes well, with his manly, no nonsense look. He was also, splendidly placed at Washington's, to launch the promotions campaign. He and Diana did it between them, helped, presumably, by Weller, who went everywhere.

There was a lot of trouble over the name. Sam said no man worth his salt was going to wear a suit with a label inside called Butterfly. In matters of this sort, Sam's judgement could be relied upon.

So the old name of Redmond & Bruce was

revived for this label.

Charlotte accepted the name gracefully, it was only fair, but it did seem to her, just for a moment, that an old ghost walked. But she pushed it away: this was the present, her today life was with James, and the old Charlotte was gone. The world in which she had lived, first with Jehan, and then with Tony, afterwards with Charles, was fast turning itself into a very different decade with a tone of its own. She could afford to revive the name of Redmond & Bruce. She was glad to do it for James.

James had no plans to separate Redmond & Bruce off from the new parent Butterfly. What he wanted to see was a company which had couture at its top end, but which extended to the market for the expensive, designer ready-to-wear clothes which Charlotte produced.

It was not a new idea, but the way the two of them had put it together was new: each part had equal status.

Only women had a choice of couture or ready-to-wear; men still had to have their suits custom-made by James. For once, sex discrimination worked against them.

*   *   *

Over breakfast, nearly a year after their marriage, and rather more than that since James had invested all his savings in Butterfly, they sat discussing business. Newspapers and fashion magazines were all around them on the floor. Charlotte had her feet on *Vogue* which had been rude about her that month.

It was Saturday, the only day they allowed themselves to relax. On Sundays both of them used the quiet to get ready for the week ahead and were more likely to be found at their drawing-boards, or folding and shaping lengths of cloth, than resting. They lived and worked, together, and had drawing-boards ready to set up side by side if necessary.

James had cooked the breakfast, saying that, although he didn't mind starving the rest of the week, on Saturdays a man must eat.

'Lovely kedgeree,' said Charlotte, her mouth full.

'It's my Scottish blood.'

'I'm getting better at cooking myself.'

'Of course, you are,' said her husband. 'This toast is splendidly black. Quite up to epicure quality. I shouldn't touch it if I were you.' He produced a tray of hot rolls.

Charlotte grabbed. 'Oh those lovely Italian ones. Where did you get them?'

'Soho. I went shopping yesterday lunchtime. I thought we'd starve if I didn't.' He didn't mind his wife's lack of interest in cooking; it amused him.

'It was *my* turn to shop,' said Charlotte, full of self-reproach. 'I forgot. Sorry.'

'Never mind. I enjoy it, really. And you were at Greenwich all day.'

'I could have shopped there all right. No excuse, there's a market.'

'How are they out there?'

'Pretty well.' Charlotte frowned. 'I have to handle them, though.'

'You depend too much on Mrs Angel.'

'I do, I do.' Charlotte grinned. 'She still thinks of it as her place, you know. And perhaps I play along with that a bit. Suits me. But if we expand *you* into ready-to-wear designer clothes for men, then we may have to think again.'

'I'm not sure if I want to spread out,' said James, buttering his roll.

'Oh, you're so naturally conservative. It's your Scottish blood.' She released *Vogue* from its prison beneath her feet and picked it up. 'But the Italians have opened the door. Look.' She pointed to a large black and white photo-spread of a beautiful young man wearing a check suit. 'You could knock spots off that.'

James said: 'Anyone could. Doesn't have to be me.'

'I can see I'm going to have trouble with you all the way.' They exchanged smiles. They were never going to quarrel over work and they both knew it.

'We will expand, though. OK on that. I am with you there. The question is which way?'

Diana had researched a series of options. 'The most promising,' she had reported, 'is bed linens, and bath towels. Charlotte designs them, and we get them made in Nottingham. You then franchise the outlets.'

Both Charlotte and James knew that this would be the way they would probably go, but occasionally Charlotte liked to kick the ball around. It was her way of thinking aloud.

She was gradually moving forward to what she had on her mind. 'I believe I'm changing the way I think about how women should dress. I believe they've been bullied too much. Even by me. We've said wear this and put this with it. I don't want to go on doing it that way.'

'Apted won't like to hear you say that.'

'And yet women need help. Advice. Guidance. It's not easy to do it for yourself.'

'He'll like *that* better.'

Through Sam, they had acquired a new business manager, a hard-headed young man called Apted. He did not succumb to the glamour of the fashion world, thinking only in terms of cash-flow, and a "good" dividend yield and a good P/E. They were not yet a quoted company, but if he had anything to do with it, they would be one day.

James looked at her slight figure bending over another fashion magazine. She was as thin as ever, still exercising energetically (she had designed a canary yellow zip-suit to wear), still watching her body anxiously for signs of ageing. At least, he supposed it was ageing that worried her. Sometimes he wondered if it was not some more subtle amalgam of fears that plagued her.

He thought a child might settle a lot of her problems. But that wasn't going to be possible.

Charlotte raised her head. 'You're looking at me.'

'I often am, my darling,' he wanted to say, but instead: 'I thought you might like some more coffee.'

Charlotte pushed her cup across, then went back to her reading.

Before they married, Charlotte had said, in a soft voice that was husky and tight with some unexpressed emotion: 'There's one thing you must understand before I become your wife; it's to be just you and me. No family.'

'I'm not marrying you for children,' he had said. Charlotte had been what he wanted; his companion for life. He was not eager for descendants.

Nor was he now. But more and more he found himself wanting all of Charlotte, her past, her present and her future. He could share in her future through a child.

He recognised it as a strand in his jealousy, but because he was a reasonable, self-regarding man he tried to accept it as part of the great love he had for her while not letting it get out of hand.

'Are you packed for tomorrow?' he queried.

Charlotte was off on a trip to Hong Kong, then back through Australia and San Francisco. Business all the way.

'Mmm.' She raised her head from the magazine. 'All done. Not taking much. Silk jersey mainly. Can't crush.'

'I'll drive you to Heathrow.'

'No. I'll take my own car, and leave it there. Then I can drive back myself. You know how often the flights are late. I hate to keep people hanging about.'

'At least have a taxi there and back.'

'No. I have so many odds and ends of luggage. I'd rather manage myself.'

She was prepared to be obstinate; James did not argue. He saved his resistance to Charlotte for big issues. This looked like a little issue.

*   *   *

Out at Greenwich a party took place nearly a week later. Officially the party was to celebrate Mrs Angel's birthday, but in fact, it was to mark the highly successful struggle out of the crisis of the year before. This was tacitly admitted by all.

Every year Mrs Angel gave a party with cake and sweet sherry, this year she had added champagne. Not proper French champagne, but something imported from Romania. 'Communist champagne,' Bea Benson noted, but she drank with the rest.

Bea was a Tory voter and an ardent royalist while maintaining an alertly critical stance. Behind her lay generations of Londoners who had done more or less what they wanted inside and out of the social conventions of their class and time. "What the eye doesn't see, the heart won't grieve over," might have been their motto.

Charlotte had been asked to the party, but had not been able to come. James had looked in, had a cheerful drink with Mrs Angel, kissed some of "the girls" goodbye and departed.

'Lovely man,' said Bea. In a wistful voice.

Her daughter, Dorothy, agreed. Everyone liked James. 'You don't have to feel guilty for liking him.'

'I don't.'

'Yes, you do. Because he's *her* husband.'

'No such thing.'

'You're loaded with guilt towards her. I think that's silly. Everyone concerned did their best. Life was cruel, that's all. Life is cruel. And she ran away from it.'

'Oh you're so young.'

'I'm not blaming her. But I'm telling you not to blame yourself. I think we ought to tell her we know who she is. Introduce ourselves. Say we're family.'

Bea was silent.

Her daughter persisted. 'After all, I've got my career to think of. It might do me some good. She might give me a push.'

Bea said: 'I think she knows if she wants to.'

'What do you mean?'

'I think she's looked at me, looked at you,

and decided not to see. She doesn't want to know us. I can understand that. Leave her be.'

Her daughter was not convinced. Everyone has a dream. In Dorothy's dream, Charlotte did the right thing by her and her career. Only she couldn't do that without being told.

Or, if her mother observed accurately, by being reminded. She did not believe that people who waited behind doors got asked to parties.

*   *   *

James was anxious about Charlotte during her entire trip. There was no special reason for it, but he felt uneasy all the time she was away. He was busy himself, but he had time enough to worry.

The fashion world was tilting unpredictably on its axis once again, again obliterating a few names, shifting some stars from the firmament altogether, while causing others to shine ever more brightly. James found that *his* was the name that was "in". Suddenly he was getting as much publicity as Charlotte herself.

'I've been around for years now,' he said to Sam, 'and they've suddenly discovered I'm a new voice in fashion.'

They were lunching together at a new wine bar in New Street Passage. James found Sam supportive company. He had a calm, wise presence, very like one of his own dogs, with a knack for saying the right thing, or even saying

301

nothing, which was sometimes even better.

'Accept it and be grateful. I should.' Thus casually would one of his Boxer dogs flick up a juicy unlooked for mouthful. 'It's the conjunction with Charlotte. She brings luck, haven't you noticed? Sometimes good, sometimes bad, but movement.'

He added, 'Mind you, don't take my word for it. I'm only repeating what Diana says. It's how she sees it.'

'Diana, you, me, even Virginia. We haven't done badly out of Charlotte, have we?' Those of us that are still alive, that is, he added to himself. 'But now I'm worried about her,' said James. 'She's off on this trip, not looking well, working too hard, as usual. And she's not communicating. Not really. I don't know what to do.'

He rang Charlotte every night: she was not always in the hotel to be spoken to. He understood that fact, but when they did speak she seemed far away. Always loving and affectionate, but abstracted in mind as well as body.

'Just love her, old boy,' said Sam easily. 'Just love her, that's all you've got to do.'

'I wonder if it's enough.'

'It's about the best you can do. The food here is lousy, isn't it? Let's leave and go round the corner and get a sandwich in the pub.'

They rose and left; they were as one on the matter of taking food seriously.

302

Over beer and sandwiches James confided: 'I never thought I'd be like this. So concentrated on her, I mean. I thought it was a thing women did and men not.'

Sam had a calm way of dealing with matters of love and women. Breeding dogs seemed to have helped him handle both easily, although he was careful to point out that parallels must not be pushed too far. 'I don't think it works like that,' he said.

'I believe I'll fly out and see her. We could meet on the West Coast. I know she's due in San Francisco on Monday.'

'I shouldn't think of it for a minute.'

'No?'

'No. Just stay home and keep the house warm. That's man's work.'

'Sam, you're letting me down,' said James reproachfully.

'Just telephone her and talk.'

'But she never says anything.'

Sam went home, vaguely worried himself by now, and said to Diana: 'Is there anything wrong with Charlotte?'

'Yes, I think there might be,' answered Diana. 'Haven't you noticed with Charlotte that as soon as her life is settling down, she muddles it up somehow?'

*　　*　　*

Charlotte lay on her bed in her hotel in San

303

Franscisco and wished James was with her. She was even more closely connected than the speakers with the phenomenon that Diana had observed and was only too aware that it was happening to her again.

Not James' fault, nor her fault, but the way things were.

Since she saw the events from the inside she knew they were not her "muddling things up" as Diana put it, but the knot in her life once again pulling all the strings tight.

This knot had, in the past, produced emotional attitudes in her which had provoked anger in Jehan. The same flaw had kept her remote from Tony so that there was no surprise if he drew away. She had long since forgiven him. You really couldn't blame him; she had been such an aloof yet vulnerable little customer. A walking invitation to be pushed off a cliff edge, especially to someone like Tony.

Charles was another matter. She had simply not been a big enough person for him; she had not measured up to his conception of the world. She had thought that her private and personal wound would not interfere with their marriage. Instead, it had shed blood over both of them.

Another life, another try at marriage, she thought. But there were no second chances for Charles.

Life had given her one with James. If she

could just hang on to it.

Thinking back to her week in Hong Kong made her realise that James was worried about her. She had felt the anxiety in his voice every time he telephoned. Just to hear that stress in his voice had made her draw back.

'I love you, James,' she wanted to say. 'Just love me. Don't ask questions.'

Questions were a threat. Husbands asked questions. Perhaps it was natural, even right, that they should, but she wished they wouldn't.

The telephone calls had been a strain; she hadn't been able to respond to James as she had wanted. He had known it, too.

'You sound tired.'

'I *am* tired. This is an exhausting city.'

'I wish I'd come with you.'

'You'd hate Hong Kong.' That was not wholly true. James was an energetic man who would enjoy the urgent vitality of the crowded, scrambling city. But what could you make of a city that built a great apartment block, sold it for use as offices, then knocked it down with the cement still damp, to erect custom-built offices? Or a city where a great architect could win a prize for a building whose beauty would never been seen because there was no room for it to be seen, so crowded in with other buildings was it?

Life was both too expensive and too cheap in Hong Kong.

'No, you wouldn't,' she had corrected

305

herself. 'You'd love it for a week. Two weeks would kill you.'

The west coast of America seemed quite calm after Hong Kong. Even a little old-fashioned.

On the flight over she had slept most of the way, except for occasional short conversations with the man across the aisle.

He initiated them; Charlotte would rather have slept. He felt he had a right to speak to her because they had stayed in the same hotel in Hong Kong, and both had British passports. After a week in Hong Kong that made them practically old buddies.

'I'm from Brum,' he opened. 'You don't have to tell me you're from the Smoke. I can tell it by the way you look. You going to 'Frisco? Me too. On business. My second visit. Your first? You'll like 'Frisco.'

Eyes closed she had wondered what pet name he had for Hong Kong. There must be one: it was his only way of feeling at home in the world outside Birmingham.

'I sell machine tools. What do you sell?' He had concluded she had to be selling something. Only sellers and buyers followed their route.

'Fashion.'

'I knew it,' he said triumphantly. 'That girl knows how to dress I said to myself. Wonder if my wife has worn anything you've made?'

'Perhaps.' Charlotte was noncommittal.

'Knows how to dress my wife does. But not a

306

heavy spender. Cheap and cheerful, that's what she says she likes. Never wears a dress more than twice. "Don't spend a lot, but spend it often is how to keep in fashion", that's what she says. Got a little dress shop of her own, of course. You must tell me your name and I'll tell her to stock you.'

Charlotte kept quiet.

'She's always glad to give a helping hand. You girls have to hang together, eh?' He all but nudged her, only then the stewardess appeared with drinks. 'Nice little shop in Edgbaston. Tax loss to me, of course.'

Two drinks later for him, and a bottle of mineral water for Charlotte, he leaned across and said: 'What about dinner with me tonight? I know you're at the same hotel. I've seen the label on your case.'

'I don't think I shall eat in San Francisco.' She had every intention of ordering dinner in her room and going to bed early. She closed her eyes, hoping he'd go away.

He went on talking to her, but she was able to ignore him. He didn't seem to mind. Perhaps he was used to it from that tax-loss wife of his.

At the airport she was able to evade him, getting a taxi straight to her hotel. She had only a blurred vision of steep, raked streets in warm rain as she drove to her hotel. The flight had been delayed, it was late, she was tired. Behind her she could see a following taxi-cab. The incoming visitor from Birmingham?

307

Two hours later, she had eaten, showered and was lying on her bed waiting for the call to James in London, to come through.

She had but a hazy idea of the time-lag, yet she knew that whenever she rang he would be glad to hear her voice.

'James? Dearest. Oh, it's lovely to hear you. How are you? Where are you?'

'Getting up. Breakfast.'

'It's night here.'

'Are you on your own?' How not to say hello to your wife.

'Someone did ask me to dinner, but I didn't go.' There was a chuckle in her voice.

'What are you doing then?'

'Lying on my bed and wishing you were here.'

There was a moment of silence, but it was a warm and loving one.

'Still, perhaps it's just as well you're not. I'm cross, and tired and my hair needs washing. I look awful.' She pulled a face at her image in the mirror on the wall by the bed.

'I love you best when you look like that. Not that you ever look awful. You couldn't. But when you look tired and in need of comfort then I love you even more than when you have that glitter you have at parties.'

'Do I have a glitter? I didn't know. Sounds exciting.'

'Of course you don't know. It wouldn't be genuine if you had to make an effort for it. The

308

best glitter is unconscious. Yes. You sparkle.'
And it was true, she did.

'You've cheered me up. I feel better already.
I shall still have to wash my hair, though.'

At the other end of the line James felt that, at
last, he was getting through to her. Perhaps he
had cracked that bleak mood which had
seemed to envelope her.

They talked for a little longer, discussing
business. She was delighted with the good
things that seemed to be developing for him in
London. She herself had done well in Hong
Kong, she reported.

After they had finished, she got up from her
bed and washed her hair.

She went back to bed feeling happier. James
had had a good affect on her. How strange it
was that this man, who was now so profoundly
important to her, should have been there in her
life for so long without her realising how deep
was the love he could call up in her.

If only she did not have the strange feeling
that her left hand had developed a life of its
own and that the right would soon follow suit.

*   *   *

Charlotte had appointments neatly spaced out
over the next day, each one so placed as to keep
her running to the next one.

Not literally running, no one ran in San
Francisco that day. The heat, the rain and the

309

humidity were too much to allow, or even permit, rapid movement.

By the time she got back to the hotel, she had done some good business, while meeting a succession of exciting, attractive people, all of whom had promised at her express invitation, to visit her in London. There seemed to be something in the air of the city that loosened her up. It would be quite a party if they all came.

She had refused various invitations to dinner that night, which she now regretted. Still, she would shower, change into one of her own dresses, and dine comfortably alone in the restaurant looking down on the lights of the city. She would eat seafood and drink the best Californian wine, and hope there would be no earthquake!

In the lift on the way up to the restaurant she ran into the engineer from Birmingham. He greeted her with cries of joy.

'So you *are* eating after all. That does it then. Dinner's on me. I've had a good day. We'll make it swish.'

He had a natural gift for the false word. It must have impeded his career as a salesman.

'I think I won't,' she began to say.

'Oh come on.' He put his hand on her arm. He had had perhaps a little more to drink than she had realised. 'We're both free agents aren't we? Everyone knows what goes on on tour. Bill Barlow's the name, in case I hadn't mentioned it. Call me Bill.'

'Please.' She tried to draw her arm away. Above all she did not want people looking at them, the last thing she wanted was a public fuss. She had had enough of that in her time. Also now she had James' feelings to consider; she knew he was jealous He tried to hide it, bless him, but the feeling was there and needed no fuel.

'Don't be shy.' He staggered slightly, pushing her forward a pace. 'Relax and have a good evening.' It was going to be difficult to get away from him neatly.

From behind a voice said: 'Charlotte. Good to see you. Of course, you are dining with me.'

She swung round surprised. A tall man, with broad shoulders, and a well-remembered face. 'Jehan . . . You?'

Jehan said to Barlow: 'This lady is dining with me. I've been waiting for her.' He put his hand firmly under Charlotte's elbow and led her to a table in the window. 'I have this reserved. Could see you were having trouble there. You didn't mind me interfering?'

It was so unlike Jehan to even ask.

Her heart was banging; she could feel the vibrations in her throat. Out of the frying-pan and into the fire was the fact of it.

'No,' she murmured. 'But I'm surprised.'

'Naturally. I knew you were here. Saw your name when I registered. But you didn't know I was around.' Politely, and even gently, for

Jehan, he said, 'You *will* dine with me? Please? Sit down.'

'I *am* sitting down.' She couldn't have got up if she had wanted to (surprisingly, alarmingly even, she didn't want to) her legs felt weak. Then, aware that this sounded ungracious, said, 'Yes. Thank you.'

He drew up a chair opposite. When their drinks appeared, he said, 'I don't blame you for looking at me with caution, as a mad monster you once lived with.'

'I never thought of you as that.'

'You ought to have done. I was. A monster to you, mad, and a drunken sot as well. You did realise that there was a lot of drinking behind it all?'

'Was there?' He was so changed. He even looked calmer and less aggressive. 'Yes, I suppose I did know.'

'You might well be nervous with me. Are you nervous?'

She shook her head. 'No.' Which was true. For the first time in years, perhaps since the first days of their relationship, she was seeing Jehan without fear and tension mounting inside her. She was free of his power over her. The pull towards him, once so strong, half desired, half hated, had gone. It would never come back. He was now just a man with whom she might, or might not, be friendly. She would have to judge whether she liked him. 'No, I'm not.'

'Good. I'll order some food for us. Leave it to me, will you? I know the best the chef does, I stay here often.' A touch of the old Jehan showed through. 'Business, of course.'

'You look as though you're doing well.' Jehan had a prosperous air, together with a new-found look of contentment.

'Yes. This life suits me. I'm not saying I'll stay for ever. Once a Londoner always a Londoner. But for now it's right. I'm married, did you know?'

So that was what had calmed him down.

'We've got a daughter. And another on the way. I'm a family man. Never have thought it of me, would you?'

'Now you mention, and looking back in safety, yes.' There had always perhaps, been a desire for solidity at the back of the old party-man, Jehan.

'I owe a lot to you, Charlotte. If it hadn't been for that terrible business over Charles, I'd might never have called a halt. That made me stop and look at myself. As did my health scare, of course. And didn't like what I saw, I can tell you.'

'I blame myself too,' said Charlotte. 'I did you nothing but harm.'

'No. We had some good times, you know we did.'

'Yes.' It would be churlish not to admit it because of painful memories of later scenes.

Their food was being served; he fumbled

with a fork. When the waiter had left, he said: 'I was envious of your talent. I knew you had ten times the creative power I had. Thank God, I've got over that now. It was rotten of me.'

Charlotte smiled. 'You were ten times better-known than I was then. I wasn't much more than an art student when we met.'

'You were a cocky little number though. Did you really have a Japanese grandfather? No, of course not. I never really believed it. But I never knew *what* to believe. You never ever quite told me the truth about yourself. That was what maddened me. You'd look so vulnerable, and so secret, and so quiet, as if you knew something you were never going to tell me. It used to make me want to hit you.'

'You *did* hit me.'

'I wanted to take you to pieces. To see what there was inside. Sometimes, I thought, nothing. Other times, I thought something rather terrible.' He was looking down at his food, not at her, but he meant her to hear what he said.

In the belief that she no longer feared him, that his influence over her had gone (not recognising that, in fact, the power remained, but now had a more benign face on it) a confidence came out: 'I do have a horror: that one day my whole physical being will collapse. Not all at once, but slowly, finger by finger, hand by hand, leg by leg, so that I have to watch it go.'

Jehan stopped drinking his wine. 'My dear girl. Stop it. This is morbid.'

'It's why I exercise so much, and watch my body so carefully in case it's started. Perhaps it has. Look.'

She held out both her hands, one of which trembled more than the other.

Jehan reached out, took them both in his and made her lay them on the table. 'Stop it, love. There's nothing in it. You're over-tired. You've been carrying heavy bags and cases. That's all.'

'I've told you more than I've ever told anyone.' Although there were some people who might know without being told.

'Once there would have been a way I could have reassured you. I could have taken you to bed. That's no way out for you and me now.' He shook his head. 'You shouldn't be out without your husband.'

But she was comforted by the reaction. He had dismissed the idea of her decay. That meant she must be acting and looking pretty normal.

Cheered up, in spite of herself, she ate her dinner and drank some wine. They gossiped about old friends over coffee.

As she repaired her lipstick, Jehan looked at her thoughtfully.

He didn't really remember much about this other husband, James, he hoped the man was up to it.

CHAPTER THIRTEEN

James was hard at work on the day of Charlotte's expected return. He would meet her at Heathrow in the early evening.

He was in his workrooms with a model, several lengths of patterned silk and a female assistant, who helped by holding pins and material in place while offering soothing and cheering comments when his anguish got too great.

Unlike Charlotte who sometimes drew her dress on the designing board, then cut a toile from it, James always worked straight from the material, moulding it onto the model's body, and only doing the toile when the blood, sweat and tears were over. He had to let the material speak to him.

The tears were coming fast. This time from the model, Matilda, who had been standing two hours and was exhausted. Sometimes the assistant wept, occasionally James. It had been known.

Big, silent tears were rolling down the girl's face. No one took any notice, work did not stop for a moment, even Matilda would have been surprised if anyone had asked her if she was tired. Still, she did hope for a pause soon.

'That's the centre point of the back collar.' James pointed to a large white pin placed on a turquoise spot. 'Remember we are working to the turquoise spots. The buttons will be turquoise.'

Then, 'Move the yoke up a quarter of an inch. So it falls better.'

'Yes. She has huge shoulder blades,' he said to his assistant, Mary Dacre. 'One shoulder is a little higher than the other, too.'

Matilda listened without taking offence; she knew all about the oddities of her body. All models got used to hearing the little imperfections of their bodies pointed out and allowed for in pursuit of the perfectly cut dress.

No one was allowed to interrupt these sessions, except under extreme pressure. The rule was well known, so it was with surprise James looked up to see Val there.

He knew it was bad news by her face. 'It's Charlotte? The plane has crashed.'

He had a vivid picture of the plane falling from the sky above some Middle-Eastern airport, then flames sweeping through the wreckage. Screams and shouts for help with no one answering.

'No.' Val swallowed. 'She's already landed at Heathrow. But she's had an accident. Crashed her car.'

James stared at her. 'What's that?' He was not taking in what she said, being still far away where the plane had crashed with Charlotte on board.

Patiently Val repeated what she had said.

Mary Dacre was taking Matilda away, carrying the dress with her.

'Heathrow? She can't be there yet.'

But it appeared she was. Charlotte had arrived at Heathrow just over an hour ago. She had gone through all the formalities quickly, then collected her case. On the out-skirts of the airport she had crashed her car into a bollard. No one else was involved, but Charlotte had been hurt.

'She's in Ashford Hospital. Yes, she's unconscious. No, I don't know how bad.' Then she said: 'I'll drive you. You're in no state to drive.'

James did not know what he answered, nor what happened next. When he surfaced he was on the motorway to Heathrow, so he must have said No.

On the seat beside him was a map of the route to the hospital. So someone had been businesslike. Val, presumably. Ashford was marked with a red arrow.

Once at the hospital it took him some minutes to locate Charlotte. There was a hiatus during which he was referred from person to person, ending with a harassed young houseman in a white coat.

'Oh, yes. Mr Bruce. Your wife's coming round. We've taken an X-ray. It doesn't look serious. Nothing broken.' He consulted some papers. 'Mrs Bruce. Just off the flight from Paris. Crashed her car. Concussed and

318

unconscious when she was brought in.'

'Not Paris.' Some confusion there, James reflected, but didn't really think about it. The important thing was Charlotte.

'No, it says Paris. Here we are,' he stood aside to let James go in.

Charlotte was in a small room with the blinds drawn down against the light.

'I'll leave you. You can have ten minutes,' said the young doctor. 'Dr Carmichael would like to see you before you go to have a word with you.'

It was doubtful if James heard. He was on his knees by Charlotte's bed.

She was wide-eyed, looking at him. 'Oh darling, it's not that bad. I seem to ache everywhere, but it all works. But it was so stupid. I think the steering of the car must have gone.' She hoped so.

'Thank God you're alive.'

'Oh I'm alive,' she said shakily. 'That is, I'm not sure if *all* of me is. I feel curiously dead in bits.'

'That's shock.'

'I believe it is. The car's a write-off, I'm afraid.'

'As if it mattered.'

They talked for a little while, but he could see she was tiring rapidly. Indeed, he was concerned about her condition. The young doctor had said 'nothing serious,' but Charlotte looked shocked and ill.

A nurse appeared at the door, silently willing him to leave.

He kissed Charlotte. 'I'll be back as soon as they let me. We'll get you moved to the London Clinic or something like it. Bless you, darling.'

Outside in the corridor, with heavy trollies rattling past, the nurse said: 'Dr Carmichael is waiting for you.'

She took him to a small room. Dr Carmichael was a young man, but not so young as the first doctor. He looked busy and overworked.

'I'm the Senior Registrar,' he said, holding out a hand. 'I thought I ought to see you. I've examined your wife; she seems all right except for the shake-up. We'll keep her overnight, but she can go home tomorrow.'

'Good. Thank you.'

However, that was not the end of it. 'What's a bit of a puzzle is why it happened. She doesn't seem to know. Has your wife any history of illness? Epilepsy or anything like that? Migraine? That can cause temporary blindness.'

'No. Nothing.' As far as he knew.

Dr Carmichael was thoughtful. 'I should get your own doctor to have a look at her. He can write to me.' He scribbled his name on a piece of hospital writing paper. 'Do anything I can.'

He hurried away, as busy and overworked as he had appeared at first.

On the way home James remembered the

comment about Charlotte having arrived on the flight from Paris. If it wasn't a mistake, it was odd. Still, she might have had last-minute business there. When she was better he would ask.

Next day, he collected Charlotte from the hospital and drove her home. She was quiet, but that was natural in the circumstances. 'I've attended to your car. They may be able to repair it, but probably better to get a new one. Safer for you.'

'Thank you.'

'There'll be no trouble with the police. No one but you was involved and no witnesses. I expect they'll want to come and talk to you, though.'

'I can't tell them anything.'

'Don't worry over it.' He took one hand off the wheel to pat hers comfortingly. 'You're all right. That's all that matters.'

'By the way, there was a silly mistake over where your flight was from. You came straight on a through trip, didn't you?'

'I was diverted to Paris.'

'Oh the weather.' He was at once relieved. But the weather had been good. 'Or was it the aircraft?'

'No. I diverted myself. I had some business there. It all blew up suddenly.'

'I see.' But he didn't. Clearly she did not wish to talk about it. He did, but dare not. What was there in Paris? Of course, she did have business

321

there, but when he came to think about it Paris came up perhaps rather too regularly in her itinerary.

He knew there were things Charlotte was not telling him; he suspected there was much she was not telling herself. He could not accept that she was guilty of any infidelity. He could not believe that the body that opened itself so joyfully and sweetly to him could have repeated this exercise with anyone else. There was naturalness and sweetness to her love-making that could not be a lie.

And yet this was the woman who had been seriously involved with four other men. He had never dared to ask if there were others, but he knew intuitively that Paris stood for something important in her life.

Don't put on horns, he told himself, they may not be there. Keep calm.

The next few days passed very quietly. To his great relief he did not have to raise the question of visiting the doctor because Charlotte herself, in a hesitating voice, said she would be going. He was surprised; she usually had to be reminded to go for things like an immunisation before travelling.

He heard her make the appointment for the next day, but she said nothing so neither did he.

Charlotte went for an early morning appointment with her doctor. She was his first patient of the day.

She recited what had happened to her in as

expressionless a voice as she could manage. Which meant just a little touch more of anxiety than she wished.

Her doctor examined her thoroughly, neatly and expeditiously, then left her to put herself together again with the aid of his nurse.

When she came back, he said: 'As usual, you are a healthy young woman. The hand tremor is very slight. There seems no organic reason for it. Nor the leg trouble. Went numb, did it? But you can use it.'

Charlotte remained silent. So far, so good...

'You may have damaged the nerve of hip and arm somewhat. Been carrying anything heavy lately?'

She nodded. 'Yes.'

He scribbled something on a pad. 'We'll keep an eye on it. You're very tense. More than usual.'

'I know.' I was blind, screaming scared because one of my legs had suddenly ceased working. Or it seemed like it. I had to drag it to the car. That's why I crashed. And you think it's hysterical. You don't say so, but you think it. And I hope you are right.

'How long have you been married?'

She told him.

'No children, of course.'

'No.'

He looked and gave her a sharp, professional stare, which suddenly made her realise that he took in a lot more than she'd guessed. Perhaps the verdict was not going to be as good as she had hoped.

'Never have had a child?' It was hardly a question, more a thoughtful aside.

'No.' She hesitated. 'There was an abortion once.'

The doctor nodded, as if she had been helpful. He rubbed his chin thoughtfully. Then took up a pencil and played with it. He did not ask the reason for the abortion.

'What age were your parents when they died?'

'My father was about forty. My mother isn't dead yet.'

'In good health is she?'

Charlotte hesitated. 'I believe so.' For some reason she had lied. She did not believe so at all.

'And what did your father die of?'

'It was in an accident, I was told. He was drowned.'

He scribbled a few more notes on his pad. 'This is a very harmless, mild sedative. Take it as from today. Come back and see me in a month's time.'

So there wasn't going to be a verdict. Not yet. Just a judgement reserved.

A month seemed a long time.

*   *   *

It was during this month that James was

mostly away from London working with a textile firm in Nottingham who were about to make silk tweed. He was advising them. Then he too was off to America to talk with the man he had worked for there.

To Charlotte he felt far away and withdrawn, just when she needed him most. For the first time she wondered if perhaps, just possibly James might have an interest in someone else. She had happened to see a letter from a silly client of his in which she wished James a happy visit to the States and went on: *"so perhaps you will find a nice American there. You deserve one. Or aren't Americans Americans when they are at home?"* A stupid letter, which Charlotte disliked, and she passionately hoped not to come true. James had laughed at it with her and said the writer was a mixed-up young character trying to be cleverer than she was. No one to be taken seriously.

But perhaps in America he *was* taking it seriously. On the telephone he sounded both discreet and detached, as if someone was always listening. Perhaps his conscience. Now *she* was jealous.

Diana, picking up a little of the atmosphere, told her off roundly and told her that James had ordered a new car as a surprise for her which she, Diana, had chosen but been sworn to secrecy. A secret she was now breaking so that Charlotte could count her blessings.

Charlotte went out to the factory at Greenwich to meet Mrs Angel in a better mood.

Business over for the day, she was packing her briefcase to go home, when there was a knock on the door.

'Come in.'

In came a small, dark girl whom she recalled seeing around.

'Good-afternoon, Miss Chaudin, I'm Dorothy Ellis, your Aunt Bea's daughter. I'm your cousin.'

Charlotte sat down, slowly, and said, 'I've seen you at work. Are you sure you are my cousin? I don't think I lay claim to any.'

'You may not lay claim, no. But you've got some all the same. Quite a few. My mother works here in the factory. She's married again since you last saw her. Mrs Benson. Bea Benson she is now. You know her.'

'I've certainly seen Mrs Benson,' said Charlotte politely.

'She says you *did* recognise her. Recognised her early on, but don't want to admit it. I can understand that, but I think it's all rubbish.'

'I am not aware of recognising Mrs Benson.' Charlotte was cold.

'We knew you'd say that. Or something like it. Mum says she understands. But it's all wrong. Everything ought to be brought out. We didn't treat you badly. I was only a kid, but I believe my mother.'

Charlotte was silent; she had gone very white.

Dorothy went on, not noticing, not caring about the anger building up in Charlotte. 'I am your cousin. You could be helpful to me in this business. You're not the only one with talent. You might think about that. Blood's thicker than water.'

'*Don't go* on,' said Charlotte.

'Why not? I won't go around talking of what I shouldn't. But remember I'm here.'

Charlotte got up and opened the door. 'Please leave. Get your cards from the office. You are dismissed.'

Dorothy said: 'You can't do that.'

'I've done it. I'll give you a reference. But get out. I don't ever want to see you again. Your mother too. You can both go.'

Dorothy went out, banging the door behind her, leaving Charlotte shaking.

She was still shaking some minutes later when an agitated Mrs Angel appeared.

'You can't just sack the girl like that,' she said at once. 'Not these days. Don't you know anything? There are all sorts of rules and regulations. Apart from anything else, we'll have a strike on our hands.'

'I've done it.'

'You'll have to undo it. Come on, now. You've had a row with her.' Mrs Angel raised a hand. 'No, don't tell me why,' she said hastily. 'I'd as soon not know. I'm not saying I like the girl. As a matter of fact, I don't. But she's a good worker. And her mother is a very decent sort.'

Seeing Charlotte looking both obstinate and unconvinced, Mrs Angel gave her a ten minute talking to on rules governing the dismissal of employees. When she showed signs of being able to go on for another ten minutes and possibly more, Charlotte said: 'All right. I get the situation. Give them their jobs back. But arrange it so that I don't see them again. Either of them.'

Dorothy said nothing to her mother, but, of course, Bea got to know. Soon the whole factory knew of the scene. Different versions circulated, none of which would have pleased Charlotte. But one and all put forward the opinion that Charlotte had not heard the last from Dorothy, no indeed. That girl would skin a cat to get what she wanted was the general opinion. Charlotte was no cat, but she might skin easily. There was that air about her.

*   *   *

Hem lines had now slid right down to the ground. The dolly-bird had ceased to be the image and the granny look was in.

Charlotte's part in this swing was unpremeditated and something of a surprise even to her. She had bought metres of a French silk printed with tiny sprigs of country flowers.

Immediately she saw the flowing, rustic, peasant style of dress that it must be used for. Sleeves must rise up to the elbow and be drawn into a puff with ribbons, skirts must be full with bodices tight. The designs flowed from her clever fingers on a happy profusion, thus proving that fashion arises from happy accidents as well as some deep response to social conditions.

To Charlotte her new styles seemed a piece of luck the more amazing in that she was not particularly happy. She was making happy clothes while feeling miserable.

'Just worries,' she said to Diana. 'Life *is* worrying, isn't it?'

'Not nearly as worrying as it used to be. I seem to be able to cope with mine better than I used to. It's heavenly to be so normal. A two-car, one-baby, twenty-dog family, that's us.' She got up, gathering her papers into her case. 'Must get back to the child. It's really Sam's turn today, but we switched. Right I get the idea for next seasons promotion. We might call the whole lot "Meadowsweet" ... Some American wants to do a profile about you, did you know? She'll want some details, autobiographical, that sort of thing.' Diana had had this remark ready to slip in sideways.

'Nothing doing.'

'Oh but the publicity!' cried Diana.

'She can do a profile of me as I am; strictly contemporary. You know my rules: no digging

329

up the past. I am not a monument. Yet.'

'You'll have to move fast then, she's digging around. You know what Americans are like.'

'Do you mean that?' She could see Diana did. 'Damn.'

Diana looked with sympathy at her friend. She had always known there was a dark area in Charlotte's life marked not to be touched. There were parts of her own life she would not have wanted digging out. But this went further.

'Where is she?'

'She rang from Geneva. You know distance means nothing to them.'

'Is she staying in Geneva?'

'Working on a story there. A tax refugee singer. The profile before you.'

'I'll go and see her. Just blow in. Give her what she wants to keep her quiet.'

'Are you sure you ought to, love? You've been looking very tired lately.'

But Charlotte was already consulting her diary of engagements while dialling Heathrow at the same time.

Diana shrugged and departed. She thought her friend was mad, but she had moments of lunacy herself, and had learnt to respect those of others.

James came into their office to read his post, passing Diana on her way out. She winked at him. Dear old James, he needed bucking up. She wasn't sure why, but a buck was definitely indicated.

James smiled at her. Good old Diana. He picked up his post.

The first letter was addressed in a rough scrawled hand, more or less clearly his name, he thought, although you had to see it with the eye of faith.

He opened the letter. Inside was another envelope with a typed address, and a Paris postmark. The envelope was addressed to Charlotte at the Greenwich factory and marked private and personal.

Accompanying the letter was a note, unsigned, saying: *"Dear Miss Chaudin, I guessed you'd want this sent on at once, and not want it kicking around the office while you were away."*

James knew at once, without any need to talk about it, that the letter had been sent to him deliberately, out of malice, and by no mischance. He had been meant to have it.

He held it in his hand for a moment, unopened. Then he passed it over to Charlotte. 'Here.'

She took it, looked at it without saying anything, then put it in her pocket.

'What the hell is it?' He shot across the table the accompanying note and envelope.

Charlotte took them and studied them. 'Just a bit of nastiness from a girl out at the factory whom I had occasion to tell off. She's just trying to make trouble.'

'Can she do that?'

'Not unless you want her to, James.' Charlotte's voice sounded on the edge of exhaustion. It was barely ten o'clock in the morning.

James was silent. With a great effort of will he refrained from forcing Charlotte to open the letter from Paris and tell him all about it. It could have been done, but it would have been the equivalent of wife-battering in his book. To Charlotte he couldn't do it.

She picked up her bag, threw it over her shoulder and said: 'I'm off to Geneva.'

'Why?'

'Business. Bloody business.'

James stood there. A voice inside said: Run after her, call out I love you, I love you. But he stayed where he was.

He didn't believe in Geneva. Or the business. All through the night, alone in their flat, he found his jealous suspicions growing stronger by the minute. It was only with difficulty he restrained himself from searching Charlotte's possessions and letters. He could have done. She left everything unlocked. For a reserved, even secretive person she was surprisingly trusting. He held back, but it was a struggle.

After a sleepless night, and breakfast of bitter black coffee, (like my mood, he told himself) he went down the staircase to work.

On the bottom flight leading to the sewing rooms he met Diana.

'Oh James, good-morning. Can I give these

to you.' She handed over an envelope. 'It's only the outline for the publicity promotion for next season. I'm in a hurry as usual.'

'Charlotte's away.'

'Yes, I know. That's why I'm giving the outline to you. Let her have it when you see her. I'm going to the country for a few days. Small holiday.' Then she looked at James. 'Are you all right? You look rotten.'

'Didn't sleep.'

'You missed Charlotte, I expect. I can never sleep now when Sam is away. I didn't know it was the same for men.'

'Charlotte says she's in Geneva,' said James grudgingly.

'Oh it's Geneva, all right. She's gone to see a journalist about an interview. I think she's mad, but it's Geneva all right.'

James did not know whether to be comforted by this evidence of truth in Charlotte or not. 'Did she tell you why she was going? She didn't say much to me.'

'Oh I know *why* she was going all right. It's to stop an American journalist writing an article about her life. The madness part is her taking off like that.' Although she was in a hurry, Diana took time to add: 'There's something wrong somewhere, only I don't know what. I think you ought to have it out with her. She needs it.'

Diana leaned forward and kissed him on the cheek. 'Get on with it, James, and good luck.

333

Bless you. Bye,' and she was gone, running down the stairs, calling out goodbye to Val, and then banging on the front door.

She left behind a thoughtful, determined man. When Charlotte came back there would be a showdown.

*   *   *

Twenty-four hours later Charlotte looked down at the city of Geneva as her departing aircraft rose above it.

The city appeared calm and clean, which just about described it. At any other time she would have enjoyed touring its important buildings, guide book in hand. This time it had been a little trip to purgatory.

The journalist, a tall, sinewy, sun-tanned woman had not been obliging.

To begin with Charlotte had had to hang around the hotel waiting for Isobel Macmaster to return. That was fair enough, for she had arrived unannounced, Charlotte admitted this. But she had not enjoyed it.

Sitting and waiting Charlotte had time to be nervous.

'Hi! Sorry to keep you waiting. What an honour! I never expected the mountain to come to Mohammed!' Isobel Macmaster towered over Charlotte, smiling amicably, professionally benign but totally unbending. Her good humour meant nothing, not even good temper.

Charlotte knew after the first few words that she had wasted her time in coming.

Worse, she had learned that this woman had discovered all there was to know about her background and would use it.

A good article would be produced, tactful, done in the best of taste, unassailable as to the facts; revealing and tragic.

'I wish you'd never heard of me.'

'You're newsworthy, Miss Chaudin. If it hadn't been me, it would have been someone else.'

'I can't think how you got on to it all.'

'There's been some speculation around for some time. But I was put on to it by Virginia, my little old friend ... She did some background work on you once for a programme she was working on.'

So that was the link, thought Charlotte. Virginia, damn her.

'Yes, Virginia always felt that she hadn't got to the bottom of Charlotte Chaudin at the time, and gave me the tip.'

There was a bit more talk, exactly what, Charlotte could not remember. She left shortly afterwards for her own room in the same hotel.

* * *

On the flight between Geneva and Heathrow she thought about what was happening to her.

335

From the close observation that she kept on her own body she believed that she was in the process of becoming seriously ill. She thought of it as a process, because she believed the seeds of her illness had been planted a long time ago. It was genetic, an inherited predisposition, not an infection.

The shadow of it had hung over her since adolescence when she first learned of the possibility. For periods in her life she had hoped that the threat had passed, that it would not strike her, that she was one of the lucky ones. But lately she had been sure she had not escaped. The insidious onset had begun.

She should never have married, it was unfair to James, but at least she would not pass on the flawed genes to another generation. She had taken that precaution.

The worst of her problems was that she had never been able to talk about it. Once she had tried, but speech had always dried on her tongue like salt.

Very soon now, once the article was published, the whole world would know.

Over the English Channel, Charlotte came to her decision. She could not go home. Once one was home, doctors and loving hands controlled one's freedom.

If what she suspected was true, for Charlotte there was only one freedom left.

*   *   *

In all loving relationships, communication goes on silently in absence as well as when together. James knew that Charlotte was suffering almost as soon as she did herself. One couldn't call it telepathy; it was too pervasive and subtle for that.

He was hardly even surprised when she failed to return. He tried to feel surprise, but he could not, a dull, inner voice had told him long ago that she might not return.

He gave her one clear day before starting enquiries. He had to do it discreetly, ringing the airport, and the airport hotels. She had arrived from Geneva safely, and that was that. No one knew more.

At this point he took Diana and Val into his confidence, only to be met with but small surprise. They had been as worried as he had been for days. He set them to ringing around. Anywhere, any name they could think of, they were down to guessing.

When he had been spurred by jealousy James had held back from searching Charlotte's desk, but now that he was moved by love, he felt no compunction.

Charlotte kept her desk in the apartment very tidy. Only personal letters and private bills were stored here; all her business records were downstairs in her Butterfly office or Greenwich.

At the bottom of one drawer, beneath a stack of drawing paper, he found a large envelope. Inside were what appeared to be a series of bills.

The bills went back over a decade; they came from what seemed to be a French clinic or private hospital. The letter heading was the Hospice Sainte Gabrielle, 89, Rue Dodart, Versailles.

The bills had been sent out quarterly, sometimes paid promptly, sometimes more slowly. Charlotte had not always had the money to hand. The sums were not small and had risen with inflation. The services being charged for were not named, but they had been regular to the present month. What ever she was being charged for, Charlotte was still paying.

*   *   *

Versailles is but a short distance from Paris. Now people lived in neat flats overlooking Le Roi Soleil's bit of extravaganza, and commuted in to Paris.

The Rue Dodart was in a turning just off the main avenue of trees leading to the palace. James found it without any difficulty. The Hospice Sainte Gabrielle was about halfway down, a solid-looking stone house of the last century, not beautiful, but clean and well painted.

James went back to a bar overlooking the palace to have a drink and think things through.

He sipped his wine, allowing himself a brief lull, a suspension from pain. The sun was shining on the trees, reflecting a pale light back from the stones of the palace. Earlier it had been raining so that the cobbled street a few yards away was wet and clean. Perhaps Versailles was always clean. Except when the tourists were there. In front of him was a large notice in German and Italian forbidding visitors to drop rubbish or to leave their bicycles propped up against the trees.

In the next few minutes he was going to find out something about Charlotte, from which he might work out where she was now.

James spoke efficient French with a strong English accent. He bought some Gaulloise, then asked the waiter for a match. 'Unusual name: Rue Dodart.'

'A joke, I think. He was a doctor in old Versailles who killed two patients, perhaps more. All the doctors killed then.' He gave a knowing shrug.

'Is that why there's a hospital in the road?'

'A private clinic. A home for incurables.'

'Geriatrics?'

The waiter shrugged. 'Some old, some young. I have seen kids there. But it's a good place. No beatings. Drugs yes, but you have to use something. And they don't know, those poor things.' He yawned, showing three splendid gold back teeth. He was in favour of heavy sedation provided the victim was old or not too bright.

James got up and left. As he walked to the clinic he wondered what he would find. A child of Charlotte's? Perhaps one with some terrible impairment that made normal life impossible? It would explain her fierce opposition to motherhood. But it was not like Charlotte to hide a child, even one crippled or retarded. He thought she would have cherished such a one proudly, defying anyone to criticise.

He had wondered exactly how he would get an entrance to the clinic, but when he arrived and announced he was Charlotte's husband, he was accepted at once and made welcome. He was so obviously exactly what he claimed to be.

The elderly woman in a white overall greeted him with a smile. 'We thought someone would call. Miss Chaudin is very regular in her visits.'

'She is ill herself.'

'I am sorry. Nothing serious, I hope?' She gave him an alert, brown stare. She did not wait for an answer. 'You want to see her, of course.'

Her? A daughter then, too sad. A girl as pretty as Charlotte but unproduceable?

'I will take you myself.' She bustled him along a short corridor. 'It is not one of her good days, poor soul. But you will forgive?'

Once again, she did not wait for an answer. She led him through a swing door and into a small, white painted room. Everything was very clean, he noticed, and smelt clean. A good place, after all.

In the room was an empty, neatly made-up bed, with an armchair turned to face a sunny window.

'Here we are,' said the nurse cheerfully. 'A visitor.'

James saw a small late-middle-aged woman crouched in one corner of the chair. Her hair was grey, her face of that pallor which suggests a long invalid life indoors. Her hands were curled in her lap. She did not look at him, or respond in any way. She looked at no one, her stare directed inside herself, where even there she seemed to see nothing.

'She won't speak, alas.'

James found his voice. 'Do you use heavy drugs?'

'For her they are not necessary. She is apathetic, alas, from the nature of the illness. Sometimes a little disturbed, but that phase is past. It's not a good sign. It distressed your wife very much to see her mother like it. Naturally.'

Her mother, thought James. Not her own child, but her mother.

'I expect Dr Roche would like to see you. He usually saw your wife.'

'I'd like to see him.'

To find out more about all this. To ask questions and to get some answers.

Dr Roche was an old man. In fact, the

341

impression was gaining on James that the whole clinic was old. Well run, clean, but founded long ago on conservative principles and still run on its own ageing lines. It needed a puff of fresh air blown through it.

A young man, probably also a doctor, was talking to Dr Roche when James arrived, but he left speedily. So there was someone young in the place. But if old, Dr Roche was welcoming and polite. James thought he was a kind, careful man. He was also aware that these bespectacled grey eyes were observing him with interest.

'So your wife is ill? Ah,' he sounded sad. 'Not seriously?'

'I hope not,' said James soberly. How did he know?

'You have a good doctor? One you trust? But don't be hasty. I know every time your wife feels ill she suspects the worst. It's bound to be her worry. But I always tell her to hope. Not every child succumbs. God is kind sometimes.'

Then he saw that James really did not understand what he was talking about. He looked shocked, embarrassed. 'Forgive me. I thought you must know.'

'Know what?'

Professional reticence held Dr Roche back, but concern for James' anxious face, pushed him into explaining.

Charlotte's mother, he said, was a victim of Huntingdon's Chorea, a progressive, deteriorating disease which gradually destroyed the body and mind. Its onset was in adulthood, by which time children had often been born to the sufferer. It was hereditary. Once embarked ... he spelt out the bleak details with clarity. James had a right to know.

How James got out of the room, he wasn't sure. He must have behaved politely. Or so he hoped. But suddenly he was outside in the fresh air, walking down the Rue Dodart.

He felt as if someone had kicked him in the stomach. He was bruised, in pain. Darling, darling Charlotte. If only she had confided in him, how he would have cherished her. But she had let herself bear this burden alone.

He still had to find her. No clues there. God alone knew where she was. But at least now, when he found her he would know how to help her.

Behind him feet were running; a voice called out to him to stop.

He turned round to see the young man who had been with Dr Roche.

'You want me?'

'Yes.' A hand was held out. 'I am Dr de Bussy.' This young man was speaking English with an American accent. 'I wanted to talk to you. I think there are things you should know.'

'Come and have a drink. Have you got time?'

'A few minutes. But it must be coffee.' He smiled. 'I am on duty.'

Over coffee in the bar looking across to the palace, Dr de Bussy said: 'I know which patient you came to visit; I want to say something that's been on my mind a long time. The diagnosis has been worrying me ... I know a little of the history. I know that the patient's husband deserted her when she first became ill and that she was looked after by her daughter, until she became too ill for her daughter to cope with.

'I don't know who made the first diagnosis, nor in what circumstances, but since they were poor, I can guess. Then she was brought here, an established case. The damage is now done, her condition irreversible—but I think it is not the result of Huntingdon's Chorea.'

'You mean she hasn't got it?'

'It is only what I think. I think she had a brain inflammation of viral origin that was never treated. It may have been untreatable. But it is not to be inherited.'

He finished his coffee. 'I think it would be in your best interest to get your mother-in-law moved elsewhere and a fresh study of her condition made. Say Paris, or London. She has been here too long. Dr Roche is a good man, but old and conservative.'

As he walked away, Dr de Bussy crossed himself. 'I hope I've done the right thing. And I hope my guess is a good one.' He had always liked Charlotte. He kept his fingers crossed.

344

When James arrived to check in at Orly
Airport he heard his name being called. He
went at once to the BEA desk. The steward
handed him a slip of paper. 'There was a
message for you if you came this way. You are
to ring that number, London.'

Diana's voice answered him at once. She
sounded as if she was crying. 'James? Thank
God. They've found Charlotte. She was lying
under a tree in a park in Greenwich. A note for
you ... One for me, too ... She said she was
going to die anyway, she knew the signs and
wanted it to be quick and soon ... An overdose
... No, James, she's still alive, but she's taken
an awful lot of stuff. They don't ... Please
come at once.'

James flew home on the first available flight,
carrying with him both hope and dread. Sam
met him at Heathrow and drove him across
London.

Charlotte was in a hospital overlooking the
Thames. The river seemed always to play a part
in her life. About her bed was the apparatus of
tubes and bottles with which doctors support a
life reluctant to continue. She was not
conscious.

A red-eyed Diana sat in a corner of the
room. It was such a tiny room that she was in
touching distance of Charlotte.

As soon as James arrived Diana said

quickly: 'I'll leave you.' He hardly heard her, did not notice when she was gone. His total attention was focused on this woman he loved so much.

Her eyes were closed, her face drained of colour, she seemed not to breathe. Here was a woman who had hidden her own private fears as well as she could, who had cared for and supported her sick mother when her father deserted them. A loving, loyal, good woman who was, as well, a creative artist of great power.

Charlotte, Charlotte, I never valued you enough.

James took the soft, limp hand in his, where it felt cold and heavy.

'Come back, Charlotte, come back to me. There's hope. Listen to me, even if you are deep under, dead to everything, hear what I say: you aren't ill. These symptoms you thought you saw don't exist, they aren't real. Come back to life, Charlotte. There's nothing for you to dread.'

As he spoke he prayed he was telling her the truth, and not recalling her to another tragedy. But he had to do it.

'Come back, Charlotte. Listen to me and come back.'

There was no response, not an eye-lid fluttered, but yet he knew that she heard. He loved her so much he could force her to attend.

He sat there beside her, repeating his

message, dragging her back, inch by inch from the dark pit.

It was not a miracle, it was work, a labour, and James sweated, groaning as if giving birth.

*   *   *

When Charlotte opened her eyes she saw James and no one else.

'I heard your voice,' she whispered. 'I was under the sea and you called to me so I swam up.'

'You did, my love.'

'Funny feeling. Am I dying, James?'

'No, not now. You're going to be all right, Charlotte.'

She began to remember her desolate wanderings around South London, through the street she had known as a student, when her mother was ill, left behind in a Paris charity hospital, and no one seemed willing to help her. She remembered lying down under a large chestnut tree near to where the Meridian announces the centre of the world. The right place to die, she had thought.

'I seemed to hear you saying *such* things. Such hope. Is it true what you said?'

'You're not supposed to talk much. You're still weak. It's true, all true, Charlotte.'

He prayed it was.

'How long have I been like this?'

'A day unconscious. One more day in

347

coming back to life.'

He knew he must explain fast, and yet be gentle. He told her how he had been to Versailles to the clinic there, and seen her mother. Then he told of what Dr de Bussy had said.

He let the importance of what he had to tell sink in. It was going to be hard for her to grasp.

'The doctors here confirm it as likely. They're as sure as they can be at the moment; you're healthy. Any symptoms you imagined—well, they probably were imagination. Because of what you feared, my love. I wish you'd told me.'

'Has that article appeared yet?' she asked.

'No, darling,' James replied. 'And we'll contact the magazine right away—tell them they must change the story.'

'Oh James. After all this time of having that terrible threat hanging over me . . . I can't quite take it in.'

But the hope was there inside her, she began to feel excited and happy. Happier than had ever seemed possible. Suddenly she felt the need to talk to James. Really talk to him.

'My parents were both artists; my father an Englishman who met my mother while studying in Paris. She was good. We lived partly in London, partly in France. And then, when I was fifteen, my mother became ill. When the doctors said they thought she had this terrible disease my father just packed up and left. He left what money he had, but he couldn't face it. I never saw him again. I heard later he had been killed.

'We were taken in by my mother's sister, my Aunt LouLou. She was a seamstress, and found me work too. When I was seventeen, my mother was admitted to the Hospice Sainte Gabrielle. And LouLou encouraged me to apply for a scholarship to Design School. I came back to London to see if I could get help from my father's family. No. They didn't want to know. Frightened I suppose. That's when I started telling lies about myself and my past. I invented a new Charlotte and took on my mother's maiden name—Chaudin.'

He knew the rest, more or less. And as she said everyone read the article soon to appear would know the superficial truth behind Butterfly. 'How brave,' people would say. 'How amazing of her to have the career she's had with that hanging over her.' Some would say with true admiration and others with a kind of titillated curiosity.

God willing, there would be a new truth to add to it soon.

He kissed her, promised to be back when she was awake again, and left her to recover.

A cool breeze blew through the window on to Charlotte. She fancied she could smell the river. Not far away must be her factory. She couldn't take in all that James had said, it would take time, but she would understand in the end.

She began to dream, half awake, half in a delicious sleep. There was a future now with James? A child even? Yes, there must be a child. Perhaps more. She was not yet so old. A whole new world was opening up before her. Work too, she could feel invention stirring again.

Dr de Bussy had to be right: such a wonderful future beckoned to her. There was hope. Hope.

Hope was like a flutter of coloured butterflies rising all around her.

She'd make it all right. Now she knew she truly could do it. With love to James.

EPILOGUE

This sunny autumn morning, in 1975, Charlotte Chaudin, who had kept her maiden name through two marriages, had decided to walk from her shop in Albemarle Street to where she was lunching. It had been raining earlier, and the pavements were still wet, but now the air was sweet and warm.

She was on her away to The Women of the Year Luncheon. She happened to know some of the other women who had been invited and a fine old collection of friends, enemies, and business rivals, it would be!

She looked down the slope to the Riverside entrance of the Savoy Hotel. A crowd had already assembled outside. Women were in the majority but then this was The Women of the Year Luncheon. The presence of television crews from several networks, together with the large number of journalists and photographers, was counted for by the chief guests: not only Charlotte, but a famous woman explorer and a young and beautiful princess.

Charlotte paused politely for a second at the entrance so that cameras could flash. She knew the value of publicity; knew she was a celebrity herself, and wanted everyone to see what she was wearing.

She had dressed for the occasion. Accordingly, she wore a soft suede skirt, bias cut, and a blue and green silk shirt, which would show to perfection when she stood up to speak. No hat, but a golden butterfly in her shining dark hair where it feel in a curve on her cheek.

The cameras followed her as she took her seat at the High Table. There was her name on a card: '*Charlotte Chaudin*', and beside it the small bag of presents each of the important guests would receive: scent, a silk handkerchief and a leather notebook with her name on it.

From where she sat she could see across the huge crowded room to the door where the princess herself would presently appear.

351

The room was full of women distinguished in all fields. She recognised quite a few of the faces; knew some of them personally. She could see Ethne Scott who had created Scott Software and Daphne Shelley, the geophysicist who worked for a big oil company. Also, the cheerful bespectacled face of Stephana Lloyd, the distinguished physician.

Diana Howden and Sophia Beauclerc came in together, which was a bit of a shock, until she remembered that, of course, they moved in the same world and always had done.

A whole troupe of memories, some painful, some good, raced in, and for a moment she was a long way away.

Charlotte looked across the room to where Diana sat. Diana who had been such a great friend, and Sophia who had for a long time been an enemy, but had now, surprisingly, dwindled into just nothing at all. Neutralised by life. Suddenly the hate was gone, leaving only emptiness. With surprise, Charlotte realised that friendliness might creep in. Understanding, certainly. They had both suffered through the same man. Charlotte saw that Sophia's face, the famous profile, seemed a shade heavier.

Why, I look better than that, she thought. She's been the beauty, but I am lasting better!

Diana looked up, smiled, mouthing a greeting. Charlotte smiled back, and assembled her notes, her heart thudding.

Was she really one of the Women of the Year?

And if so, what year?

I know, she thought. I'll be a Woman of Next Year. Because hope is my best chance.

Presently, she would rise, turn to face the TV cameras and begin.

'Your Royal Highness, Madam Chairman, ladies—My theme today is "Fashion for a Life..."' A taxi delivered her back to Albemarle Street in time to hear from her secretary that she had missed a telephone call from Tokyo.

'But I said you'd ring back.'

Charlotte nodded assent.

'And then there was a telephone call from a man in Manchester. He wanted a batch of dresses. Just like that. Name and order on the pad.' Val sounded ruffled. 'I don't think he knows who you are.'

Charlotte laughed. 'I won't lose his order.'

Down below she could hear the murmur of clients and vendeuses in the shop. Above was the subdued noise of the work-rooms. Occasionally feet ran on the stairs from one to the other, but in her office all was quiet. They had been trained not to disturb her. Peace and quiet to work in was the luxury she had bought for herself at last.

She had put off telephoning her doctor. So he called her first.

'Do you want to know the result of your test

or not?'

'I'm frightened.'

'Let's make this easy for each other. I'll tell you when it's time to be frightened. You aren't the first woman to face this, I'll give you the statistics if you like.' He knew the right line to take with her.

'Does that mean what I think it means?' Charlotte asked, grinning.

'Yes, my dear. You're pregnant,' her doctor confirmed.

Charlotte hugged the knowledge to herself for a minute or two, then went to find James. She'd come a long way since he'd given her back her future eight months ago. They had so nearly lost each other.

Desertion. Death. Sex without love. Love without sex. She'd had the lot. And each had a face and a story; they walked towards her. Beginning in 1964. That was the archway through which all characters trooped.

She found him in the cutting room.

His eyes lit up when he saw her. 'Darling! How did it go?'

'Oh, very well, thank you.' She went and put her arms around him, then continued: 'But I've something much more interesting to tell you about...'

We hope you have enjoyed this Large Print book. Other Chivers Press or Thorndike Press Large Print books are available at your library or directly from the publishers.

For more information about current and forthcoming titles, please call or write, without obligation, to:

Chivers Press Limited
Windsor Bridge Road
Bath BA2 3AX
England
Tel. (01225) 335336

OR

Thorndike Press
P.O. Box 159
Thorndike, Maine 04986
USA
Tel. (800) 223–2336

All our Large Print titles are designed for easy reading, and all our books are made to last.